BY ANNE PERRY

FEATURING ELENA STANDISH

Death in Focus
A Question of Betrayal
A Darker Reality
A Truth to Lie For
The Traitor Among Us

FEATURING WILLIAM MONK

The Face of a Stranger
A Dangerous Mourning
Defend and Betray
A Sudden, Fearful Death
The Sins of the Wolf
Cain His Brother
Weighed in the Balance
The Silent Cry
A Breach of Promise
The Twisted Root
Slaves of Obsession
Funeral in Blue
Death of a Stranger
The Shifting Tide
Dark Assassin
Execution Dock
Acceptable Loss
A Sunless Sea
Blind Justice
Blood on the Water
Corridors of the Night
Revenge in a Cold River
An Echo of Murder
Dark Tide Rising

FEATURING CHARLOTTTE AND THOMAS PITT

The Cater Street Hangman
Callander Square
Paragon Walk
Resurrection Row
Rutland Place
Bluegate Fields
Death in the Devil's Acre
Cardington Crescent
Silence in Hanover Close
Bethlehem Road
Highgate Rise
Belgrave Square
Farriers' Lane
The Hyde Park Headsman
Traitors Gate
Pentecost Alley
Ashworth Hall
Brunswick Gardens
Bedford Square
Half Moon Street
The Whitechapel Conspiracy
Southampton Row
Seven Dials
Long Spoon Lane
Buckingham Palace Gardens
Treason at Lisson Grove
Dorchester Terrace
Midnight at Marble Arch
Death on Blackheath
The Angel Court Affair
Treachery at Lancaster Gate
Murder on the Serpentine

FEATURING DANIEL PITT

Twenty-one Days
Triple Jeopardy
One Fatal Flaw
Death with a Double Edge
Three Debts Paid
The Fourth Enemy

DEATH TIMES SEVEN

DEATH TIMES SEVEN

A Daniel Pitt Novel

Anne Perry
and
Victoria Zackheim

BALLANTINE BOOKS • NEW YORK

Ballantine Books
An imprint of Random House
A division of Penguin Random House LLC
1745 Broadway, New York, NY 10019
randomhousebooks.com
penguinrandomhouse.com

Hardcover ISBN 978-0-593-98251-8
Ebook ISBN 978-0-593-98252-5

Printed in the United States of America

1st Printing

First Edition

Book Team: Production editor: Jennifer Rodriguez • Managing editor: Pam Alders • Production manager: Nathalie Mairena • Copy editor: Pam Feinstein • Proofreaders: Andrea Gordon, Amy Harned, Lisa Grimenstein

To Susanna Porter, Meg Davis, Donald Maass, and Ken Sherman

And for Anne, with love

DEATH TIMES SEVEN

CHAPTER

One

THERE WAS A knock at the office door and Daniel looked up to see Impney, the chief clerk, already inside. Daniel was working on a complicated brief and was getting increasingly frustrated by its wording.

Impney closed the door quietly behind him and drew in his breath. His face was so white, he looked as if he might faint.

Daniel swallowed hard. "What is it, Impney?"

"Mr. Kitteridge is in court today, sir."

"I know," Daniel said before pausing. "Sit down," he ordered, "before you fall over."

"No thank you, sir. I'm perfectly all right." Impney held up a hand to stop further comment.

Daniel said nothing and waited. He noticed a sheen of perspiration rising on the clerk's forehead.

"Sir, we have just had a telephone call from Suffolk, where Mr. Kitteridge's parents live . . . lived." He drew a shaky breath. "Sir, they have both been shot. Mrs. Kitteridge is dead. Mr. Kitteridge, or I suppose I should say Reverend Kitteridge, is badly injured, but it is just possible he might live. Possible but . . . unlikely."

Daniel sat motionless in his chair. He felt sick. It was too horrible to believe. Toby Kitteridge was senior to Daniel, but he had become his closest friend since joining the law firm of fford Croft and Gibson fresh from university. In his mind, he pictured Toby, lanky, awkward, and always looking untidy, even when he made an effort. He was shy, modest . . . and brilliant.

"Sir." Impney's voice broke into Daniel's thoughts. "I've checked with the Suffolk police, in case it was some kind of obscene joke or a cruelty." Impney took another deep breath. "I'm afraid there is no mistake."

Daniel stared at Impney for a long moment before speaking. "Have you told anyone else? Mr. Hunter?" Gideon Hunter, KC, was their new chief lawyer. *KC* stood for *King's Counsel*, a much-coveted title. But it was Toby who had been named the new Head of Chambers, since the retirement of Marcus fford Croft less than nine months ago. "Or Marcus?"

"No, sir," Impney replied. "Mr. Hunter is leaving later today for a brief holiday, but I will tell him when he comes in. I'm not certain about Mr. fford Croft. Perhaps your wife should break the news to him? And I'm sorry, sir, but I think you should tell Mr. Kitteridge. He has to know, and best it comes from you."

Daniel rubbed his hands over his face. "Yes, of course, I'll go and tell him." He returned his gaze to Impney, who remained distraught. The clerk had served chambers long enough that he considered its members to be his family. Actually, more like his children, and he was fiercely protective of them all.

"What on earth do they say occurred?" Daniel asked. "I have to be able to tell Toby something. Was it a ridiculous accident? For heaven's sake, Toby's father is a village priest! The local vicar! Church of England, I think. Yes, he would be. Or nonconformist of some kind, I suppose." Again, he noticed the pallor of Impney's skin, and his very obvious distress, and the hollow feeling inside Daniel was made even worse. "Well?" he said hoarsely.

"There was apparently no one else there, Mr. Pitt. They are saying that Mr. Kitteridge shot his wife and then turned the gun on himself. Maybe something made him stop, or at the last moment he lost his nerve. He is very badly wounded, in his head, but as of a few minutes ago, when I got the news, he was still alive. Possibly, in the circumstances, it would be better if he slipped away. I'm sorry, sir, but that is the sum of what they were able to tell me."

"Who is *they*?" Daniel demanded. It was pointless being angry, but so much easier than believing news like this. Toby's father, a vicar! Why on earth would a vicar kill his wife of nearly forty years and then himself? It could not be true, not like this—not on an ordinary Wednesday morning.

"Police from the local station, sir," Impney replied. "In Ipswich. They said they couldn't reveal more than that. Except that Mr. Kitteridge is in Suffolk General Hospital, in Bury St Edmunds. I'm sorry, sir. Shall I cancel your appointments for the rest of the day? And perhaps tomorrow as well? I'll find someone to take your place, temporarily. And, of course, Mr. Kitteridge's." Impney closed his eyes. "And please give Mr. Kitteridge our deepest sympathy, sir. I hardly know what to say."

Daniel understood, searching for words befitting of this tragedy. "I don't think there is anything we can say, Impney. I'm not engaged in a case at the moment," he added, placing his hand on the brief he had been examining when the clerk entered. "Or nothing pressing, so you'll have to excuse me, too. I may end up taking Mr. Kitteridge to Suffolk. Of course, he'll want to go. I think he has a right to be there. He'll be beside himself to know what to do, or where to turn." The thought of how Toby would react increased Daniel's sense of feeling ill.

Impney nodded, and then ran his hands across his jacket, as if making sure he was properly attired. "Yes, sir. Don't you worry about anything here. I assume you'll tell your own family where you are, but if you want me to do that, of course I will."

"No, no thank you," Daniel replied, getting to his feet slowly, as if unsure of keeping his balance. "I'll go to court and tell Toby. It's the Old Bailey, isn't it?"

"Yes, sir, a big trial, for the murder of Miss Alexandra Stanton. Very nasty business. Murder and attempted rape."

Daniel well knew what Impney was telling him: that if found guilty, Toby's client would end up on the gallows, probably within a week or so of the verdict. Time, it was almost always one of the elements. No room to make mistakes. Vindication was no use to the dead.

"I'll ask for a week's adjournment," he said to Impney. "If Toby needs longer, and he may well do, we'll figure it out. Sometimes, work distracts from grief, but nothing—" He stopped, searching for words powerful enough, and ended by merely shaking his head. "Someone else will have to take over, or at the very least, be there, if it's needed."

"Yes, sir. I dare say that Mr. Hunter would do that himself." He did not add the reasons. The firm of fford Croft and Gibson was small, but highly thought of from the days when Marcus fford Croft had been a star of the court, passionate, articulate, ethical, a fighter who occasionally was beaten, but who never gave up. Those who took over from him must act the same.

There was a moment's silence, then Daniel thanked Impney again, collected his jacket from the stand in the corner, and went out. He walked briskly across the street and hailed a taxi. It would be far quicker than driving himself, or even trusting the underground railway. Besides, he daren't think how he was going to deal with this. He had neither time nor attention to give to driving.

"Yes, sir," the cabby said. It was one of those brand-new black automobiles, neatly designed to give the driver a separate compartment of his own, and safe from the passengers, if necessary. These vehicles were a bit like square boxes on wheels, but they could turn on a sixpence, and the drivers knew the streets of London as if the maps were imprinted on their brain.

"The Old Bailey, please," Daniel directed, as he climbed in and closed the door sharply.

"You in a hurry, sir?" the driver asked.

Was he? No. He needed time to think how he was going to tell Toby that there had been a murder-suicide in his family, and that he must leave Peter Ward and his defense to someone else. There was no good way to say that. "Not really," he replied. "I have bad news. Nothing is going to make that better."

"Yes, sir, I'm sorry, sir." The driver put the car into gear and they shot forward into the traffic with ease.

Twenty minutes later, Daniel was climbing the steps of the most famous courthouse in London, perhaps all of Great Britain, still with no better idea of what he would say. He went inside. He was startled when one of the ushers recognized him.

"Mr. Pitt, sir. You look disturbed. Are you all right?"

"Yes. Yes, thank you." Daniel shook his head as if to get rid of something that was clinging to him. "Which court is Mr. Kitteridge in? The trial of Peter Ward."

The corridor was almost empty, nevertheless the man conducted Daniel as if he were likely to get lost on his own. Thanking the usher, Daniel gently opened the door in front of him.

The room was exactly like any other in this building: magnificent carved benches, high ceilings, the judge on a raised platform in the center of the far wall. The jury was to one side of the room, while the high witness box was to the left of the judge's chair. The elevated dock, where the defendant remained, was directly across from the judge, on the other side of the chamber.

The gallery was packed. It would have been impossible to cram in another person.

Toby was standing up, his back to the gallery.

Daniel stood inside the door quietly, anxious not to interrupt proceedings more than was necessary.

A young man was in the witness box.

No one moved, and Daniel was careful not to be noticed. And, in fact, no one did, because all eyes were on Toby's lanky figure and that of the striking-looking young man who was being questioned.

The witness was not traditionally handsome, there was too much bone in his face, but it was powerful, and in its own way, attractive. His hair was thick and dark, and he was immaculately dressed. He did not grip the rails of the witness box, as many frightened people did, but stood straight, respectful—or perhaps *attentive* would have been a better word.

"And you knew Miss Stanton, the victim?" Toby asked.

"I had been introduced to her, but no, sir, I could hardly say I knew her. I made the usual niceties, the weather, some seasonal play that I had seen, and it turned out that she had seen it also. I bumped into her later in the evening. Some fellow was annoying her—persistent, you know? Like . . . he had hold of her arm and she pulled it away. I told him to leave her alone. He looked at me, and her, then I repeated it, and he took himself off."

"Did you know his name?" Toby asked.

The witness, Martin Flynt, who Daniel guessed must have been in his mid-twenties, shrugged very slightly. It was a graceful gesture of regret. "Sorry," he said. "I don't recall ever having seen him before. Or since, for that matter."

"But you go to a lot of these parties, Mr. Flynt," Toby insisted.

"Sir, I would help you if I could, but I am called as a witness only because my name was on the guest list. And yes, I do go to a lot of these parties, all held by the society set I know. But I couldn't tell you the name of the young man. He was nobody I had seen before."

"Did he stand out in your memory for that reason?" Toby asked.

"What reason? That I did not know him?"

"Yes. You seem to recall the encounter."

The young man looked momentarily surprised. "Yes, I suppose that is the reason. I couldn't place him . . . I'm fairly good at faces. One of the scout skills, you know?" He smiled.

Daniel told himself to be patient. The uninterrupted questioning of a witness was critical to the success of the case. But what he was about to tell Toby was far more critical. Toby's world was about to be shattered.

Why was the gallery so full? What were they all here for? The tragedy? To see justice done . . . or justice miscarried? Was it the fact that if you know the details of something horrid, you can manage it better, can reduce the horror to human proportions? Or was it to feel gratitude that this had happened to someone else, and not you? Daniel knew that Toby dreaded what was sure to follow: the prosecution presenting forensic evidence that proved Peter Ward's guilt. Perhaps the delay of this trial, if it was to be delayed, would allow the defense to order another look at the evidence. That would mean handing it over to Miriam and Dr. Evelyn Hall. Since Miriam was Daniel's wife, and the daughter of the founder of fford Croft and Gibson, there would be a mighty challenge coming from the prosecution. These challenges had been overcome in the past, several with dramatic results leading to acquittals.

Daniel realized that he must have moved, because half a dozen people suddenly turned their heads to see him. One of them caught his attention because he bore a considerable resemblance to the witness currently on the stand. He had the same prominent bones in the face, a sinister balance of nose and jaw, and the same thick, dark brown hair, except his was sprinkled with gray. Or, more accurately, white. His was also a powerful face, and Daniel remembered having seen this man's photograph in the newspaper. Sir Anthony Flynt he was, and with quite a different social status than either Toby's or Daniel's father. Daniel was the son of Sir Thomas Pitt, a gamekeeper's son who rose through the police force to become head of Special Branch. Daniel knew enough about the senior Flynt to understand that he pulled the strings attached to several members of Parliament. It was all very discreet, of course, but Daniel could discern the weight he wielded over others. It was in the angle of his head, the slight smile, as if he knew that in the end all would go as he wanted it to.

Toby followed the spectators' glances and his expression changed when he noticed Daniel. At first, he appeared to be curious, but a longer glance shifted his appearance to confusion and then worry.

The judge watched the movements of now many in the courtroom, turning his attention from Toby to Daniel. "There is no room for you, sir," he said briskly. "And you are interrupting the proceedings. Unless you have some other purpose, please take yourself outside at once."

Daniel did not answer. Instead, he was running words through his mind that would cause the least drama. "I do have some purpose, My Lord," Daniel finally said, his voice louder than he had intended it to be. "With your permission, I would like to tell you before I speak to anyone else."

"As I said, you are interrupting the proceedings where a man's life hangs on the jury's decision. What is it you want?"

Daniel walked slowly up the aisle, passing the gallery seats and continuing between the defendant's table and the prosecutor's table. Every eye seemed to be upon him. He nearly glanced at Toby, but could not.

"What is the nature of your business, sir?" the judge demanded.

"May I speak with you privately, My Lord?" He did not want to tell the whole room of Toby's tragedy.

"For heaven's sake . . . Mr. Pitt, isn't it? This is a piece of exhibitionism I will not tolerate."

Daniel kept walking, right up to the judge's elevated bench, still meeting the man's eyes as if there were just the two of them in the room.

The silence was ominous.

He spoke as quietly as he could. "My Lord, I have come to tell Mr. Kitteridge the news that his mother has been murdered and his father is close to death. Under these circumstances, he will not be able to continue on . . ."

The judge's face drained of color. "My God, are . . . are you sure? If this is some grandstand—" He removed his eyeglasses and looked more intently at Daniel. "They . . . God, how awful," he said quietly.

Daniel could barely hear the judge from just a few feet away, so he knew that Toby could not hear their exchange.

"Of course," the judge replied. He gave a single rap with the gavel. "Court is adjourned for today. Mr. Kitteridge, sir, if you would be so good as to come with Mr. Pitt, we will deal with this matter in my chambers." He made a gesture with his hand for Daniel and Toby to follow him, ignoring the buzz of curiosity and irritation in the crowd. Several of the men on the prosecutor's side rose as if to protest, but the demeanor of both the judge and Daniel gave them pause.

Once the three men were in the judge's chambers and the door was closed, the judge nodded to Daniel.

There was no point in waiting, prevaricating and drawing out the pain. Nothing he could think of would alleviate it. He sat in one of the chairs and motioned for Toby to sit in the other. The judge was already seated behind his desk, and seemed to shrink into himself. He said not one word, clearly having decided to leave everything to Daniel.

It was time.

"I'm sorry, Toby, but a very terrible thing has happened, and I have to tell you about it, and then help do whatever you think is best."

Toby looked nonplussed. "What? What has happened? Is Marcus dead?" Daniel was keenly aware of Toby's relationship with Marcus fford Croft, the former head of the firm. And, as it happened, Daniel's father-in-law.

"No, it's worse than that, Toby. I'm afraid your mother is dead, and your father is very seriously injured, and in hospital."

Toby sat frozen for several seconds, and when he did speak, his voice was almost unrecognizable. "What . . . What happened? Were they in the car, or in the road walking? Surely . . ." He struggled and could not find the words.

His body seemed about to fold over, and Daniel feared he might fall from the chair. He reached out and placed his hand on his friend's arm, but there was no need: Toby pulled himself upright, torment in his face.

Justin and Delia Kitteridge had been attacked, his mother dead. There was no way to soften what had to be said. Daniel cared too much for Toby to be evasive. "I'm sorry, but it seems they were both shot."

"Shot? What on earth do you mean? Some local with a grudge . . . against my father?"

Daniel closed his eyes for a moment, preparing himself for what he was about to reveal. "The police think that your father shot your mother, and then himself. He was severely wounded, but is still alive."

"That's ridiculous!" Toby protested, rising abruptly and then, as if wondering how he had come to be standing, lowered himself into the chair. "They never even have a decent quarrel! I've never heard my mother raise her voice. It was infuriating sometimes, how she kept her temper, no matter what. Somebody's playing a horrible practical joke. It's—"

"Toby, no," Daniel cut across him. "Do you think I'd come here without checking? Impney called the police in Ipswich and they said that the basic facts are correct. They don't know yet exactly what happened, and there are no witnesses to the actual event."

"Where?" Toby interrupted. "I mean, where did it—"

"In the kitchen of their home. Early this morning."

Toby looked lost, his brow creased, and then he closed his eyes. "Why do they think that . . ." He opened his eyes and looked imploringly at Daniel, and then he swallowed as if there were a huge lump blocking his throat. "Why would my father do such a thing? It's mad, insane."

"We don't know," Daniel replied. "At least, when I left chambers, that was all they could tell us. I don't know if there has been anything else—any more to report."

Toby started to stand again, only this time he staggered a little, and Daniel caught him and eased him back into the seat.

"I need to go!" Toby protested. "I have to—"

"Of course," Daniel agreed. "I'll drive you."

Toby shook his head sharply. "You've got to take over this case. Peter Ward is innocent, and I have a new line of proof. I can drive myself."

At that point, the judge leaned forward, forearms on his desk. "Mr. Kitteridge," he said.

Both Daniel and Toby turned their eyes to the judge, as if noticing him for the first time.

"I will put the case on temporary adjournment for a week. That will give you a chance to think through what you must do. As of right now, it seems very little is certain, except that there has been a tragedy. And you have had an appalling shock. I suggest you don't drive yourself." He turned to Daniel. "Where are they? That is, where is his father?"

"Suffolk, My Lord. And I'll drive him." Daniel turned to face Toby, although he was still speaking to the judge. "Of course, the firm will find someone to take over the case, if necessary. I think it would be wise to assume that will happen. Mr. Ward deserves the best defense that can be had."

He looked directly at the judge and saw how his lips tightened and his eyes narrowed. Daniel drew a breath, and then said, "I'm sure the last thing any of us wants is for a claim to be made that he was not given a fair trial."

The judge raised his hands above the desk, as if conjuring up an object. "All right, I take your point, Mr. Pitt. We must not only be fair, we must be seen to be fair, or justice itself is not served." His eyes moved to Toby. "Mr. Kitteridge, I am deeply shocked by the tragedy that has struck you, and the things you will have to face in the immediate future. I release you of responsibility in this case, and I wish you the best possible outcome of your tragedy. Your family will need you. You have siblings, sir?"

"A sister," Toby answered. "And I suppose her husband will also be of some comfort to us. I . . ." Clearly, he did not know how to continue.

"Indeed." The judge made it a word of closure. "My clerk will bring you a cup of tea. A stiff whiskey might do more good. If you prefer that, let me know. I will go back to court and you, Mr. Pitt, will go to your client and explain to him what has occurred, and that he will not be left unrepresented." He fixed Daniel with a sharp eye.

Toby opened his mouth, but it seemed that he could not find the words.

Daniel rose to his feet. "Thank you, My Lord. I shall return as soon as I have spoken with him."

"My clerk will take you."

Some minutes later, Daniel was sitting in a bare interview room when Peter Ward was brought in manacled, but with his hands in front of him, not behind his back. The warden saw him inside, removed the manacles, then withdrew.

Ward was in his mid-to-late twenties and was dressed in his own clothes for the trial. He looked not unlike Daniel himself—they were about the same age—except for the fear in his eyes. He was a little over average height, slender, with a pleasant face and a good head of black hair. At the moment, the pallor of his skin made him look sickly. He started to speak, and then stopped, as if Daniel's expression foretold something he did not want to hear.

Daniel could feel the man's suspense, almost like the presence of an unexpected bomb in the room. He dismissed diplomacy in the matter as an unnecessary torture. "I'm sorry to tell you that I've come with terrible news for Mr. Kitteridge," he began, watching Ward closely. Daniel knew that Toby believed the man was innocent, and he did not want Ward to misunderstand the situation and think that Toby had deserted him, or that the company had lost faith in his innocence and refused to let Toby continue. Ward had very little money, which Daniel learned when Impney had briefed him.

"His parents have met with a disaster," he continued, looking at Ward, meeting his eyes. "They have been shot. His mother is dead, and his father is hanging on, but he is not expected to survive." He saw a quick flash of pity in Ward's eyes, unmistakably real. "Which may be as well," Daniel hurried on, "because the police seem to think that he shot Mrs. Kitteridge, and then himself." It sounded awful, being said aloud, and in a voice almost dispassionate, as if it meant little.

Ward started to speak, then perhaps took stock of what it all meant and said nothing.

"I understand," Daniel said. He could see from Ward's face that there was a momentary softening of his expression. "And I am sure you understand that Mr. Kitteridge has to go home to Suffolk, immediately."

"You'll go with him?" It was only half a question. "You can't let him—"

"Of course I will," Daniel cut him off. "And if he is able to return in a week's time and resume the case, he will do."

For a moment, Ward appeared shaken. He was facing prison, and now he was being told that the man putting forth his defense was leaving. "Yes, I see," he said, although the words sounded trapped in his throat.

"If he isn't able to continue," Daniel went on, softening his voice, "then someone else will, someone from the firm. We have excellent lawyers."

"But will they believe me?" Ward said. There was quiet despair in his voice, as if he had to force the question. "Mr. Kitteridge does! He believes me!"

"I know. I promise, we will not leave you alone." He gave a bleak smile. "It would be disastrous for our company's reputation to abandon a client because of our own tragedy. More than that, it's not who we are. Ethics is important; compassion, too. Mr. Kitteridge is one of our best barristers, but Mr. Gideon Hunter is a silk, a King's Counsel. You don't get that far if you aren't good," Daniel told him. "He's newly head of the firm, and he has to make his mark. Who would trust him if he quit, just because the going is a little rough for a while? I can assure you, we will not abandon you."

Ward gave a slight smile, but his eyes filled with sudden tears that were clearly beyond his control. "Will you tell Mr. Kitteridge how sorry I am for his loss, and his—" He could not go any further.

For Daniel, the only decent thing was to promise to do that, then leave the man alone to try to compose himself. He rose to his feet and held out his hand.

Slowly, Ward gave his hand, too. It was a firm grip, two men shaking hands in a moment's understanding of grief.

Daniel sensed that this was not the grip of a drowning man, as he let go of Ward's hand. He silently vowed to take the case himself if Toby did not recover sufficiently to resume, although he had no idea how he would manage it.

CHAPTER

Two

DANIEL WALKED OUT of the courthouse and down the steps, keeping his hand on Toby's arm, almost as if he were leading a blind man, or someone walking in his sleep. Toby did not stumble, thanks to Daniel's guidance, and also because this flight of stairs was as familiar to him as those in his own home. Daniel gave him a quick glance and saw a curious blankness to his face, and then he realized that Toby's mind was far away.

Daniel understood this. Had such a tragedy happened to him, it would have been impossible to grasp. His parents were the background to everything in his life, the foundation upon which it was built, as he believed it must be with most people. He searched bleakly for something to say that would ease any part of his friend's pain. Nothing came.

They stood at the curb and hailed the first taxi they saw. Daniel stood on the street and gave the driver Toby's home address, a pleasant boardinghouse, no more than a couple of miles away.

Toby's family had never had a great deal of money. They had saved, gone without to pay their son's living expenses while at university, which would never have been more than a dream without his scholarship. That had all disappeared now, like a reflection in a puddle when the water is disturbed by footsteps.

Toby climbed awkwardly into the taxi, banging his elbow on the door handle, without seeming to notice it. Daniel followed him, and the instant he settled into the seat the taxi moved off.

Daniel wanted to speak, to give his friend some comfort or reassurance, but he remained silent. Toby didn't need platitudes, and the last thing Daniel wished was to come off as an insensitive intrusion, like mindless chatter at a graveside.

The taxi made its way through a busy intersection. A newsboy stood nearby calling out the headlines. With the windows closed, Daniel could not hear him, but the headlines spoke loudly. It was 1913, and the country was still in the throes of a labor revolt that had begun two years earlier. From the coal miners' strike to repeated walkouts among skilled metalworkers, there had been at least a thousand shutdowns. And now warnings of the East End docks being locked down threatened to bring the country to its knees.

Seeing the boy, the raised paper, brought back the most terrible memory. It was only a year and a half earlier that the indestructible and unsinkable *Titanic* went down, taking more than fifteen hundred people to their grave.

Yet, none of this seemed to matter today, not with the grief awaiting his good friend only a few hours north of London. Another world, it was.

As Daniel thought this, a bright-red Model T Ford pulled up next to them. The driver undoubtedly considered himself fashionable in his pinstripe suit and top hat. Daniel could not see what his passenger, a woman, was wearing, but he guessed she was constricting her waistline with a corset, an article of clothing Miriam believed to be not only unnecessary as a fashion statement, but dangerous. Several times, Daniel and Miriam had been present when a woman suffered a loss of oxygen and fell to her knees. "Oh, she swooned!" said her husband, helping his wife to her feet as if this happened often.

"She didn't swoon," Miriam whispered to Daniel. "She fainted . . . This happens when your diaphragm is so constricted that you cannot breathe!"

The taxi arrived at Toby's house and Daniel asked the driver to wait, promising they would not be more than fifteen minutes.

Daniel followed Toby inside and straight up the stairs to his large bedroom looking onto the back garden. It was the nicest room in the house.

"Pack just what you need," Daniel said at the door to the bedroom. "And a good coat. It will be colder on the coast. I'll go downstairs and find your landlady. What's her name?"

Toby looked at him blankly.

"It would be courteous to address her by name," Daniel prompted.

"Oh, yes, of course. Mrs. Dassam." Toby looked around him, as if seeing this room for the first time. "I'll . . . I'll pack."

Daniel went downstairs and walked toward the back of the house. He hoped Mrs. Dassam was at home. He did not want to write about this in a letter to her.

She was ironing on a board in the kitchen and looked up sharply at the sound of a step unfamiliar to her. "Yes?" she said, her voice cutting. "Ow'd you get in?"

"I am with Mr. Kitteridge, Mrs. Dassam." He did not smile, as he would normally have done. He saw her immediate worry.

"And who are you?" she asked, her face now creased with concern.

"Sorry, I'm Daniel Pitt. I work with Mr. Kitteridge. I'm afraid he received news that is very bad." He told her in the simplest terms what he knew, and saw her face blanch with shock, and then her eyes fill with tears.

"Oh, poor lamb," she said softly. "You're going with him, aren't you?" It was more a demand than a question.

"Yes, Mrs. Dassam. And I'll stay with him as long as I can." He fished in the small breast pocket of his jacket and pulled out a card case. He removed a card and handed it to her. "If you need me, that is my telephone number at the firm. But I will go with Mr. Kitteridge and stay with him. If there—"

There was so much pain etched in her face that he wondered if he should go on speaking. He nearly apologized, but swallowed, took a deep breath, and then released it slowly. "If you need to contact him for any reason, please call the firm and Mr. Impney, our chief clerk, will get in touch with Mr. Kitteridge or with me."

"Thank you, Mister . . ."—she glanced at the card—"Mr. Pitt."

He had not noticed a telephone in the hall, nor was there one here in the kitchen. Would he chance to ask if there was one in the house? He would wait until Toby was ready.

"I'll go upstairs, if I may," he said. "In case he can't gather his wits together to pack. I don't think I could remember much, were I in the same state."

"I know I couldn't, if it were me," she said. "Don't let him worry about anything 'ere. I'll tidy up and keep it all safe."

Daniel understood her desire to help, to do anything she could. "Thank you, Mrs. Dassam, I'm sure it will help greatly that he doesn't have to think about it. I'll tell him."

He moved quickly, leaving the kitchen, going out into the hallway and up the stairs. There were other doors on the landing, but only one of them was open, and he could see Toby standing in the center of the floor, two hangers with shirts on them in one hand, and a casual pair of boots in the other, a contrast to the polished city shoes on his feet.

"Good idea," Daniel said quietly, gesturing toward the boots. "I'd wear those and pack the ones you have on, just in case you need them." He did not say *for your mother's funeral*, but the words hung in the air. "Clean shirt, clean underwear," he went on. He was aware that Toby was looking at him but not really listening.

"Yes," Toby finally said.

Daniel walked over to him and took the shirts out of his hand. He folded them neatly, taking care of the collars. He packed up the other things Toby had laid out, and then checked what was already in the case. "Shaving kit," Daniel told him. "And your hairbrush. Perhaps another shirt, casual, and extra socks. That's about it."

When Toby didn't reply, Daniel gathered those toiletries, chose more clothing, and tucked them all into the case. "I'm sure you can buy whatever more is needed," he said. When Toby said nothing, he added, "I still have to pack as well. And telephone Miriam to let her know that I won't be home for a little while." There was no need to say all the words. It was understood.

The taxi dropped them at the house where Daniel and Miriam had lived since their marriage. And like their marriage, their house still seemed as exciting and new as it was in the beginning, and yet as familiar as if, in some part of him, it had always been theirs.

Daniel paid the driver and thanked him. As the taxi drove away, he guided Toby, carrying his case as if his friend had forgotten what it was, up to the front door. He opened it and entered, with Toby following him mindlessly, automatically.

Inside, Daniel turned and faced him. Toby looked like a lost child, not knowing what to do next, struggling with a profound grief that was working its way through every part of his body.

The tidy kitchen with its dining table, a vase of flowers sitting on it, the range of pots and pans on the shelves beyond the cooking stove, had such meaning for Daniel. They had a maid, so the house was always clean and orderly. Miriam worked as hard at her profession as Daniel did at his. And as Toby did, for that matter.

"Perhaps we should eat something, and have a cup of tea," Daniel suggested.

Toby shook his head, almost as if the words had no meaning.

"You'll need your strength," Daniel said. "You need to be alert, Toby. You must eat something. I don't know the area; I'll need you to guide me."

Toby nodded.

"Fine," Daniel said. "Then I'll put the kettle on and pack." He put the action to the words, leaving Toby sitting very still at the table by the window.

Daniel walked up the stairs to the furthest bedroom. He looked at the bed; it was so comfortable. He closed his eyes a moment and saw Miriam's red hair spread across the pillow, and then shook away the distraction and put into his case clean underwear, socks, two shirts, a warm sweater, and an extra pair of trousers. Then he collected his toothbrush, shaving kit, and hairbrushes, put them into his case, and closed it. As an afterthought, he opened it again and put in a pair of more casual and comfortable shoes. There were no items appropriate for a funeral; there would be time to collect them later.

Downstairs, in the hallway, he lifted the telephone from its cradle. When the operator answered and requested the number, he gave her the number of the morgue where Miriam worked.

The call was answered by the laboratory assistant.

"Joe? It's Daniel Pitt. I need to speak to Dr. fford Croft. It's pretty urgent; I can't afford to wait."

"You all right, sir?" Joe's anxious voice came across the line.

"I am, but I'm afraid something terrible has happened, and I have to leave London. I don't know how long I'll be gone. Can you bring her to the phone now . . . please?"

"Yes, sir. I'm very sorry, sir."

The line was open, and Daniel heard a murmur of voices, and then Miriam on the other end.

"Daniel? What's happened?"

He did not try to soften the words, or prevaricate in any way. Miriam was as direct as any man. "We just received news that something appalling has happened to Toby's parents." After explaining the news, he heard the intake of breath on the line, but continued. "The police seem to think it was a murder-suicide. His father is not expected to live, but if he does, then there is every possibility that he will be tried for murder. I don't know more than that. Impney came and told me, and I went straight to the Old Bailey where Toby was defending Peter Ward. I told you about that case, I'm sure you remember."

"I do remember," she said, speaking quite clearly, as if she were completely composed, but he knew her well enough to hear the strain in her voice, the suppressed emotion. "Are you taking him there now, to Suffolk?"

"Yes." Inwardly he thanked her for understanding. She was familiar with violent death, but it was only after the event itself that her vivid imagination would fill in the pain and the loss, the confusion Toby must be feeling. "I'll stay as long as I can," he continued. "The judge gave us a week's adjournment."

"Do you think that's enough?" Her voice was filled with doubt.

"No, but it's all we can expect. Someone else will have to take over, maybe Gideon Hunter will return in time to do it himself, we'll see. I'm afraid Peter Ward will feel lost without Toby, but—" He ran out of words to say what he meant. Gideon Hunter, KC, was the finest barrister they had, one of the very best in England, but Toby was the new Head of Chambers since Marcus fford Croft, Miriam's father, had finally retired, before his age, his eccentricities, and his gradual loss of memory led to an embarrassment, a blot on his almost legendary reputation. Toby was not quite used to his new position, and Daniel was aware that he was too modest to see his great value to the firm.

"I'm sorry." He wanted to apologize for leaving her without a proper goodbye.

"You must go," she said. "For a week anyway. You can't let Toby face this alone. What about the rest of the family? Will they look after him?"

"Not from what I've heard," he replied. "They are not close, and nothing is going to heal the shock. His father, as you know, is a local vicar." He paused, needing to keep his voice calm, level. "Miriam, I don't know what really happened, but we have to prepare for accepting the fact that it's a nightmare, whatever transpired. I'm sorry," he repeated. "I'm not sure—"

"Daniel, I understand," she said, interrupting him, her voice soft and insistent. "You don't know yet what happened, or what the situation is, but Toby has to be there, and you must be with him. The only thing that could make it worse is for him to have to go alone."

"I know," he said quickly. "Don't worry, I'll take care."

"Call me when you're there," she said. "And Daniel?"

"Yes?"

"Look after him, and look after yourself, too. Do you want me to tell Father or not?"

Daniel thought of Marcus fford Croft, brilliant, and far more fragile than he looked. "There's nothing he can do. But I'll leave that up to you. Better from you than someone else. I expect Hunter will pick up the case if Toby can't get back in time, which is very likely. Impney will see that Hunter knows all there is to the situation. But I must go now, darling," he said. "I want to get there, or at least most of the way there, while it's still daylight."

Miriam drew in a quick breath, as if to say something, then let it out. "I love you," she said.

"I'm banking on it," he replied with a lightness he did not feel. Then he hung up the telephone and went to share a quick pot of tea and the rest of a ginger cake with Toby, and be on their way.

Daniel drove his own car. It was far from new, but it was still a luxury, a gift from his parents. The one thing they had insisted on was reliability. He felt strongly that Toby did not need the public torment of a crowded train, the anxiety of changing at Ipswich, and then catching a small line north to the village, and then getting a taxi. Or leaving the train at Ipswich and taking a taxi to the hospital. All of this travel would possibly require going to the bank and getting more change than he usually carried. And delays. More delays, if they missed a connection. One thing he could happily offer was for Toby to sit in the passenger seat and allow Daniel to make the decisions. The drive would be around two hours, if all went as planned. It was not until they were on the road north of Ipswich that he would need directions to the hospital. And if the road signs were good enough, not even then.

It was late afternoon, a beautiful October day. As soon as they were out of the city, driving was a pleasure. The countryside opened up to fields, some with stooks of corn still standing, the lowering sun casting long shadows. Copses of trees were turning color into golds and early reds that would deepen in the weeks ahead.

Daniel wanted more than anything to comfort his friend, but every word tumbling through his head felt meaningless. And how not? Whatever happened in his own life, whether he sought the shelter of his family or forgiveness for his faults, there was always the presence of love, the protection of his parents. There were shadows now and then, of course there were. He remembered being younger and hungry for independence, occasionally resentful of things so trivial he could not name them now. He had even been afraid, particularly on those two occasions when his mother had been kidnapped and his wife taken hostage. But they were both safe now, so he could not say to Toby that he understood what he was going through. Words of misunderstanding, no matter how well meant, could only be upsetting, making Toby feel even more desolate and isolated.

They drove in silence through the golden light of the lowering sun. They nearly stopped near Chelmsford for a short break and a light meal, but it was late dusk and Toby asked that they continue.

As they reached the outskirts of Ipswich, Daniel was about to ask Toby for directions. However, before he could speak, Toby guided him to the hospital.

They pulled up in front of the old building, small and plain by London standards.

Daniel inquired at Reception and they were directed to follow the nearby hallway to where it ended at a locked door.

"The Security ward," the man at the desk explained.

Daniel and Toby exchanged glances. Was Reverend Kitteridge there to protect the world from him, or to protect him from himself?

Daniel knocked at the door.

A man opened it. "Patient's name," he demanded.

Toby stepped forward and identified himself.

The man nodded and held the door wide open. "Family only," he said, blocking Daniel's way. "Take a seat in Reception and your friend will meet you there."

Daniel nearly argued, but Toby gave him a quick nod and stepped through the door, which closed firmly behind him.

It was nearly an hour before Toby reappeared, his face reflecting deep sorrow.

Daniel stood, but said nothing. Toby would speak when he was ready.

As they headed toward the exit, Toby said, "The doctor wasn't there; he will be later. We need to go to the police station."

Daniel drew in a breath to ask if Toby would not prefer to see his sister first, then looked at his friend's face, the rigid set of it, barely in control, and changed his mind. Toby was in a world of pain to which no one else, even those with all the wishes in the world to be of help, could enter, never mind understand.

In the car, Toby directed Daniel to the station. Daniel parked, but Toby spoke before he could leave the car.

"The police seem convinced that my father killed my mother

and then tried to kill himself." He stopped, as if gathering his thoughts and controlling his emotions.

Daniel waited, understanding that his friend was grappling with fear, grief, anger, all thrown together into a terrible confusion.

"Father's injuries are serious," Toby went on, "but the doctor feels that he might survive. Still, the bullet penetrated his skull and caused considerable bleeding. We're hoping that his brain might not be permanently damaged. The only blessing seems to be that Mother died instantly."

They walked into the police station. There was a sergeant at the desk who recognized Toby. He rose to his feet and came forward, his face filled with distress.

"Mr. Kitteridge, I'm . . . I'm so sorry." He turned to Daniel, requesting proof of his identity. "Sorry, sir, but I'm required to ask."

"Daniel Pitt. Mr. Kitteridge and I have been friends for years; we also work together."

The sergeant glanced at Toby, saw anguish in his face, and turned back to Daniel. "Good. There'll be room for both of you at one of the guesthouses, Mrs. Prestor's. Just around the corner. It's late in the season; she's got no one else at the moment."

Toby looked confused.

"Your parents' home is a crime scene," the sergeant explained.

"Thank you," Daniel said quickly. "That's very good of you. May we see whoever is in charge of—" He did not know how to phrase it without it sounding brutal.

"Yes, sir, if you'll come with me."

They followed him out of the public part of the station and into a private office, where the lights were already on and a middle-aged man with a thin, ascetic face was sitting behind a large, almost empty desk. He looked up as they came in.

"Mr. Kitteridge and Mr. Pitt," said the desk sergeant.

The man rose quickly to his feet. "Inspector Ridgeway," he said, extending a hand to both men.

After they were all introduced and sympathies expressed, the sergeant left and Toby and Daniel sat down.

"I'm sorry, sir," Ridgeway said quietly. "I'm not really local, so I didn't know your parents, but the village is stunned. Everyone speaks well of them both. We have to investigate this tragedy, you understand? We cannot simply assume—"

"I know that!" Toby said abruptly. "It doesn't make any sense! It can't be . . . I mean, there must be some . . ." His voice trailed off.

Daniel looked at his friend, saw how his shoulders were hunched and his body appeared stiff, as if every muscle in his chest seemed so tight that it took an effort to breathe. He wondered if he should step in and manage this meeting for Toby. Would that help, or would it annoy him? He didn't want Toby to feel closed out of this investigation, of the one thing he could do to feel as if he were in control, at least of himself, his voice, his mind.

"We are looking into it very carefully," Ridgeway told Toby. "So far, we know only the most obvious facts. I'm sure the doctor will speak to you, if you ask. You don't need to see their bodies. That is, unless you want to. Your brother-in-law, Mr. Esmond Walsh, identified them."

A jolt ran through Daniel. Was he saying that both of Toby's parents were dead? Before he could ask, Toby spoke.

"Both? Has my father died? But . . . I just saw him and he was very much alive . . . and now he's dead?"

Ridgeway shook his head dramatically. "No! Forgive me! I meant that he identified your parents. Your father is still alive. And for this we're all grateful." Ridgeway's voice was rough, as if fighting to control his emotions. "They thought he might be placed in the local nursing home for treatment and observation, but then it was realized that his injury was more severe than first assumed and that the nursing home was unable to treat such a serious case. I'm sure they've told you—that is, no one can say whether there is any hope of his surviving, or what one may reasonably hope. His injuries are very bad."

Daniel thought he was withholding the words that hung in the air: *It might be more merciful if he had died.*

Silence filled the room, as if grief had sucked the air out of it.

Somewhere outside, a dog barked.

Daniel was compelled to speak. "If Mr. Kitteridge wishes to see his mother, where is she?" It was an awful question, but Toby had the right to choose whether to see her or not. Some people feel it is an opportunity to say goodbye, while others prefer to remember them as they were. He looked at Toby for some sign of his thoughts, but his friend looked stunned.

Daniel decided for him. "Not this evening anyway. Thank you. I know it's getting late, and Mr. Kitteridge had a long and difficult day in the Old Bailey before the news came through. And we have been in the car for more than three hours. Nobody is hungry, but we need to eat."

Toby turned toward him and started to say something, then stopped.

Daniel wasn't sure if he had changed his mind, or perhaps had forgotten what it was he was going to say.

"Of course," Ridgeway agreed. "I suggest you go to your lodgings and have something to eat before you sleep. And if you feel compelled to see your father during the night, I'll be sure they let you in, regardless of the time. In these circumstances, I—" He stopped, as though at a loss for words.

"As long as I can continue to see my father," Toby said. "I must—"

Daniel took Toby's arm and felt the muscle tighten under his hand.

"We'll take a break first." Daniel paused. "We'll get settled and then we'll see." He met Ridgeway's eyes and saw the pity in them.

There was no need to explain. It was going to be a long, restless night, and waking in the morning would bring no relief.

═══

During the short drive to their rooms, Toby wondered aloud why they were not staying in his family home. Daniel struggled with the words to explain, but then Toby said, "I know, yes. It's a . . . crime scene."

Nothing more was said.

Mrs. Prestor turned out to be a large, comfortable woman who took pleasure in making other people feel at home in her house. The lines in her face suggested a smiling personality, but this evening she was tearstained and keeping her composure, presumably for the sake of her two guests. She was probably of an age to be mother to both Toby and Daniel, and she seemed to take to them instantly. They arrived to find that she had prepared a hot, thick vegetable soup, and she did not bother to ask if they wanted some or not.

As if in a dream, they accepted and ate absentmindedly. It was only when buttering a thick slice of bread and spreading homemade plum jam on it that Daniel realized how hungry he had been.

Whether he was enjoying it or not, Toby also ate. He flashed Daniel a rueful smile, a silent thanks.

Daniel wanted to acknowledge it, but Toby instantly looked away. Perhaps speaking even one word would break this hard-won calm.

They were sitting in Mrs. Prestor's front room, Daniel wondering if it was wise to do anything more today, let alone make the drive to the hospital and back, when there were voices in the hallway. It was a man and woman, voices raised, choked with emotion.

Toby stiffened and turned in his chair.

The sitting room door flew open and a woman strode in. She was taller than average, thin to the point of gauntness, but also oddly elegant. She moved with an old grace, not as a dancer might move, more like an athlete. Her hair was carefully styled, flattering her face. It was shining brown, with a heavy natural-looking wave, and it softened her rather angular face. She looked so like Toby that she had to be his sister. Her features and coloring were like his, but she had none of the awkwardness that he had. And her clothes looked as if they had been made especially for her. It occurred to Daniel that perhaps they had been. They were quite original. In his eyes, she appeared to be a leader, never a follower. Toby was in his mid-thirties, several years older than Daniel, and he knew that Alberta Walsh was two years younger than Toby. At perhaps thirty-two, there was already a hardness to her mouth.

"Well, at least you came," she said to Toby. "Not that there's anything you can do now!"

There was a moment of stunned silence, then Daniel stood and strode forward, holding out his hand. "How do you do, Mrs. Walsh, I'm Daniel Pitt. I work in the same law firm as Toby, and I drove him here to be sure he arrived safely."

"Kind of you," she replied, taking his hand in a gesture so brief he barely felt it before she let go. "I suppose you will go back tomorrow morning. You have no interest in this tragedy."

"I didn't come out of *interest*, Mrs. Walsh. I came as Toby's friend and to do whatever he wishes me to. I expect there will be several duties he will have to perform."

Her expression was one of skepticism. "A little late, aren't you? The people here will do all that is necessary. Toby left years ago to pursue his career away from us, from the village, the family."

Daniel looked at the bitterness in her face, the grief turned temporarily into anger. "I doubt you have need of a lawyer of Toby's quality in a village of this size," he said, trying to keep his voice gentle.

"Not as you have in London, thanks be to the Lord," she replied. Then she turned to her brother, as if she had finished with Daniel. "Of course, you are the executor of the will," she said. "You being the lawyer, and the son, even though you knew nothing of his work, their friends."

The man behind her moved forward and stepped beside her. He was not more than an inch or so taller than she, but far more solid. He had a wide face, his fair hair was receding slightly, and he had blue eyes, bright and clear, remarkable in an otherwise forgettable appearance. He held out his hand. "Esmond Walsh."

Daniel took it. "How do you do. Daniel Pitt. Whatever I can do in this tragic situation, I'm here."

Esmond's face filled with relief. "Good of you. Are you a lawyer, too?"

"We don't need more lawyers!" Alberta snapped. "What we need is arrests!" She shot a look of blame at Toby.

"Ross is taking care of all services and other immediate needs," Esmond said gently. "He really is very good," he added, looking at Toby.

"Ross . . ." Toby seemed confused.

"For heaven's sake, Father's curate," she explained. "Of course, he's competent, but he can't do everything!"

"Nobody expects him to do everything, dear," said her husband. "Just the immediate things, until the bishop sends someone else. Be reasonable. Toby's just as bereaved as you are."

"We don't need a lawyer," she repeated, looking at Daniel. "And we certainly don't need two!"

"You haven't got two!" Daniel snapped back. "Toby's here because he's lost his mother, just as you have. I'm here because I'm his friend, and it looks as if he could jolly well use one! Doesn't seem as if you are going to fill that space!"

She blanched and drew in her breath sharply.

He continued without giving her a chance to respond. "And if what you have said so far is accurate, you may well be glad of a lawyer before this is all settled." He had torn the bandages off. Should he leave?

"What the devil," Esmond began.

"And what is it you imagine you can do?" Alberta demanded.

"Do you understand what happened, and why?" He wasn't at all sure if it was a question he should ask her, and it was possibly badly timed. But she had asked. "Do you know your father well? Were you close to him?"

"Of course I was! I was *here*! Not off in London chasing money and fame!" Her voice was wobbly and she struggled to hang on to anger when grief threatened to drown her.

"Do you know why this happened?" he asked more gently.

She gulped. "No, of course not. Don't you think if I saw this coming, I would have done something to stop it?" She made a gasping sound for breath.

Esmond put out his hand to touch her, and then pulled it back, as if consoling her would not help.

Daniel watched this, saw how intrusive any gesture of kindness would be. In truth, he could not remember Toby ever having mentioned Alberta, other than in a passing reference to having a sister. But then, he could not recall ever having told Toby much about his own elder sister, Jemima, married to an Irish American policeman and now living in Washington, D.C. If this were Jemima, what would he do? Best to leave old quarrels forgotten, at least for now.

"Perhaps we could discuss the reason for it?" Daniel suggested, his tone no longer angry. "None of you who knows him can understand it. Maybe there is something we've been aware of, and can perhaps try to make sense of."

Alberta stared at him. "Like what? What on earth could make a sane man suddenly—" If she knew what she had meant to say, she could not say it. At least, not aloud.

"What happened yesterday afternoon?" Daniel asked.

Alberta looked at her husband, her eyes pleading for his help.

Esmond nodded, a silent gesture that he would handle this. "Apparently, the vicar spent at least a couple of hours showing some tourists around the old church building. He told them stories about the former church at Dunwich, right on the coast, a church and a community lost to ravages of the sea. They say if the wind is right, and the tide, you can hear the bells ringing. It's rubbish, of course, but it spins a good yarn."

"Has anyone spoken to those tourists?" Daniel asked, wishing Esmond to get to the point of all this.

"Not that I know of. There was no one else in the house," Alberta replied. "No one but Mother and Father." She shook her head. "There's no point in trying to blame someone else. They were strangers passing through. Father often used to talk to people, he liked all sorts, and he was so trusting."

"He thought people were better than they were," Esmond added. "But why would a complete stranger do this appalling thing? Are you suggesting that some tourist, after getting your father to show him around the ruins of the old church, followed him home, shot him, and killed his wife? Nobody's going to believe that, much as we would like to. By the way, as far as I can tell, nothing valuable was stolen. And there were valuables there, around the house. Besides, several people saw him, this tourist, including my wife, and they say he was older. Dark hair, streaked with gray, very well dressed."

"Who just happened to be carrying a gun?" Daniel asked.

"No," Esmond said quietly, looking down and away from them. "It is Justin's gun."

Toby spoke for the first time. "He had a gun? Why? How do you know? I didn't know." He said it sharply, as if it offered some kind of hope.

"It's very old," Alberta said. "I don't know where it came from."

"Army days," Esmond offered.

Toby started to respond, but his sister cut him off.

"He hardly spoke about it, but we know he served in the army, in Africa somewhere. It was years ago. A long time. When he was a young man. He rarely mentioned it. He hated violence."

"I wonder why he kept it," Toby said.

"I don't know!" Alberta snapped. "Perhaps if you'd been here, you would have asked him! Leave this alone, will you? Isn't this bad enough?"

"You're sure he didn't know this man?" Daniel asked, ignoring her. "Could it be an old quarrel reignited? Not your father's fault, but something that got out of hand?"

"They were strangers," Alberta put in. "Don't you listen? I saw a man that day, a tourist, and I'd never seen him before. Neither had Father."

Esmond stared at her. "Are you sure?"

"Yes, because he didn't know his name to introduce him. You know Father, he was being friendly. He loves showing people the old ruins. Raked up all the Invasion Coast stories, from the Romans to the Vikings, and the Spanish Armada."

"They never invaded," Toby pointed out.

"Of course they didn't, because the storms drowned most of them. What has this to do with anything?" she demanded.

"Just that he wouldn't get it wrong," Toby said hastily. "He loved the history of the coast. It was as if it was all still alive to him, still relevant."

"So it is," Alberta said quickly. "It's who we are, but—"

"It's relevant now," Esmond interrupted. "Obviously, he had a breakdown of some sort. Something broke inside him. We have to face it, he did it himself. I've seen him get annoyed, even refuse to discuss a subject, but never lash out in anger, even in words, never mind actions. He'd just go silent."

"It must have been more than that," Daniel pointed out. "He went and retrieved his gun—where did he keep it?" He looked from one to the other of them, puzzled. "Surely, not in the open where anyone could find it? And would they even know to look? Who is he expecting to attack him? That doesn't make any sense."

"Of course it doesn't," Alberta snapped. "He's a vicar, for heaven's sake! Why on earth would he walk around with a loaded gun?" She was standing stiff-backed, as if to brace herself from falling, and her hands were clenched, clearly using every ounce of her strength to stop herself from accepting any of this.

Daniel could understand. He felt he would do the same if someone had said it about his father. But his brain had to believe that someone had shot Delia to her death, and then shot Justin. And not to death, but missing only by a fraction of an inch. He turned to

Toby, who was sitting awkwardly on one of the kitchen chairs, as if he knew his legs could not hold him. "Do you want to go back and see him again? He may not know you are there, but you will know that you were by his side." Even as he said it, it did not sound sensible, but sense was not the point now. Daniel wanted to help ease Toby's mind by doing all he could.

Toby hauled himself to his feet, using the back of another chair to bolster himself. "Yes, please. Can you drive? I don't think I'm steady enough."

"Yes, of course I'll drive," Daniel replied. He did not ask Alberta or Esmond if they wanted to come. It was not an option. He apologized to Mrs. Prestor for the inconvenience, and she brushed it aside and gave Daniel a key to the front door. He thanked her and put the key in his pocket, then took Toby by the arm and went out to the car.

THEY DROVE IN near silence for miles in the dark, past assorted traffic to the hospital. There was nothing to hold on to. Perhaps hope, and all the hopeful words that had been uttered.

Daniel needed all his concentration to keep the car steady on the road. It was hard to believe that only a matter of hours ago Toby had been in court trying to defend a difficult, maybe impossible case, and that all was well with his world. It seemed as if his family had always been safe, secure in their beliefs, their life's work, and that they were a known quantity, not prone to drama or making unreasonable demands on their son. Was it possible that violent passions lay so well concealed, just below the surface, that no one had any idea about, or even guessed at, their existence?

Daniel glanced at Toby's face in the glow from the headlights of the oncoming car, then he wished he had not. Without meaning to, he had intruded on a moment of naked grief, filled with confusion, like that of a little child. Perhaps Daniel would feel the same if the very foundation of his life suddenly shattered, leaving only the broken pieces, sharp edges cutting. And all made even more painful if his sister turned on him with vitriol, every word dripping with contempt.

Certainly, they had had their moments, Daniel and Jemima, and it wasn't until he was out of Cambridge and quite established in chambers before he began to understand her anger. But only recently, during her visit to London, was Jemima able to talk about it, acknowledging that while it had been her choice to marry and move to the States, the distance had created in her a sense of isolation from her family. There were times when this was expressed as resentment, particularly toward her brother for living in London and spending so much time with their parents. As much as that conversation had softened the hard edge between them, they both now understood that it could never be fully resolved, not with Jemima living thousands of miles away.

He thought for an instant whether Toby would rather see his father alone again, then dismissed it. He shouldn't leave him that choice. He climbed out and waited as Toby got out, getting his balance as he stood up.

"Come on," Daniel said quietly, and started to walk toward the lighted doorway—slowly, so Toby didn't have to catch up with him.

Despite the very late hour, they had not many minutes to wait before a doctor came into the waiting area to speak with them. Daniel was surprised to find him on duty, and then realized that a larger hospital might have sleeping quarters for overnight staff.

He introduced himself and then Toby.

At first glance, Dr. Vidams was what one might call nondescript: medium height, medium build, neither handsome nor plain. But when he turned toward the light, everything seemed to change. His eyes were nearly black, yet kindness shone through them, and he had a gentle face. "I am sorry, Mr. Kitteridge, but your father has not regained consciousness. It is still possible that he may. With this kind of injury, any degree of recovery is possible, but we have to prepare you for the worst. It was just a single shot, but he lost quite a lot of blood, and scalp injuries tend to bleed quite badly."

"I saw him earlier. May I . . . may I see him again?" Toby kept his voice steady with obvious difficulty.

"Of course." The doctor held out his hand, as if to guide Toby in the right direction. Then he glanced at Daniel.

"Would you prefer to be alone?" Daniel asked Toby.

Toby appeared to be confused. "What?"

Daniel glanced at Dr. Vidams, who nodded with so slight a movement of the head that Daniel hesitated. Then the doctor walked forward along the corridor, leaving Daniel and Toby to follow.

The place had an antiseptic smell, but it was at least warm, and at this time of the evening it was almost silent. Daniel could hear only the slight shuffling of their own footsteps.

They passed a nurse in a stiff white uniform, skirt just above her ankles. She acknowledged the doctor but not Toby, suggesting that she was not the same nurse who had spoken to Toby earlier.

They reached the door to Justin Kitteridge's room. It was closed, but not locked. The nurse inside rose to her feet from her chair near the foot of the bed.

"No change," she said to the doctor, barely glancing at Toby or Daniel.

"Thank you," Dr. Vidams acknowledged, then he turned to look intently at the man who lay there, his head swathed in bandages, with a thicker bandage over one eye. The rest of him seemed to be completely unharmed, but he was so pale he looked bloodless. The doctor placed a hand on his shoulder, as if to give comfort, despite Justin's unconscious state.

The thought forced itself into Daniel's mind that they were too late: he was already dead. And then he wondered, too late for what? It was obvious there was nothing they could do that would affect him. They could neither hinder nor help. He was alone with his pain, or his guilt. At this moment, there were no answers to be found.

Daniel stared at Justin Kitteridge, as if the man's blank expression could tell him something. The only thing it made plain was his identity. From what Daniel could see of the vicar's face, he looked like a picture of Toby, only older, grayer. His jaw was like Toby's, the same angular shape, but the stubble, like the hair on his head, was also gray. His hand lying on top of the sheet was exactly like Toby's: big, slender fingers and knuckles that were too large for elegance, even when the hand was at rest. The nails were clipped, the skin smooth.

For God's sake, what had happened to him?

Without thinking, Daniel turned to Toby and saw tears wet on his cheeks, and turned away again. He wouldn't intrude, but must find the truth, though when he did, he would have to think hard whom he told, if anyone at all.

He touched Toby's arm and then followed the doctor into the corridor, leaving Toby alone with his father. As much as he wanted to be there for his friend, he was painfully aware that Toby's grief was private.

CHAPTER

Three

MIRIAM WAS BUSY working in the morgue, catching up with notes on the autopsy she had just finished on an elderly man who had died unexpectedly. Her tests proved that his heart had been in a worse condition than his doctor had suggested. Death of someone who was loved was always a blow, but this one at least had been sudden, and the man's pain short-lived.

She put the pen down and looked across the benches and sinks of the clean, spacious morgue, to where Evelyn Hall was filling half-empty containers and making sure everything was in its correct place, labels showing. Eve, as those close to her called her, was stocky, of average height, yet she was far from average once one noticed the air of certainty about her, the vivid concentration that hinted at the extraordinary mind within; the furious dedication. She was not particularly pretty. In fact, considering her short, curly hair that seldom looked as if it had been brushed, never mind styled, and her shapeless clothes, she could as easily have been mistaken for an aging man. In her world of science and research, she was considered a woman of great skill and dedication, a student of matters of the mind, a professional who gave total dedication not only to the science of pathology, but to the art of it as well. She was the first, and as yet only, woman to be at the top of her field, respected by all—and, one might add, feared by them.

Then the attack had happened. Miriam would never forget, not only because it was recent, but because it was so brutal. A man crazed by imagined threats to his life had broken into the morgue, flung Eve against the wall, knocking her senseless, and kidnapped Miriam, who was freed in a drama worthy of one of those adventure movies that were beginning to appear in London cinemas. It had been a seemingly endless time in hospital before Eve had even regained consciousness, and longer still before she had regained her mind and her memory. Miriam was not sure if Eve now realized she sometimes suffered moments of absentmindedness, or whether she thought that, because these lapses were only two or three seconds in duration, such as anyone might have, they were normal.

Miriam had wanted desperately to believe that the injury to Eve's brain was minimal, but these episodes had become more frequent and their intervals shorter. It pained her to admit that she needed to watch for them, as discreetly as possible. What was far more difficult was Miriam's belief that she had to check Eve's work. Even thinking this, letting the idea cross her mind, was painful.

At this moment, Eve was not engaged in complicated, scientific work, which proved frustrating to her and, in Miriam's judgment, humiliating. At least Eve seemed to understand the necessity of removing herself from analytic work that required intensive thought and complete comprehension. Her emotions seemed to be assuaged by Miriam's promise that, although it would take time, she would be back to her old self soon.

Before they met, Miriam had only ever worked with a teacher who was also a mentor, and a personal friend of her father. He was a skilled man, a scientist who believed in Miriam absolutely, but was not in a position, whether academically or in research, to help her. Then she met Eve, called in as an irrefutable forensic expert and scientist, who was working in a field reserved for men, yet was prepared to hold her own among them; a woman who pulled magic out of what seemed to be the most unlikely sources, while producing new evidence, much of it either unknown to other scientists or misinterpreted. She was like a force of nature, hurtling over old beliefs and revealing new and difficult conclusions. She fascinated everyone with her ability to take the most advanced scientific theories and explain them to jurors, prosecutors, and defenders, even the police. They saw her as different, certainly unique. They were not only used to such people being men—old and young, handsome and polished, plain and awkward—but unequivocally masculine. Of course, she did not always convince a jury: there were many jurors who were suspicious of any scientific answers they could not understand, which inevitably was the majority of them. And if these scientific answers were delivered by a woman? Suspicion often quickly turned to distrust.

If Eve ever doubted herself, she was faultless at hiding it. No lawyer, however learned or clever, made her contradict herself. And she never lost her temper, except when lawyers made little of someone's pain or indignity—when they spoke of a dead human body as if it had never been alive, passionate, excited about life, or capable of pain or fear.

Miriam smiled now as she remembered Eve listening to a police officer who was in the witness box and describing the body of a dead woman with disrespect. She had used no harsh words when she later confronted the man, but the contempt on her face, in her voice, had driven him to apologize. Eve later explained to Miriam that nothing was more important to her, as a pathologist and as a human being, than showing respect for the dignity of a person, any person, alive or dead. Laid out in the pathology lab, they could not protect even the most private part of themselves on full view. And to have someone, no matter in the lab or in the witness box, speak of them as a piece of meat, this was unforgivable. "We are all vulnerable," she told Miriam. "And it is our responsibility that privacy and dignity follow these people long after their death."

Please heaven that she herself would never become so used to bodies that she would lose that same desire to protect! There was no doubt that this desire extended to her need to protect Eve's dignity, should her problems increase. Miriam had seen the momentary confusion in Eve's eyes when this brilliant scientist had felt the need to repeat a test she had run after an unforeseen result. A few days earlier, when Eve had left for home, Miriam had doubled back to check her mentor's work. It had been accurate, which made her ashamed that she had felt the need to check it at all. Eve was not lacking in mental acuity. It was simply a matter of age. Certainly, no one could expect a woman thirty years Miriam's senior to show the same vigor!

Miriam reminded herself that there were tests she wanted to run on Alexandra Stanton. They had the results of other tests, already done by another lab, after they had been requested mid-trial by Toby Kitteridge. That is, before this tragedy required that he leave London and tend to his family in Suffolk. Daniel had told her how Toby was convinced of Peter Ward's innocence, and nearly frantic to uncover forensic proof of it. But now Daniel was suggesting—and Miriam concurred—that if proof could be gleaned from a further examination of the forensic evidence found at the scene of Stanton's death, it would clear the young man of guilt and allow him a long, normal life.

Miriam understood that one error, one oversight, no matter how seemingly insignificant, could send Peter Ward to the gallows.

"What is it?" Eve's voice cut across Miriam's thoughts.

Surprised, she answered. "What makes you ask?"

"Evasiveness," Eve said tartly. "Answering a question with another question. That's not the way you usually behave. So, what is it?" This was said with a sharp-edged voice, more as a demand than a question.

Miriam heard fear. "It's Toby," she said. "Daniel has driven him to Suffolk because something terrible has happened."

"You see?" Eve said. "That's what I mean: evasive." She drew breath, as if needing to take control of this conversation, and then said, with all the old curiosity Miriam was accustomed to hearing, "So, again I ask: What is it?"

Miriam leaned against the bench, taking a moment to collect her thoughts. "Eve, there's been a tragedy. Toby's mother is dead and his father is badly injured." She saw Eve's face shift from wariness to surprise . . . and then something that Miriam interpreted as purpose. "The police are saying it was a murder and an attempted suicide." She stared at Eve and it struck her that, in this moment, their roles were reversed from the way they had recently become. Eve was the strong one, and Miriam the one needing help.

"Poor man," Eve said quietly. "If it is true, he must have had a medical event of some kind. A stroke or an aneurism in the brain can do that. But are the police necessarily right? That is, that he killed his wife and then tried to kill himself? There could be indications, but not proof."

"Daniel is with Toby now, and knowing him, I'm sure he's looking for proof." She paused for a moment. "I can't even begin to imagine the grief of it."

"It wouldn't help if you could," Eve said quickly. "If he dies, poor man, make sure there is a proper autopsy, into the skull. It won't help him, but it will help the family—Toby, and whoever else is left—if it proves he was not responsible. In fact, that is about all we can do to help now."

Of course it was. Why had she not thought of it immediately? "I will, Eve. I expect Daniel will call soon."

"Then you had better join him now, be close by and ready to act, and not here, where you can only wait," she said firmly. "If there's anything you can do to help, Joe and I can manage here. There probably won't be anything urgent. And if there is a sudden rush of bodies, a train accident, or whatever, we'll call the Suffolk police and ask for our pathologist back."

Miriam smiled in spite of herself. Then suddenly her throat tightened. Before, she had only performed autopsies on strangers. What if she was called on by Toby to perform one on his mother? She pushed that thought away. The Alexandra Stanton case had to remain in the forefront.

Eve was staring at her and her gaze was growing shadowed, uneasy.

"If it comes to the point where I can be of any help, then I will go to Suffolk," Miriam answered. Was that the truth? "But I don't need to without a reason. I wouldn't like it if another pathologist came into one of my cases when there was no apparent need. It suggests I don't know what I'm doing!"

Eve continued to stare, the look both long and steady.

Miriam felt uneasy, but remained silent.

"You're right," Eve conceded finally. "And perhaps whoever is there is capable, but this is a terrible tragedy. Maybe their pathologist will find only what he expects to find, and then looks no further. But they're in a village in Suffolk, yes?"

"It's not far from a bigger town, and within an hour or so from Ipswich, so I'm sure there are trained scientists. I'm also confident that—"

"We know what they can do," Eve finished for her. "But Ipswich is a rather provincial city, not known for violence, let alone a possible double murder."

Miriam felt as if a vise were tightening around her chest, and it might stop her from breathing. She inhaled deeply, then released the breath slowly. "It's too early to know. They will hardly be there yet, and there will be so much to do. Toby has a sister, although I gather they are not close. I've been told that his family was proud of him, but they also resented his leaving them and coming to London. And according to—"

"Families always resent the one that's different," Eve said, as if Miriam had not spoken. "You know about the peculiar chicken?"

Miriam was lost. "I've no idea what . . ." Her voice trailed off in confusion.

"Didn't look like the others. Had to stand in the yard and stare up at the air. Annoyed to be left out, so different from the others. Joined a new family, too."

Miriam ran her hand across her eyes. "Eve, what are you talking about?"

Eve gave her a little smile. "And then one day, instead of scratching around the yard, it took flight, soaring straight up into the sky, and into the sun."

"What?"

"Miriam, it wasn't a chicken at all," she said. "It was an eagle!"

Miriam sank into the chair next to the table and put her head in her hands. That so perfectly described Toby, like some awkward chicken, his arms and legs too long, untidy, unlike the rest of the young men in chambers. The analogy worked only in that one respect, but it helped Miriam to let go, to both laugh and cry.

She felt Eve's hand on her shoulder, gently.

"Miriam, my dear, you are so clever with the dead, it's time you learned to see the living a little more clearly. Go and help Toby and Daniel, if there's anything you can do. Before it's too late."

"I will, yes, when I've tidied up here." She looked at Eve with gratitude in her expression. "I've a few more notes to finish up. If I don't go over them now, I'll not be able to read them tomorrow. They were pretty scribbled. I might be late, so I'll leave it to you to open up in the morning. I hope that's all right with you?"

Eve hesitated only a moment. "Right," she said and gave a slight smile, which added warmth to her face.

"Thank you."

Eve returned to her reports and left Miriam to her work.

Minutes before Eve left the lab, she did something she had never done. She walked over to where Miriam was examining something under the microscope and hugged her. And then she whispered, "Don't worry, please."

Miriam held on to Eve, not sure if she meant not to worry about Toby's situation, or about the possibility of Eve botching the examination of an important piece of forensic material.

AFTER EVE LEFT the lab, Miriam set about tidying up the few odd dishes that needed cleaning and putting away. There was not much else to do, apart from checking all the paperwork and seeing that it went into the correct file. This particular grouping related to the earlier reports regarding Alexandra Stanton.

Miriam was reviewing the fifth page of Eve's notes on an autopsy she had recently performed, when she realized that she had no understanding of what Eve had written. Had she been so stricken this day by Toby's tragedy and, by extension, Daniel's grief as well, that she had written the wrong conclusion? Perhaps Eve had misplaced a page. Or had she lost her concentration?

Miriam went back to the beginning and reread the report.

To anyone not trained in medicine, chemistry, or any allied science, it made sense, but the conclusions were off. Or were they? Miriam was upset and distracted when she thought of what could have happened to the Kitteridge family, so perhaps Eve felt this as well.

Toby had described his mother as a woman private enough to let only a few people know how perceptive she was. He thought she was beautiful. But surely to any happy child, their mother was beautiful? Beauty was more honestly seen in gentleness, grace in the soft touch of a hand, a smile. Love itself transfigured everyone. We choose to remember that which tells us we are safe, that gives us joy.

Still holding Eve's report, Miriam's mind continued its focus on what could possibly have happened to Justin Kitteridge. Some form of madness heretofore unseen?

Miriam had never met him, but she visualized him looking very much like Toby, but without his flaming red hair. She imagined that Justin's was white now. Whatever his appearance, these allegations would make it impossible for him to mourn the death of his wife, much less keep the memory of her close throughout his remaining years. Whether Toby's father was guilty or innocent, Miriam was confident someone loved is never forgotten, whatever the cause of death.

She read the pages yet again, and this time she saw the error that made a nonsense of Eve's conclusion, but only to someone trained in pathology. It was as if Eve had begun with one set of facts relating to this case, and then halfway through had switched to a different case, making her conclusion irrelevant, worthless. Or, as Eve would be the first to say, rubbish.

Miriam passed her hand across her eyes and reminded herself that she might be in need of eyeglasses. She was more than a decade older than Daniel, which placed her as middle-aged . . . which was far from old!

Before judging Eve, she gave the report another careful read and was soon quite sure that pages from one case were mixed in with pages of the second. It would be easy enough to do, for anyone who had put in the many hours Eve had and was overcome by fatigue. At the end of a long day, Miriam paid special attention to her own work, knowing that a moment's lapse of concentration could mar the results of a test. Nevertheless, confusing two cases? This was an error that could not be excused. It could lead to an innocent person whose guilt was in question spending life in prison. Or . . . being hanged.

But what if this kind of error happened the other way around? What if a guilty man had been freed? And then his guilt was later proven? Could they try him again? The words of witnesses, and even more important the testimony of experts in science, were all that lay between a verdict of guilty or innocent. One error could send an innocent man to prison, or a guilty man home to his family.

Whatever the cost, no error could be allowed to stand as the deciding factor in any trial, whether for petty theft or murder. This was a common fear among pathologists, that an error went unidentified and resulted in a false conviction. And women in her field? Their skills were sometimes ignored, even mocked. At the same time, Miriam was beset by her responsibilities. Not only to her profession, but to all those women scientists whose careers would be adversely affected by one of their own accused of being lax, or of some lapse of precision or judgment with terrible consequences. It would not only set every woman's progress back, it would be as if the race had never been run. Any women aspiring to positions of skill and trust, and to the power, the respect that went with such a position, would be afraid. And the woman who had erred? Her name would become a byword for incompetence and tragedy, and not for everything that had come before, when she had broken into a man's world and had defeated many of them at their own skill, but for her actions now. There would be no mercy for her in the future as well.

What would Miriam want, if it were her own legacy in question? She and Eve were as unalike as two women could be, and in a dozen different ways, but when it came to professional skills, dedication, and courage, Eve was everything Miriam aspired to be. Miriam asked herself what she would want to happen if she ever reached such eminence, such legendary achievement.

She did not have to imagine it. She would know when it was time to retire, while she was still being honored. She would not expect anyone who cared for her to feel the need to rescue her from herself, while her honor, her own self, were still intact.

She placed the flawed report in a folder and slipped it under several other folders on her desk. Whatever would she say to Eve? She thought of her own mother who had died many years ago, twenty years younger than Eve was today. She was never given the chance, like Eve and her father, Marcus, to grow old and worry about such things as aging.

Miriam sat for a moment and then retrieved the folder. She spent the next few hours studying the two cases and rewriting the pages that needed altering. When she was finished, she locked the files in the safe and left for home.

CHAPTER

Four

Daniel awoke in the morning after his first night in Suffolk and felt Miriam's absence. He had so easily become accustomed to the warmth of having her beside him. Now he was in this strange room, in a single bed, reminded that pain was not restricted to the body; the mind could suffer it as well.

Throwing off the bedclothes, he washed, shaved, and dressed, the room chilly enough to hurry him along. This was not going to be an easy day. He wanted to find Toby and see if his friend was in any shape to face the world. He remembered saying goodnight and leaving him at the door to his room.

He found the same door on the landing, opposite his own, and knocked.

There was no immediate answer.

He knocked again, far more loudly than he had intended. There was no reason to fear, but his heart was hammering in his chest when the handle turned and Toby pulled the door open. He was half dressed, and with shaving soap covering most of his face.

"Oh, Daniel." His voice sounded as if he were choking. "Are you all right?"

"Yes, and you? Did you sleep?" Without being invited, Daniel walked past Toby, who closed the door behind him. "Finish shaving and dressing," he said. "And then we'll go to breakfast."

"I don't want any, I'm—"

"Doesn't matter," Daniel said. "You'll need your strength. Alberta seems pretty competent, but you can't leave it all to your sister. And she's—"

"I know," Toby interrupted. "I . . . She's my sister, but I can't seem to think of the right thing to say to her."

"There probably isn't a right thing," Daniel replied. "Especially now. She's angry, because she's confused and desperately grieving. Her world has suddenly fallen apart in a way that is completely inexplicable. Anger is so much easier to handle than grief, and then there's the fear that she herself might have done something wrong."

"Rubbish!" Toby said angrily. "How could she possibly be to blame for all this?" He swung his arm around to include everything. "It—"

"Now *you're* doing it!" Daniel pointed out. "Anger is so much less painful than grief, and searching for where you yourself might have gone wrong."

Toby froze with his arm midair, then he let it drop to his side. "Yes, of course. You're right. I just don't know what to say to her." After a long moment, he added, "I never have."

"There isn't anything you can say that will change this," Daniel replied. "Just be there. Do you know Esmond very well?"

"What? Oh, her husband. No, not really. Mother liked him. I . . . I don't really know why."

"Is Alberta happy with him?"

"Yes, I think so. They have three children, and Mother—" He

swallowed hard. "Mother got a great deal of happiness out of that. So yes, I can say that Alberta is as happy as anyone is." He paused, as if considering something for the first time. "There are things she would have liked, I think. She's bright, you know? Nothing like Miriam, but she would have liked to have furthered her education. English, or perhaps history, something like that. But there wasn't enough money to educate both of us up to that level." He looked away. "In fact, I know our parents went without quite a lot, to put me through university. Scholarships only take care of certain things. There's always . . ." His voice trailed off, his face reflecting emotions that Daniel could not fully read.

"I know," Daniel said, his own voice softer, gentle. "I went to university, and my sister didn't. Difference is, I don't think she wanted to. Your sister may lash out at you, and you'll just have to put up with it, and do what you think is right. But you don't need me to tell you that, do you?"

"I don't know what I need," Toby said ruefully, half apologetic. "I need to wake up and find I'm late for work and this was all a bad dream."

"If you're late for work, it is a dream," Daniel replied. "You're never late."

Toby's face softened, as if a smile might form. Almost.

"Get dressed, then we'll go down for breakfast." Daniel held up his hand, as if to stop whatever protest Toby was about to voice. "Just finish shaving and we'll move forward. It's going to be a trying day."

Toby nodded without answering, his face still quite bleached of color.

Daniel was concerned that his friend lacked the energy to face the day, but there were decisions that had to be made. And if Toby did not make them, then Alberta and her husband would, while claiming that any decisions were also in Toby's best interest, and in their parents', which might or might not be accurate. Daniel knew enough about the rivalry between Toby and Alberta to understand that she would wield her power wherever possible. If she said she knew her parents better than Toby did, that was almost certainly true. But it did not mean she was the expert, the last word. He feared that she might be one of those siblings who lords it over the others. She was already arguing that she was the child who was there, nearby, and not the one who had abandoned their parents and taken himself off to London.

Daniel waited as Toby finished getting ready, then watched how he brushed his hair with such concentration and determination that it lay almost flat. This saddened Daniel. He wanted his friend to do as he always did. That is, run his fingers through his hair and create a tangled mess. But wishing this was ridiculous, as well as useless. No one, and particularly Toby, could make it look as if everything were normal, when it wasn't. Perhaps life would never actually be the same. No, of course not, how could it?

Mrs. Prestor was an unusually tactful woman, despite the bad reputation often assigned to landladies. She brought them breakfast plates, each with eggs, bacon, mushrooms, and a good helping of tomatoes, then left the room and returned with a rack of fresh toast. There was butter already on the table, and a jar of thick, dark homemade marmalade. Naturally, there was a fresh pot of tea. She made no suggestions, no comments on how they would need their strength, or other true but unhelpful advice.

"Thank you," Daniel said, as he glanced at her and smiled. She might or might not have realized that the smile was for the silence as well as the food. Like Toby, he was not hungry, but he knew he would need all his courage and tact to get through this nightmare without fumbling, missing something important, or making the grief any worse for his friend. And the energy derived from a good meal provided the required fuel.

The two men ate in silence for several minutes. It was a refuge from conversation, at least for a while.

Daniel ate everything on his plate, then went on to the toast, applying a good amount of butter and marmalade. He took a bite and its distinctive tartness sent a current of pleasure across his tongue. "Do you believe what the police are saying happened?" he said at last.

Toby looked up. "What?"

It was a delaying tactic, and they both knew it.

"Do you believe that out of the blue, with no warning, your father suddenly produced and loaded a gun and shot your mother, then shot himself, not quite fatally?" It sounded brutal, put like that, but there was no point in skirting around it with a plethora of words. Toby was too smart for such circumlocution and would resent Daniel's attempt at it.

Toby winced, but he met Daniel's eyes. "No, there must have been something more than that."

"Such as what?" Daniel asked.

"I don't know, Daniel! Something terrible, but I can't imagine what."

"Neither can I," Daniel agreed. "And I don't think that anyone else can either. From everything I've ever heard about your father, and everything they are saying now, he was a good man, a gentle man. He still is."

"I want to think so," Toby said miserably, putting his knife and fork neatly on his plate, with only a mouthful left, then pushing it away from him. "But it won't change anything."

"We don't know that happened for certain," Daniel said. "And we won't know, once your mother is buried, and if your father dies. If he recovers, we can only hope he'll be able to remember and then—"

"And then what?" Toby said, his voice nearly choked in his throat. "He'll be hanged? You don't need to remind me of that. Did you imagine I had forgotten?"

"That's nothing like the man you know, is it?" Daniel said, skirting the question. "Are you just going to accept it, without trying to learn anything?"

"What difference would it make now?" Toby sounded as if he were so exhausted he could barely form the words.

Daniel leaned forward a little across the breakfast table. "It isn't over until you say it's over, Toby. You are his son—if you won't fight to learn the truth, who will? I'll help you all I can, but I haven't the authority to demand anything."

"Demand what?" Toby asked, his face creased with uncertainty.

"To begin with, a thorough autopsy by a professional pathologist, someone who would be able to tell us more than what the police seem to think is the obvious."

Toby's face screwed up in confusion. "A pathologist can't tell us why he did it, and that's the only thing that'll make any real difference." He pushed his fingers through his hair, leaving it messy, as it usually was. "It might tell us something, such as where she was standing when she was shot, but it doesn't put anyone else there. It doesn't change anything that matters. What could even the best pathologist alive find? Are you saying that Eve Hall would come here? And would that help . . . or hinder?"

"I don't know," Daniel replied, unwilling to give any explanations. "But Miriam would certainly come here." He was going out on a limb by saying something like that. He looked at the helplessness in Toby's eyes. "I don't know what she'll find, Toby, but don't we owe it to your parents to look? Can you even imagine your father shooting your mother?"

"No," Toby conceded. "But Father's not dead. If he has a brain tumor, something that made him hallucinate, or whatever, we won't know it, because unless it kills him, we can't go inside his head to look. And then it would be too late for him, for—" He stopped, helpless to find the thought he was seeking.

Daniel picked up his napkin and wiped the corner of his mouth. "Can you afford not to know? Would you always wonder if there was something we missed, a truth that would explain what really happened? How else can we understand, without an expert autopsy on your mother?"

"Yes, I know," Toby said quietly. "But I think Alberta will be against it. In fact, I know she will."

"Do you want it enough to fight for it?" Daniel asked. "When the shock is past, the grief will go on, of course, but it will be worse if you think there was a truth better than this, and you didn't look for it. You may not find everything, Toby, but that you don't look says a lot about what you think of your father."

"Stop it!" Toby said with a sudden flare of temper. "I'll think about it. But it runs counter to what my sister believes, and she'll consider it totally without respect for the person we've lost. Even now, Daniel, it's terrible to look at my mother. An autopsy is so—there's no way to protect her privacy, her dignity. This isn't just another case that requires investigation. Would you agree to it, if it were your mother? Would you not try to protect her dignity, even in death? No," he quickly added, "*especially* in death, when she can't speak for herself?"

Daniel drew breath to argue, but Toby had more that needed to be said.

"Could you, or anyone with the expertise and training, take a knife, even a razor-sharp scalpel, and cut into her?" Toby stared at Daniel for a moment. "It's an element of respect that's born into you." He studied Daniel's eyes, as if expecting him to answer.

The silence became almost like a solid object in the room, a barrier between these two men who cared for and appreciated each other.

"There's another point," Daniel finally said. "What if your father recovers, and is charged with murder?"

It seemed that every last drop of blood drained from Toby's skin, leaving him pasty white.

"There's no point in telling you less than the truth," Daniel said quietly. "You need to know what happened." He wanted to add that not knowing was often worse than knowing, but he sensed that would be too much for Toby to process.

Toby scowled at him, his eyes reflecting his struggle, as if he were desperate to know but could not bear the truth. Shock contorted his face.

Daniel sensed that Toby had still not grasped the entirety of it all. Did he understand that this crime would affect every part of his life yet to come? And everything he had taken for granted? He had to face it.

"Toby," Daniel said, his voice low, "you have everything about your life that was planned, and you have fulfilled those plans, but now much of that foundation has to be rebuilt. Not a lot, perhaps, but some of what you always knew would be there must now be reconsidered. The only way you can do that is to learn the truth, or else it will all fall apart again. We can leave things that are—" He did not want to say *secret*, which implied a will to deceive. "That are private."

Toby was staring at him.

"We owe it to your mother—and yes, your father, too—to find out something of what happened to her . . . as much as we can," Daniel said. "That is, the truth, and not just what's being assumed. It looks like a quarrel that ended in tragedy, but that may not be the truth at all. If your father recovers, he may remember what happened, but we need to know, beyond what he says. We may need it to defend him." He nearly added *in the courtroom*, but he held back those words.

"I do see that," Toby responded. And indeed, there was a look of comprehension in his eyes. "But Alberta won't allow it, and Esmond will go along with whatever she wishes."

"Good. But you are also Delia's child, and if you insist, I think you'll prevail. You're older, and the executor of their estate. Alberta won't appreciate your imposing your will on her, but this is one time you must. It's the only way to learn the truth. An autopsy might save your father from being condemned."

Daniel heard a loud noise outside and turned in time to see a procession of cars and buggies following a four-horse-drawn funeral hearse. He turned back, relieved to see that Toby had not noticed. A sadness swept over Daniel, knowing the distress his friend was suffering.

Toby's eyes were tightly closed and his body shuddered, as if a shiver of ice were running through him. "The last thing I want is a quarrel with my sister. She's always been so close to our parents. This has to be far beyond the worst nightmare she's ever had. It's so awful that I cannot see how she's not buckling under the weight of it . . . collapsing." He shook his head. "I can't add to her pain, Daniel, I just . . . can't." He looked at Daniel, his eyes imploring. "She'll never forgive me for it. We aren't as close as we should be, and pushing for an autopsy will—" He paused, as if gathering his emotions. "This will pretty much cut me off from her altogether." And then he stopped, as if uncertain as to what he wanted to say next.

Daniel imagined ripping plasters off old wounds that still bled, and now new wounds that needed treatment. This thought made him feel insensitive, as if he had caused his friend unnecessary pain. But he could not let this go. It wasn't because he was being callous—he had known Toby's mother, albeit only briefly, and he knew well the depth of Toby's love and respect for her. What would *he* want, if this conversation were about Charlotte, his own mother? He couldn't imagine it, nor could he bear to even try. But if that were the case, if Charlotte had been murdered, he would be ferocious in his instinct to protect the woman who had protected his life from the day he was born. She was his friend, his teacher in many things, but she would always be, first and foremost, his mother. "I'm sorry," he said softly. "Your mother is unquestionably special to you and Alberta, but she deserves the truth, just as much as anyone else. Are you afraid that if there is an autopsy done, it will show something . . . ugly?"

Toby stiffened. "No!" Now there was real anger in his face. "Of course not! It's—it's just the intrusion! The lack of respect."

"And your father? If he dies, don't you want to know if he was afflicted in some way, and it wasn't his fault that he shot her? Do you care enough to face the truth, and have him buried with honor, and the respect he has earned all his life, rather than as a man who suddenly, one day and without warning, went against everything he taught his children and others all his life and shot his wife . . . dead? There may be an explanation, if we look for it."

"An explanation for murder . . . and suicide?" Toby could barely force the words out of his mouth. "Such as what, for God's sake?" He stood from the table, as if ready to bolt out the door, and then sat just as suddenly, covering his face with his hands.

"I don't know!" said Daniel, working hard to control the frustration building in his mind, yet painfully aware of his friend's distress. "I can't think of anything, sane or not." He took a deep breath. He felt horribly guilty. Would it really help to know? What if everything Justin and Delia Kitteridge had seemed to be, the people everyone knew them to be, was a lie, and the tragedy had been predictable? Were his children better off for knowing that? And perhaps not only Toby and Alberta, but the whole parish? He couldn't imagine that anything could be worse than what they were left with now.

He said as much to Toby, expecting resistance.

"She won't agree," Toby answered.

As much as Daniel had anticipated this reply, he took a moment before responding. "Your sister doesn't have to agree, Toby, if you make this decision." He heard argument in his voice and told himself to tone it down, but there were realities that Toby needed to face. "Would Alberta really prefer that your father be hanged, rather than find out the truth? There may be a physical explanation—some brain anomaly, perhaps a tumor—which means he's not morally responsible. Toby, he spent his life protecting other people! Doesn't he deserve everything you can do to find why this happened?" Daniel realized that he was focusing his argument on Toby's father, when the only one who might provide even the smallest answer was his mother.

"Yes," Toby said very quietly, as if just realizing the weight of the word as he spoke it. "But I'm afraid of what I shall learn if there's an autopsy. That's a terrible thing to say, isn't it?"

"Yes," Daniel agreed. "But it's honest, and I share your feelings. I don't want to see anyone as clearly as that, especially if it's someone I love and admire, and then learn that someone else was hiding inside. And as for me—I don't want to be seen, to have all of my faults on view—I'm not ready for that. Whether it's to myself, my mother, father, or wife, it's unimaginable to have everything exposed, displayed. But then, perhaps that's what love really is, yes? Being able to accept the whole person, not just the best bits. I know there are many sides to me that I'd rather Miriam didn't see, in case she thought much less of me. And yet, I wouldn't look away from any part of her, because I love the very fact that she is vulnerable, imperfect. I'm contradicting myself, aren't I? Perhaps I need to stop talking!"

Toby smiled a real smile for the first time since Daniel had told him the news in the courthouse, a time that now seemed like ages ago. "Stop talking? You?" He sat a bit straighter. "I do know that Miriam would love you the same, even if you were perfect," he said, still smiling. "And think about it, Daniel; you'd be less realistic, less vulnerable, less tolerant of anybody's weakness if you had none yourself. Certainly less tolerant of theirs, whatever and whoever they are. If you were perfect—and God knows you are not!—you would have no need of Miriam. It would be simply that you liked her, and that's pretty tame, really."

"You are wiser than you look," said Daniel. "I think my comments suggest that I've not realized your shock, but I have. And I'm sorry. So," he concluded, as if a decision had just been made, "we'll go and find Alberta and tell her of your decision."

"You mean ask her."

"No, Toby, I mean tell her. With the firm and logical explanation that it's the only way to find as much of the truth as we can." He was not sure if the expression on Toby's face was surrender or uncertainty.

"Nobody wins every case, you know that," Daniel continued. "You just do everything you can. If your father really did shoot your mother, we need to know why. And if he did it for no reason—"

Toby started shaking his head.

"—then we'll find that out, too," Daniel finished. One thought raced through his head; he questioned the benefit of sharing it with Toby. But then, if he did not, what kind of friend would he be? And what kind of attorney? "Toby, there's one element we need to explore, and only a thorough autopsy on your mother, and the most comprehensive forensics examination possible, will give us the answer."

Toby started to speak, and then closed his mouth.

Daniel squared his shoulders, as if about to make a formal proclamation, and then reminded himself that they were alone, two friends, and not seated side by side in a court of law. "Toby, we need to leave open the possibility that someone else did this, shot your mother and then your father." Before Toby could respond, he held up his hand. "It's a remote possibility, but it's not impossible, and we owe it to your parents to explore that."

As if realizing for the first time how terribly hard these dining chairs were, Daniel shifted, hoping to find a more comfortable position. When none could be found, he settled back and waited for Toby to respond, watching him, but remaining silent. What was Toby afraid of? Of how well he thought he knew his parents and now he was questioning this? Justin Kitteridge seemed, in some ways, an older version of Toby himself, a man who loved the church as much as Toby loved the law, and probably was just as humane and honorable. But was he everything he appeared to be when looked at honestly, and not seen through a foggy lens, the lens of his children who loved and admired him? Alberta might be able to help her brother see their parents more clearly, especially their father, but Toby wouldn't even ask. Only because she seemed to view their father even more idealistically than did Toby. But then, it would make sense that she would be open to the possibility that the man was innocent, and someone else had committed these crimes. That should give her some hope, and yet Daniel sensed that she was closed to even considering that.

Was that an accurate assumption on his part? Would she refute the idea that her father might be innocent? Or would she refuse to consider it because it could rely on having to perform an autopsy on her mother? Daniel wondered if this was something inherent with women, that fierce instinct to protect those they believed were vulnerable. Was it part of their makeup? He needed to convince Alberta that the autopsy of her mother was a powerful way to protect her father, now that the man could not protect himself.

Daniel thought back to Jemima, his own sister, older by three years. She was generally quite reasonable, fun at times, civilized. But patronize their father, or attack him in any way, and she was a tiger! Thomas Pitt was vulnerable in very few areas, but if he were under attack, or questioned in terms of his integrity, Jemima would not think about it—she would charge in! Come to think of it, when Daniel was a child, she had protected him in the same way.

Daniel had seen firsthand how a mother cat would box the ears of one of her own kittens, but would stand up with ferocity to anybody, human or dog, for that matter, she considered a threat to her offspring. With a strange feeling that caught him by surprise, he remembered how this same mother cat had protected him when he was small and easily frightened. She would climb into his lap and sit there purring, as if to tell him that he was safe.

CHAPTER

Five

Daniel understood that Toby could not afford to wait for a precipitous time to ask Alberta whether or not they should request a further and more expert opinion on the cause of death of their mother. Some local doctor's written report was insufficient, considering that Delia Kitteridge was murdered. They needed to go to Alberta's home at once and get this resolved. Her three children were being looked after by their other grandmother, Esmond's mother, Penna Walsh. Daniel assumed that the children were staying at her home, and it was important to resolve this while they were away from the drama.

Esmond and Alberta's house was a short distance from the vicarage, almost in the shadow of the church itself, and made of the same weathered stone blocks. It was four or five hundred years old, Saxon in style, a square tower, with stained-glass windows that caught the sun here and there. Trees reached up into the sky from the adjacent graveyard, leaves whispering in the wind. The vicarage, where Justin Kitteridge was believed to have shot his wife, was less than a hundred yards away. It looked abandoned. Its doors were closed, the windows curtained.

Daniel was surprised, and not at all pleased, to find Penna at Alberta's house with the children. He introduced himself, thinking how her appearance suggested she was quite matronly, with curly gray hair and a robust bosom. A practical woman, he thought, with a kind face. He liked her at once.

"Thank you for stepping in," Toby said.

"Stepping in?" she repeated. "Of course I'm stepping in, I'm their grandmother! And as soon as Alberta returns from the market, I'll take my poor wee mites home with me. They know there's something wrong. Best explain it to them, if we have to at all, that there's sad business to attend to, and their parents will be back soon. I've looked after them many times," she assured Toby. "They are comfortable with me." Her voice left no room for confusion: the issue was settled.

While Penna was collecting the children's clothing and putting it into a satchel, Daniel took her aside and explained the need for an autopsy on Delia Kitteridge, and how he was quite certain that Alberta would try to stop this.

Penna made it clear that the situation was more serious even than the shooting and death that had already occurred, grave as this was. "The little ones are sad and frightened," she said, her eyes filling with tears. "The last thing they need is to see the family quarreling. Even to think of an autopsy at all would be horrifying to them, little as they might understand what that actually entailed."

The older children were only six and four, and the baby eighteen months. Daniel was not sure how much they had been told, but Penna was right: what little they did understand, judging by their expressions, they found brutal beyond explanation. Everyone was hopeful that the older two understood almost nothing.

It was when the children were ready to leave for their grandmother's home that Penna turned at the foot of the stairs and spoke to Daniel. "He is a very fine man, Reverend Kitteridge is, and I shall always think of him as that. I hope you're going to find out what really happened?" She looked levelly at Daniel.

Daniel sensed this was more than mere politeness, or even a generosity of thought. This was an outright challenge. "Thank you," he replied. "I shall stay here as long as I can, and when I have to go back, it will be to fill in for Toby at the firm, in whatever way needs doing."

She seemed satisfied. She gave Daniel a brief, warm smile, turned to Toby and offered him the same, but with a sympathetic tilt of her head, and then went to help the children pack whatever else they would need for the next few days, or perhaps even weeks.

Daniel had no idea when Alberta would appear, but waiting in the stone-cold foyer was no longer an option.

He and Toby walked into the sitting room. It was modestly furnished, with comfort more the focus than décor. Toby settled on the sofa and Daniel chose a well-cushioned chair angled toward Toby.

The room was quiet, peaceful, but having been built centuries earlier, there were little gusts of cold running through the air. Daniel was hoping that Alberta would arrive soon. Had he felt more comfortable, he would have ignited the logs in the fireplace to add some warmth to the room.

Toby swallowed hard and turned to Daniel. "I suppose it's the right time to speak to Alberta. She'll not agree, no matter what her mother-in-law thinks, or what I'm certain our mother would have wanted. And yes," he quickly added, "I know that as well as if I had heard her say so."

Daniel did not hesitate. "Are you prepared to accept the judgment, without knowledge, that your father killed your mother without reason, and let him stand trial, if he lives, and then be found guilty, and hanged publicly, on the end of a rope, until he is dead?" As he spoke, his voice raised in pitch. When Toby stared at him in what could only be described as a jaw-dropping pose, Daniel immediately regretted his words. But how to say them without equivocating? And in a way that his friend would hear? He took a deep breath and tried again. "Toby, are you all right with letting every good thing he did be forgotten and this black mark on his reputation remain, without even trying to explain it?" When Toby again said nothing, Daniel leaned closer to his friend and asked, "Be honest, are you?"

Toby looked as if Daniel had struck him. There was something in his eyes, perhaps a resigned expression, and it told Daniel that what he said was a blow half expected. It pained him deeply to see his friend hurting so much.

"You would want to fight, all the way, no matter what it turned up?" Toby asked quietly. "Is that what you would do, if it was your father?"

"I think so," Daniel replied, yet there was an unmistakable certainty in his voice. He wanted to announce that he would fight until he reached the very last ditch on the battlefield, to prove his father was the man he believed him to be—not infallible, on rare occasions crushed by fear, even misjudgment—a man like anyone else. But not cruel, never running from a challenge.

Despite Daniel's admiration for his father, Thomas Pitt, and his accomplishments, he had chosen a different path for himself. The world of a policeman and that of a lawyer were often in conflict, but his father accepted his son's choice. Would he have grown distant from his father if he had chosen to be an artist of some sort? Or a butcher? Or a greengrocer? This thought had not entered his mind for a very long time, a sign of the trust and mutual respect shared by father and son. "Toby, if the roles were reversed, wouldn't your father do everything in his power to defend you?"

"Yes," Toby said quietly, and without hesitation. "But Alberta thinks she is defending both Father and Mother, by keeping whatever nightmare this was as private as possible. She'll do anything she can to protect their reputation. I do understand that, but—"

"You can't keep this private," Daniel insisted. "Sooner or later every newspaper in the country will have the story. And they'll all put their own speculation and twist on it. If they don't have any facts, they'll make them up."

"I know!" Toby said sharply, throwing up his hands. There was anger in that gesture, as well as in his face and his voice, and unmistakable pain.

The first time Daniel had met Toby, he had been reminded of a scarecrow, angular and lanky. Over the next few years, he learned that his friend was made not of straw, but of something far tougher. For the moment, however, there was only fragility, and it touched Daniel's heart to see it so clearly.

"They'll all claim to have the truth," Daniel said, "but they'll go into the most sordid descriptions, imagining all sorts of grim vignettes, until some other poor devil takes their attention and they rush off to create the next sensation for a bloodthirsty public."

"But they'll still nip at us, Daniel, and they'll continue to do so for years! Every time this village is mentioned anywhere, people will say, 'Oh, yes, isn't that the place where the vicar shot his wife, and then himself? I wonder why!' And then the speculation will start all over again." Toby ran his hand across his forehead, as if trying to wipe away these thoughts. "I don't read the gutter press, Daniel, but I know what they say. And the better the life someone lived, the further they fall . . . and the larger the story. Like crabs in a bucket!"

Daniel was lost. "Crabs?"

Toby gave a little shrug. "Anyone who grows up by the sea knows this. If you catch a crab and put it in a bucket, you must have a lid on it or the crab will climb out. But if you put more than one crab in that bucket, they will each stop the other from escaping. You don't need a lid."

Something flashed across Daniel's mind. "I've heard that somewhere before, maybe from you. But, Toby, you are not alone. I'm with you, and I intend to find out what really happened. And I don't believe your father is an evil man. Whatever he did, or did not do, there is something that explains it. Unless you forbid it—in fact, even if you do—I mean to find out what really happened."

A ghost of a smile covered Toby's face. "Good luck with Alberta."

When Daniel saw how Toby wrapped his arms around himself, he stood and crossed to the hearth. "What good is a fireplace without a fire?" he said, and began putting bits of wood and newspaper onto the iron rack in the hearth. He was quite sure that this fireplace was constructed centuries earlier; the heavy draft warned him that there was probably no chimney flue. He needed to stack the wood onto the raised grate with care. It would do no good to make a warm fire that filled the room with black smoke.

"I've got a sister," Daniel said over his shoulder. "I know that sibling relationships can be awkward. What I haven't got—in terms of what I can or cannot say to your sister, or do on behalf of you and your parents—is authority. You'll have to step forward and give me that. We have to act now, Toby."

He looked around for matches and found them on the far end of the mantel. He struck one, held it to the paper, and the fireplace was quickly throwing heat into the room.

"Let's bite the bullet and find out what really happened . . . and why," he said, returning to his chair.

"Bite the bullet," Toby repeated with a touch of irony. "Unfortunately, well put."

Daniel thought of apologizing, but decided to remain quiet.

They had been seated for only minutes when they heard sounds coming from the kitchen. They entered the room and found Alberta placing a chicken in a large pot.

Daniel coughed lightly to announce their presence and she turned around. Daniel knew they were interrupting her; the grimace she showed them confirmed this. But then, he suspected that an appearance by anyone and for whatever reason would result in the same grimace.

He looked around at the many ingredients and bowls strewn across the counter, a sign that she was baking not to feed her family, but to keep busy. She was cooking food she didn't need, some of it bubbling in large pots. Her children were away, and there were only herself and Esmond in the house. This food was enough to feed a dozen hungry people.

It was too early for the midmorning break, known as elevenses, but Alberta did offer them tea, which they declined. The kitchen table was taken up by various cooking utensils, as well as flour, sultanas, and a bowl of dried orange peel. Daniel looked around, uncertain where he and Toby should stand. Even the chairs around the table were covered with cooking items.

"You'd better come through to the sitting room," Alberta said, wiping her hands on her apron and leading the way. She did not invite them to sit down, but they did anyway, and then she, too, sat down, seemingly reluctantly, in what was fairly clearly Esmond's chair, near what was now a glowing blaze.

"We didn't know you were here," Daniel said, "so I made a little fire."

"I don't know what there is to talk about," she said, ignoring his explanation. "We've made all the arrangements. Mr. Cattermole will make the assignments. He's the curate." She looked at Toby. "I don't think you know him. He's been here quite a while. But then, it's been ages since you last came."

"I remember him," Toby said quickly. "Very thin young man, with a beautiful voice."

"He doesn't sing!" she said tartly.

"Speaking voice," Toby corrected her.

"What does that have to do with anything?" she asked.

"Nothing," he replied. "It was you who mentioned him, so I . . . Listen, Bertie, can we just—"

"I'm not *Bertie*, not to you!"

"I've always—"

"Mother and Father called me that; you don't have the right."

"Mr. Cattermole," Daniel said, cutting across them both. "I assume he will take care of the service. He knew your mother and thought very well of her?"

"Of course he did," Alberta said tartly. "Everyone did!"

"Then we will leave him to do it," Daniel said, his voice indicating that they had closed the subject. "What we have come to talk about is quite different."

She raised her eyebrows, and Daniel sensed something inside her hardening, as if she were bracing for a blow.

Toby drew a breath to speak, then bit it back.

Daniel filled the silence before it could descend into something more difficult. "Toby feels that we do not yet know exactly what happened, and I agree. Your father was a remarkably good man, as anyone in the village knows."

Alberta suddenly sat forward, her hands clenched into fists, as if she were about to lunge at Daniel. "Are you suggesting my mother in some way deserved to be murdered? How dare you!"

"No!" Daniel said, startled by her outburst. "That's not at all what I'm saying! Your brother and I—"

She cut him off with an abrupt hand gesture, her eyes flashing anger, and then narrowing, as though warning him to stop. "Who are you to come here, intruding on our family grief, and make such a suggestion?" Raising her voice, she continued, "You've never even met my mother! It was kind of you to drive Toby here, but you have no business remaining, and even less putting in your opinions." As if having exhausted all of her energy, she leaned back into the chair and pushed a handful of hair from her forehead.

Daniel looked at her. As annoying as she was, he wasn't unmindful of her emotional state and knew it was best if he remained quiet. He thought of Miriam's belief that if we look at a person, especially when they are under stress, or experiencing grief, we can get a good sense of who they really are. That is, under the face created for the world to see. In a voice barely above a whisper, he said, "In fact, I have met your mother and found her to be a warm and intelligent woman."

After having said this, he sat quietly and studied Alberta. He noted the obvious first: light brown hair, quite straight, reaching nearly to her shoulders, in a style more for younger girls, not the mother of three. Whether it was her desire to feel more youthful, or simply that, as a mother, she lacked the time to deal with it, he had no idea. But far more telling than her hairstyle was her mouth, the way it curved down, and not when she was speaking in an agitated manner, but when her face was at rest. A permanent frown is what he saw, and it made him sad. His thoughts were interrupted by Toby's voice.

"Alberta," he said. "Please."

As if finding a new well of energy, she sat straighter. "We didn't ask for your opinions," she said to her brother, "and we don't want them. Do you hear me?"

The compassion Daniel had seen in Toby only moments earlier was slipping away.

"Half the village can hear you!" Toby snapped before Daniel could think of the right words to assure her. "And I asked him to stay, because he is my friend. I could use someone with a cool head and a kind heart."

"Are you suggesting I haven't?" she said tartly.

"I hardly need to," Toby replied. "He can hear that for himself." He did not even glance at Daniel. "It seems as if you want to hide as much as you can. Just bury her and don't look too hard, in case—"

"I look with dismay!" she spat back. "And with respect." She stopped. "What are you saying?"

"There's only one way to know what happened," Daniel explained. "I know it's difficult to consider, but there must be an autopsy."

"No!" she nearly shrieked. "I will not allow some strange man poking around inside her, cutting bits off. She was a happy woman." She suddenly paled. "A person with dignity, and a love of privacy. She wasn't a deer to be killed and then cut up and examined!"

"It doesn't have to be a man doing the autopsy," Daniel said, without looking at Toby. "We can send for a woman, if it would help you feel less uncomfortable. But I think—"

"I don't care what you think!" she declared. "This is all none of your business. Perhaps you're without care if your mother died and some stranger cut into her body and opened it with . . . with cold-blooded detachment."

"I don't know how I would . . ." Daniel said. "But if my father were accused of having killed her, I believe I would want to know if he really had killed her. And if so, why. Why do you kill someone you love?"

"You don't! Unless you've gone raving mad," she replied. "The only decent thing about it is he shot himself, even if not very efficiently."

Toby moaned and closed his eyes. "I didn't realize you were so bitter." He shook his head, then opened his eyes and stared at her. "Who is it you hate? Me, because I got the education and you didn't? Did you really want to be a lawyer? Or a doctor, or to teach something, instead of marrying and having children?"

"Nobody asked me," she replied bitterly. "I'd known since I was eleven or twelve that the money was being saved to send you to university. So don't—"

"I got a scholarship," he interrupted.

"You still had to live! To eat! To sleep somewhere. To buy books. You weren't earning anything."

"I know!" Toby said sharply, his voice thick with emotion. "I—"

"No, you don't know," she interrupted. "You don't know the pretty clothes the other girls had, and I didn't, because we were saving all the money we could to provide for you! A village vicar doesn't earn much, you know. The phrase *poor as a church mouse* has more meaning than you seem to realize."

"Should I have sent it back?" Toby looked hurt, angered.

Nobody was looking at Daniel, but he answered. "No, they saved it because they wanted you to be like the other students. They were proud of you then, and even more so now, that you are Head of Chambers."

"How can you say that?" Alberta glared at him. "You spent, what, a few hours with them?"

"Are you saying they weren't proud?" Daniel snapped back. "How do you know they weren't? Did you open their letters to Toby and read them?"

"No, of course not! Did you?"

"He showed me," he replied, stretching the truth a little. "It mattered to him. But what does it have to do with this? Do you want to know what happened, or are you afraid it was even worse than it looks?"

Alberta leaned back, as if having been shoved. "She's helpless—she can't even cover herself from the prying eyes of people who never knew her, never cared for her; never knew her life, her love, the beliefs that she had . . . who she was! A person with laughter and tears, with love, who expressed anger at waste and at cruelty. She was—" Alberta covered her face with her hands. "I just want to bury her in peace, without violating her body." Her shoulders shook with the depth of her grief.

Toby got up from his chair awkwardly and went over to her. He didn't speak, didn't ask her permission, he just put his arm around her and held her close to him, letting her cry.

Daniel also rose to his feet, leaving them alone to make whatever peace they could.

He walked outside into the fresh air. It was a perfect, bright autumn day, and the wind was off the sea, a bare few miles away, strong enough to take the yellow leaves from the trees nearby and send them hurtling through the air to land on the grass still summer green, and with the last of the bright asters and purple Michaelmas daisies forming the borders.

Daniel's stroll relaxed him somewhat, but questions buzzed in his head. Why did it always seem that tragedy happened in an ordinary home? And why were people so quick to hide old betrayals and family secrets in the basement, as if never to be revealed? Surely someone held information that explained this tragedy. It was absurd to believe that some marital squabble was cause for a bullet in the head. None of this seemed to fit—but Daniel was afraid that it might. It so often did.

As he approached the village green, he wondered if the police had looked at the possibility that some terrible secret was suddenly exposed. What could Delia Kitteridge have done that was so unforgivable that murder was the only answer? How could she have betrayed her husband? Or *had* she?

In so many ways, Toby was his father's son. He had that strong core that was kept almost hidden, until such strength was called upon.

Daniel and Toby had talked about the Kitteridges occasionally, but the state of their marriage had never come up. Perhaps Daniel had not really been listening. Perhaps Toby had told him things about his father that concerned him, that he couldn't now remember, but he doubted that. There might have been differences between father and son in philosophy, in how they viewed their lives. Did Daniel believe as his father did? Probably not. Thomas Pitt had lost his father, a gamekeeper, when he was deported to Australia for a poaching crime of which he had not been guilty. But innocent or guilty, it didn't change the fact that his mother had been left alone as a laundrymaid on a large country estate. Young Thomas had been educated alongside the son of the house, partly out of charity, but also in great part to spur on a lazy boy who was not to be outdone by a servant's son.

Daniel had always had a father in his life. He had been given a first-class education, beginning at a good school and then at university. He could not remember his father ever pushing his own views on him. But he should not judge Toby and his father by the same measure.

He wondered if this was a question of religious belief. Anything was possible, even Toby's father losing his faith. Such a loss would be nearly impossible for a preacher to bear. It would result in an anger that would seek release, be directed at someone, anyone . . . even a wife.

Another question Daniel could not shake was the matter of this stranger Justin had shown around the old church and its graveyard, sharing with this man the inscriptions on the graves of the dead, family histories etched in stone. Was he a local fellow, interested because his roots were here? Maybe he had said something to Kitteridge that was a critical clue to this tragedy. Or was it just a coincidence of timing that he happened to be there on that particular day?

How could they find out? Daniel needed to know if that visit was relevant, or merely a coincidence.

DANIEL ASKED THESE questions when he met Toby for lunch back at their boardinghouse. Neither of them was hungry. Daniel's mind was still on Alberta and her outburst against him. She could not make a rational argument for avoiding a proper autopsy on the body of Delia Kitteridge. Yet he could understand her feelings, and he could not honestly say how he would feel if it were his mother. It was not reason she had used to make her argument; it was the depth of her emotions.

He sat at the table and waited for Toby to speak. In the end, he finally asked, "Do you want to have the autopsy done or not?"

"Want to? No," Toby said gently. "But need to? Yes, I think so. Whatever it costs, I think we have to know. What happened between the time he showed that man around, whoever he was, and the . . . the end. I looked, but I can't find any letter or papers, or any person who called after that. What changed? What was it?

How could a lifetime of every day together end in gunfire?" He shook his head, as if the thought remained incomprehensible. Or perhaps he was trying to shake it out of his thoughts.

"It's good that you haven't changed your mind," Daniel said. "And—"

"We have to do it," Toby interrupted. "My mother is not in her body anymore. That body . . . don't ask me where she is, I don't know. I know what she believed, and I wish I could believe it, too." He looked at Daniel intently. "We have to think of the living." His voice was hoarse. "For lots of reasons. I know that she believed, and Father, too. They had differences on some things. My mother wasn't just some obedient housewife." His words were strained, as though he had to force each one out. He swallowed hard. "She believes—believed—I don't know! I wish I knew what I believed." There was desperation in his voice now. "I have the responsibility given to the son. I grew up with it and have learned more about it, but the cost of it was— I can see how Alberta has always felt second best." He fell silent for a moment, and then said, "Daniel, my father was the most honest person I have ever known. And—" He stopped abruptly, as if he could not finish the sentence. But the rest of it, the suffering and the confusion, they lay in the air as heavily as if he had spoken the words.

"Not saying something is not the same as not meaning it," Daniel said quietly. "Perhaps, if he was as honest as you believe, he had times of doubt. Most people do. Allow him the ordinary doubts of having known how the world is. Open your eyes, Toby, and look at what you believe, and then question it. That's how we'll find the truth."

Toby said nothing.

"Whatever it is inside you, it makes you gentle with others, honest with yourself, willing to share, keeping hope even when you don't see any reason to. Those are qualities I believe you shared with your father. My father questions himself every day. I don't think he believes in God—not the God of the Bible anyway, as interpreted by man."

Toby looked up. "You know your father pretty well though, don't you? I'm not sure how much I really know mine. He wanted me to go into the church, as he had. He never actually said so, but I knew it from a hundred small things, mostly unspoken. But I just couldn't."

"Maybe you couldn't follow what the church teaches, and the obedience it requires," Daniel suggested. "But I know you, and I know that you have faith on your own, and in something good."

Toby looked at Daniel closely for a moment and nearly smiled. "As you know, I don't respond well to being told what to believe."

"Then believe that," Daniel responded. "Use the skills you do have, and remember all that he entrusted in you, and find out what on earth happened to him. He didn't stop loving you, or defending you because he didn't always understand you."

"I know! I do know," Toby responded. He rose to his feet a little unsteadily. "I have to talk to Alberta again. I don't think I can change her mind, but I won't do this behind her back."

At Toby's request, Daniel went with him. Alberta received them courteously enough, although she looked tired and strained as soon as they entered her house. Seeing her in the clear morning light, he realized how young she was. She was not expecting visitors and was wearing a very ordinary housedress, with her hair brushed and hanging loose, a little disheveled around her neck and shoulders. Previously, she had looked, if anything, older than Toby. Now she was very clearly younger. Her skin was pale, her lips colorless. Standing there, with Toby nearby, Daniel could see an even stronger resemblance than he had noticed earlier.

Daniel felt that she was all but ignoring his presence. Instead, she was watching Toby, apprehension in her face.

"What do you want?" she demanded "The funeral is the day after tomorrow. Are you saying you can't stay for it?"

"No, of course not," Toby replied instantly. "I'll stay for . . . I don't know . . . as long as it helps."

"Helps who?" she asked. "It doesn't help me. You want to rake everything up, no matter how private it is. I don't know what happened, or why Father did what he did! I don't know where to look. The police seem to accept just what they can see. But they didn't know him!"

"No, but we did."

"I did," she said sharply. "You weren't here to know him. You were here half a dozen times a year, or less, and didn't stay more than a day at a time. What do you expect to know in that time? You talked mostly about yourself! Did you even talk with him alone? You asked how he was, and he said he was fine. What does that mean? You have to do more than ask, Toby! You have to listen, to watch, to hear what isn't real, or work out what is."

He looked at her as though she were speaking a language he had never learned. "You can't ask people questions about things like that, about what they believe!" he protested.

"He said what you wanted him to say," she replied, before he could continue. "What he knew you wanted him to say."

"You're saying he had doubts?"

"Of course he had doubts!" She was almost shouting now. "Everybody has doubts. At least, everybody who is capable of thinking. We all must see them. Face them. Find an answer we can live with until an answer comes . . . or it doesn't. It was Father's job to seem as if he was always sure of everything. That doesn't mean it was easy. There were times when it was difficult . . . very difficult."

"I don't understand. Are you saying some kind of . . . of religious doubt?"

She gestured with her hand, as though to dismiss everything he was saying. "Oh, don't be so stupid! Of course, no, I'm not. Sometimes he'd get tired, fed up with the same old questions time after time. It's his job to help us, not to carry us! And some things can't be mended, they just have to be endured." She shook her head, as if she had walked into a cobweb and wanted to get rid of it, get it out of her hair. "Don't you have clients you can't save, because they're guilty? And knowing they're guilty, would you want to save them? Father faced that dilemma often."

"It's not my job to decide whether they're innocent or guilty," he began.

"And you haven't the wits to work it out? Really?"

He shook his head, clearly confused. "What's that got to do with Father, and what happened. He didn't—"

"I don't know!" she said. "I don't know anything, except that cutting open Mother's body, as if she were some inanimate object, isn't going to help anything. We know how she died. She was shot. And we know who did it: Father. Cutting her open like a piece of meat isn't going to change any of that!"

Daniel interrupted for the first time. "How are you so certain it was your father who did this? Or . . . have you considered that your mother was dying, and he wanted to spare her suffering great pain?"

Alberta's face was wrought with emotion. She swung around to Toby. "She never said anything about being ill. And if she was—" She shook her head. "Oh, no, you can't just say that and expect me to accept it. Did she tell you that? Why didn't she tell me?"

"I didn't say that," Daniel said. "I was just—"

Alberta took a step closer to her brother. "Well, you are not going to cut her up. I won't allow it."

Toby rose to his feet slowly, as if dragging a weight. "Then we'll just have to take it before the magistrate, and see what he says."

"She's being buried the day after tomorrow!"

"No, she isn't," he said firmly. "Not if the magistrate agrees to an autopsy."

"I can't agree!"

"Alberta, don't."

"I won't allow it!"

DANIEL TOOK A short break in his room before their appointment with the magistrate, who, considering the circumstances, had granted them a quick hearing. The courtroom where such matters were decided was available that same afternoon.

When Daniel and Toby arrived, they sat in a corridor and awaited Alberta and Esmond. A few minutes later, they appeared. She was dressed somberly in black, with a white blouse under her jacket, and white pearl earrings. She was so tense with emotion that she walked awkwardly, without any grace at all. Beside her, Esmond seemed acutely aware of her distress.

Daniel saw how Toby acknowledged his sister, with his face placid. On the contrary, her venomous stare was brutal. Daniel could not help but be aware that, from the outset, this was going to be ugly.

Since theirs was primarily a family affair, no one was intended to be present except for Esmond, Alberta, and Toby. When the magistrate arrived, Toby explained Daniel was his legal representative and the man agreed that Daniel could join them.

Everyone entered the magistrate's chambers. Introductions were brief and informal. The magistrate, a local man who, along with his wife, had known the Kitteridge family for many years, was also dressed in somber black, and after introducing himself to Daniel he expressed his grief and concern, and then went straight to the matter.

"Mr. Kitteridge." He addressed Toby gravely. "I believe you wish to have the body of your mother, Delia Kitteridge, autopsied before her burial. Since the cause of her death is quite plain, and it is against the wishes of her daughter, your sister, Mrs. Esmond Walsh, please give me the reason for this unusual request." The tone of his voice made it quite clear that this was against his own consideration.

Toby stood up from the bare wooden seat he had taken. “Yes, sir. It is as you said: quite clear that she died from a gunshot wound. And that there has been no suggestion whatsoever that anyone but my father, her husband, was present. We could believe that, but what if there is an alternative explanation? None of us knows what it might be, but I believe it’s imperative that we investigate. An expert autopsy might clarify the circumstances, including who, if not my father, is responsible for these crimes against my parents.”

Alberta drew in her breath, as if to speak, and then remained silent.

The magistrate leaned forward a little. “Do you truly believe an autopsy might reveal that, Mr. Kitteridge? I don’t, I do not see how. Surely your father is the only one who can answer that. That is, if he lives. I’m deeply sorry for the whole tragedy. I have known Justin Kitteridge nearly all my life, and I never met a better man, a more honest, genuine, or kind man. But you surely do not expect to find some explanation of this tragedy in your mother’s body?” He drew a breath. “If your father survives this, he may tell us why. But I doubt it will make sense to us, and it will change nothing for your mother. Can’t you let her rest in peace, as your sister wishes? Indeed, as we all wish.”

“No, sir,” Toby said quietly. “If my father dies, as the doctors seem to think is likely, then he must carry this darkness, this shame with him.” He swallowed and took a moment or two to regain his composure.

Daniel wished to help Toby, but to intervene now would be to rob his friend of his own dignity. At the same time, Toby might remember only that Daniel did not speak up.

“Had something changed in my father?” Toby began again. “Or had it changed in my mother?”

“Such as what?” Esmond broke in. He clasped Alberta’s hand

and held it tightly, as if he would give her some of his own strength. "What on earth could justify his shooting her?"

Toby's face was ashen. "Perhaps she had some illness that was going to end in appalling pain."

"Rubbish!" Alberta hurled out. "She was well, very well. And even if she had something wrong, you shoot an animal that's in terrible pain, you don't shoot a human being! You understand nothing, if you can even imagine he would do such a thing!"

"I don't know what we'll find," Toby said. Clearly, he was not going to let it lie. He simply was not able to. "Perhaps there may be a different answer."

"Of course you wish there was," she retorted. "We all do! But grow up, Toby. Not everything can be argued out or battled in court. It is not a matter of what we want, or what we can persuade anyone of. Mother is dead. Father shot her, and only God knows why. But the least we can all do is not fight about it, and let her rest in peace. Have some respect, some sense of decency! Don't destroy her any more than she has been."

Toby looked so distressed that Daniel longed to take over and argue for him, help him somehow or other. But if he took it out of Toby's hands now, Toby might think of himself as a failure, and that Daniel had needed to rescue him.

The silence prickled in the room.

Daniel swung around to Alberta. "Do you believe in resurrection?" he asked.

She looked indignant, and then confused. "I do! What a thing to ask! Toby might not be a believer. He questions and argues about everything, but I believe."

Daniel looked at Toby, waiting for him to respond.

"I don't know," Toby said honestly, looking beyond Daniel and Alberta. And then he picked up the thread of Daniel's question. "But if you do, then you know she's not in her body, not anymore. What about people who are burned? Or—or drowned? Or eaten by tigers?"

"We don't have tigers in Suffolk!" Alberta said, the tears running down her cheeks. "Idiot! And you don't believe in the resurrection. You think she's just gone! Poof! As if she had never existed."

"That's not fair, Alberta," Esmond said, his voice gentle. "She was Toby's mother, too. You were closer to her because you saw her nearly every day. That doesn't mean Toby didn't love her. He did, just differently, that's all. Do you think she'd want you to shut him out?"

She turned and stared at him, as though seeing him for the first time, but the anger drained out of her. She turned to Daniel. "If it was your mother—"

"I don't know," he said. The thought was one he could not answer, not now, perhaps not ever. "But I would want to know as much of the truth as I could. If it looked as if my father had done it, I would do anything at all to know how and why. What happened? I would need to at least try to understand. And if a further inspection—an autopsy, in this case—proved that he didn't do it, then his name and his reputation will have been salvaged."

"Do you honestly believe that this will tell us anything?" she asked, her voice no longer shrill. "Can you tell me what we will learn that we don't already know?"

Daniel sensed that his response could be a deciding factor, so he took a moment to form the words in his head. "I honestly can't say, Alberta, but this is thc only chance we have to find out."

She looked at him squarely, unflinching. "I'm not sure I want to know."

"You don't have to be told," he replied. "Perhaps your father doesn't want you to know the truth. But on the other hand, perhaps he does." He drew breath to add something about it being better than she thought, and then knew that would sound trite and changed his mind.

For several seconds, no one spoke.

"If we don't look," Daniel said, breaking the silence much as a pebble breaks the surface on a pool of water, "we will always wonder, and so will other people."

"It may be terrible," Alberta started.

"It may," he agreed. "But it may not. Is that what you would tell him, if he lives? *I was afraid to look for the truth, because it could be terrible?* Would you say, *You are my father and I couldn't bear to look at you without your church robes on, your clerical collar, because I need you to be damn near perfect or I can't love you?*"

"No!" Now she was shouting at him. "That's . . . you know that's not what I mean at all. How dare you say such a thing!"

"Then look for the truth," Toby cut in. "If we find it, and it's something we need to hide, then we will. I don't believe it will be. I think it might be something tragic, but it won't be wicked."

Daniel knew that Toby was speaking to himself, half hoping, and he promised himself yet again that he would protect his friend, whatever had caused these events. He looked at Alberta and gave a slight smile. Nothing suggesting happiness, just a bit of warmth to soften the shadows ahead.

Alberta looked at the magistrate and nodded. She was too clenched with tension to speak.

Daniel heard Toby release an almost inaudible sigh, a sense of relief that he shared with his friend. He turned to Toby and saw the pain and uncertainty in his face. He knew that the truth might prove difficult to accept, but Delia Kitteridge was due the truth. Delia, Justin, their children and grandchildren, and the many friends and villagers who loved and respected them.

CHAPTER

Six

Miriam was in the morgue when she received the telephone call from Daniel, asking her to come to Suffolk and perform an autopsy on the body of Delia Kitteridge.

"Why?" she asked. Not to be argumentative, but because she did not see the purpose of such a thing, which to most families almost always seemed intrusive. "Is there a question as to the cause of death?" That was doubtful. Any doctor fit to practice could identify a gunshot wound.

"Not the cause," Daniel said. "But there are doubts about who committed the crime. The whole thing seems inexplicable," he added quietly, as if he were out of earshot of everyone else, but only just. "A most-loved parish vicar quite suddenly shoots his wife dead, and then himself. Thoroughly devoid of any remorse at all. That is, if you believe the opinion among the investigating officers. There was no quarrel. At least, not that anyone knows of. They have no debt, live modestly, and no one in the parish sees any reason for these violent acts. Any . . . motive. Miriam, if we don't find something, either he will die of his injuries and be marked as a suicide, meaning he'll be buried outside holy ground . . . or he will live, be tried for murder, and probably hanged."

She heard the pain running through his voice and ached to be able to help, to alleviate it any way at all. And Toby? He was probably in a hell of his own, his emotions beyond anyone's reach. No, it was not sympathy the Kitteridge family needed, it was practical help. Medical investigative help.

"Yes, I'll come," she said gently. "We're not especially busy. I can let Eve handle whatever arrives at the lab." That was so easy to say, the words slipping out as though without any need to weigh them.

As if he had not just spoken these words, Daniel said, "We need to find out what happened, or they will try him for murder. I know that I'm belaboring this, but if he's found guilty, they'll hang him." In spite of his efforts, his voice broke. "Listen to me, sounding like some . . . what? I'm not sure. All I know is that it's a desperate thought, thinking of the likely consequences, and a hideous thought for Toby and his sister. So, anything you find that could put a light on this, anything at all . . ." He took a deep breath and exhaled loudly.

"I'll come," she repeated, before he could finish his thought. Not because she believed she would find anything of help, but because she hoped to ease the pain she was hearing in his voice. "I'll set out tonight."

"No!" he declared. "Don't drive in the dark alone, please. Come tomorrow morning. And watch for ice on the road."

"It's early for ice, Daniel, but I'll drive carefully, I promise. I'll collect my instruments and start out in the morning. Tell Toby that if there is anything there, I'll find it. We may learn something that helps," she said, though she could barely think of anything that would make it easier. "I'll do what I can."

"I know," he said quietly, but this time she heard his desperation. "He either shot himself, or he was shot, and in the brain. I don't know how he's managed to survive. Still, we don't know the extent of the wound. We might never know, while he's alive, and it won't matter knowing when he's dead. Even if they let us do an autopsy on him after he's hanged, what good will that do? God, Miriam, this is awful!"

She heard him take another deep breath, as if this would supply him with sufficient oxygen to continue speaking.

"What I'm really afraid of," he said, "is that the police have committed themselves to a course—that is, there's no doubt that it's a murder-suicide—and I'm afraid they'll never retreat from it. They can't admit they were wrong. Ordinary people can so easily lose faith in the law. And so many people become frightened if the law is found at fault. Miriam, we've got to find the answer . . . and soon."

"Tomorrow morning," she said. "I'll be there. Please assure Toby that I'll do everything I can." She wanted to tell him again that she loved him, but it seemed odd when she couldn't even see him. She hoped that, just now, any expression of love could be taken for granted.

"Thank you," he said softly, then the telephone clicked off at the other end.

Miriam put the receiver down, rubbed the fatigue from her eyes, and set about planning. First, she must tell Eve, who had stopped her own work and was staring at her, waiting.

"They want a proper autopsy," Miriam said, as straight to the point as Eve had always been with her. Among the many things this scientist had taught Miriam was how to address a problem, any problem, and do so straightforwardly. If debate or questioning was necessary, that could come after the initial decision, which was the starting point, the basis from which the next steps would be taken, steps leading to a solid and scientifically proven conclusion. It was not always easy—in fact, it rarely was—but the effort, if, in fact, that conclusion was reached, was immensely satisfying.

As always, Eve went to the very heart of it. "They think it might have been a mercy killing? There are some diseases it would seem kinder to end early, before the pain becomes beyond unbearable, or the mind stops altogether. I can understand those who believe that keeping someone alive who can no longer function, think, move, make decisions about their own lives, is unnecessary torture. Let someone die swiftly, and with dignity still left intact. Are you thinking it could be the case this time? That he killed his wife to avoid, or even to end, her suffering?"

"I don't know. Honestly, I think they are clutching at any straw they can see or imagine," Miriam admitted. "But I must go."

"When do we leave?" Eve asked.

The question caught Miriam by surprise, although it should not have. There was such pressure in her chest that her heart skipped a few beats. "Daniel has asked that I do this."

Eve looked first at Miriam and then away. "I see."

"Eve—"

"No, better it be you," she said. Her voice was curt, yet positive. "Of course you must," she said in a softer voice, as if recognizing the importance of this task and ready to hand it off to her disciple. "Joe will help me. We can manage for a few days."

Eve turned to Joe, who had known her long before Miriam had arrived to work as an assistant. He was perhaps ten years younger than Eve, and she felt as comfortable having him by her side as anyone she could name.

"We can," he agreed.

Miriam looked at him and saw something in his eyes. Perhaps he, too, had picked up on the changes in Eve's performance at the lab. Miriam hadn't said anything to him about it, but she guessed he had noticed. His dedication to finding the truth, weighted against his loyalty to a woman for whom he felt a profound fondness and respect, were destined to clash one day soon. The only question was when that would happen.

"We've got nothing much pending," he told Miriam. "If anything comes in, and it's not urgent, we'll hold it for a day or two.

I'm taking it you'll be right back, after you do what you have to do for them in Suffolk?" There was a slight shadow of doubt in his eyes. It was a question, but it was one tinted with hope.

"If I go early tomorrow morning," she replied, "I should be back by lunchtime or early afternoon the next day."

"Make that the day after, Doctor," he responded. "Don't like you driving when you're tired out. Some adherence to duty means common sense as well. Learned that from Dr. Hall here. Not that she follows it, mind you, but she's right to say so."

Miriam smiled. She liked Joe, his ease around two strong women and with never a derogatory word or glance. It could not be easy, a man working for Eve and Miriam. "And you are also right to say so. I'll remember that. Thank you."

He nodded and appeared pleased to be part of her decisions.

Miriam set out early the following morning, as soon as there was sufficient light to see any ice remaining on the road. She knew that thin, black ice was the most dangerous, because by the time a driver was aware of it, it was often too late, the car's wheels having already lost their grip and both car and driver skating, rather than driving. But it was a bit early in the year for that. There was perhaps another month, or even six weeks, before autumn gave way to winter and the slippery patches were hazardous. Today promised to be a fine day, with patchy sunshine and high fluffy clouds casting shifting shadows across the ground.

It was the kind of day that made her want to take a walk, smell the flowers around her, feel the warmth of the sun on her face, hear that gentle rush of wind moving through the trees. Unlike the busy and challenging, and sometimes unpleasant, world around her, a walk in the country would be peaceful, nurturing.

Miriam drove with the pleasure she always felt when behind the wheel of her car, a sense of freedom, a place where there was no phone, no cadaver to examine. She was determined not to think ahead to the task that lay before her, and how she would almost certainly have to inform Toby and his family that while the body of Delia Kitteridge had told them the cause of death, it was unlikely that it would reveal the reason for her having been killed, or by whom.

She soon left the main northbound road and swung east toward the sea. It was a lovely, gentle land and the roads were completely clear, so early on this weekday. Most heavy freight to the seaports was transported by rail, and the inland goods were carried along the main trunk roads heading north to cities like Birmingham and Manchester, or even Glasgow, the industrial heart of Scotland.

Another hour and she could smell the sea's wind in the air, salty and bracing, and found herself smiling again. It was almost an odd feeling, unfamiliar, what with the worries about Eve, and now this tragedy that had befallen Toby.

It was flat land around her, the road not rising into any hills from which to catch a glimpse of the shining water beyond the fields and copses of trees, but it would come soon enough, she knew that. She was not here to find pleasure in her surroundings, but to work, to find reasons and explanations for this catastrophic event in Toby's life.

She gripped the steering wheel and then felt the force of that grip. Easing her fingers a bit, she reminded herself that the times were changing, and dramatically so for women. It was not so many years ago that it was unthinkable for women to drive, yet here she was. And not only driving, but behind the wheel of her own car, and with no father, brother, husband—or any male chaperone—accompanying her.

The fields of corn gently swaying, clusters of sheep appearing as white dots on the green, and the harvested fields, straw gold with the steeply pointed stooks standing watch, soldiers protecting the calm of the land, all of this made the final minutes of her drive serene.

Miriam arrived in the village and reminded herself that difficult work lay ahead. She had the address that Daniel had left with her before he had driven off. Had it been only two days ago? It felt so much longer. Weeks, not days.

The church was easy to see, even from so far away, its spire high above the trees. The vicarage would be close to it, and she had the instructions from there to the boardinghouse where Daniel and Toby were staying.

She stopped to have her car refueled with petrol and retrieved the address from her bag. When she asked directions from the fellow who was filling her car, he pointed up the road.

"Can't miss it," he said. "Watch for the spire. Boardinghouse is on the road behind the vicarage."

Miriam smiled, paid the man, thanked him, and drove off.

When she pulled up in front of the boardinghouse, Daniel was waiting for her on the doorstep. Before she had a chance to switch off the engine, he was rushing toward her. She climbed out of the car and nearly fell into his arms.

She was at first surprised to see him dressed in a suit, and his hair brushed as if he were about to enter the courtroom. She stepped back for a better look and saw that his face was lit with pleasure at seeing her. But even with his smile, he could not hide the tension running through him.

After a moment's hesitation, he put his arms around her yet again and held her so hard that she winced. When he finally released her, she reached up and touched his face. "How is Toby?" she asked. "Do you know anything more about what happened?"

"No, and it doesn't make any sense, nothing does. Unless there's some dark secret we know nothing about. Something in the—"

"If there is," she said quickly, "I'll find it."

"It's the only thing we can think of," he said, removing her bag from the car. "I didn't send for you just because we're out of our depth here, although that certainly is the case. Toby and I want you here because, well, there just doesn't seem to be any reason for this tragedy. His parents have no enemies that we can find, nor that anyone else seems to know of. They don't owe money, and nobody owes them. It just doesn't make any sense." He gave an almost imperceptible gesture of resignation. "And it's safe to say that there's no madman running around in the village, or anywhere else in the county."

"But he's a priest," she said. "Perhaps someone told him something—"

"More accurately, he's a minister. Anglican, not Catholic. His parishioners can talk to him, if they want, but there's no obligatory confession, as the Catholics have, and no oath of silence."

They walked toward the guesthouse, Miriam thinking about this. "True," she finally said, as they reached the front door. "But this doesn't mean somebody didn't confide in him, sharing a secret they then regretted telling him. Or that he knew about it some other way, and they felt compelled to silence him."

Daniel reached to open the door, but Miriam placed her hand on his arm. "What is it?" he asked.

Miriam thought for a moment, and then looked away, as if searching for some elusive answer. "It's the only thing so far that makes sense." She drew in her breath slowly. "Unless he suffered a brain injury of some sort, and he didn't recognize Delia as his wife, but as some monster, and so he shot her. An autopsy isn't going to help with that. I'm sorry, Daniel, but I can't promise I'll find anything that will explain his behavior." She moved closer and leaned lightly against his arm. "I will certainly look, and very carefully."

She nearly mentioned how serious the situation had become with Eve, and then reminded herself that this could wait. Daniel had enough on his plate.

They entered the guesthouse and Daniel introduced Miriam to Mrs. Prestor. The landlady looked at her through narrowed eyes.

"Miss fford Croft," she repeated, shifting her gaze to Daniel. "I'm sorry, sir, but this is a respectable place."

Before Miriam could defend her honor, Daniel stepped forward.

"It's Dr. ffrord Croft," he said, just enough of an edge in his voice to signal Miriam to say nothing. "That is her professional name. She is my wife."

Mrs. Prestor offered him a rather forced smile, nodded to Miriam, and then turned and disappeared into the kitchen.

"I guess I should use your married name," he said with a little shrug.

"Or perhaps you can magically make me fifteen years younger," Miriam replied with a rather mischievous smile. "No doubt she suspects an older woman is corrupting the morals of a fine young man."

With that, Daniel led her upstairs to their room. Once inside, he held her closely. "A fine young man, you say," he teased, kissing her yet again. "And decidedly corruptible."

An hour later, Miriam and Daniel met up with Toby at the vicarage. She gave him a hug, saying only that she was sorry for the terrible loss to his family. She did not make more of it than she would have with anybody, understanding that this was not the time to express her emotions. Toby needed to see her as the expert, the woman who would perform the autopsy on his mother, go to thc hospital and examine his father, and hopefully uncover the information needed to either clear Justin Kitteridge or explain his behavior. She saw at a glance that he was struggling to meet the situation, and restraint was the only way he had to maintain any degree of courage.

She met his eyes for a moment, and realized she was in no way understanding the depth of his loss. Some people thought it was heartless to confront something so emotionally wrenching with logic and reason, but it was not. Miriam understood that, for many, it was the only way of keeping control, coming through any kind of a crisis and with emotional dignity, so as to deal with what had to be done. Even Miriam, with all of her medical training, sometimes found her work so painful that it took every ounce of professionalism she could muster to do her job.

There was one situation that occurred too often between some well-meaning person when speaking to a grieving friend. She had conducted an autopsy on a child who had died unexpectedly. As she discovered, the little boy had a badly deformed heart. His mother asked if Miriam would attend the church service, which she did. Standing on the steps after the service, she watched a woman approach the grieving mother and say, "I know how you feel." Miriam understood that this was meant to show sympathy and compassion, but she found herself unable to hold back, "Oh, you've lost a child, too? I'm so sorry."

The woman had appeared startled. "Oh, no, I haven't, thank God!"

"Then you have the good fortune of not knowing how she feels," Miriam answered.

The woman seemed at first confused, and then realized what she had said. Without a word, she turned and walked away.

"Thank you," said the boy's mother. "Until my son died, I never understood how we can choose the wrong words to convey sympathy."

"It's a fine line," Miriam had said. "But I'm sure most people have the best intentions."

The woman had given Miriam a little smile that conveyed both gratitude and understanding.

Miriam pushed that memory away and glanced at Toby, reminding herself that there were so many ways one feels pain. One could always weep alone, afterward, or in the company of someone whose understanding, and even silence, were both loving and empathetic. And, above all, someone whose expressions of compassion one could trust. It comforted her that, for this, Toby could rely on the unwavering support of Daniel. Knowing this about her husband, she loved him all the more.

Miriam understood that there were formalities to be observed. Shortly after she arrived, she was introduced to Toby's sister, Alberta Walsh, who spoke stiffly, and tried to smile, but could not manage it. To her, Miriam was clearly an intruder who was going to add even more indignity to a tragedy that was already unbearable. Miriam wondered if her presence might be seen by Alberta as an added insult because Miriam was a woman doing what many believed was a man's job. Did this make it an even greater betrayal?

When she met Alberta's husband, Esmond, Miriam saw at once that he was in pain, hurting as much for his wife as for himself. Still, he seemed to lack the hostility she sensed from his wife.

Miriam noticed how Toby was watching everyone, as if trying to determine who was friend and who was foe. Whatever he observed or was feeling, she could see that he was in no shape to do anything about it. The expression on his face reminded her of soldiers returning from the front: shock, disbelief, even disorientation, dissociation.

"I suspect you'll want to get to it," Alberta said, directing her steely stare at Miriam.

The woman's tone of voice and glowering expression brought to Miriam's mind a line from *Macbeth: If it were done when 'tis done, then 'twere well it were done quickly.* "Yes," Miriam said. "And I promise that I will be the least invasive possible."

Alberta opened her mouth to speak, but said nothing. Tears came to her eyes.

"And with the greatest respect for your mother's privacy and dignity," Miriam added.

Again, Alberta said nothing. Miriam noted how her face softened a bit and she felt a deep sadness for what this bereaved daughter must be suffering.

Daniel, Miriam, and Toby excused themselves and went to the local police station, where they introduced themselves to Officer Thorpe, the policeman on duty. Toby took the lead, as was his right and his duty, and then introduced Daniel as the family attorney.

Miriam presented her credentials, which Thorpe received with some reluctance, and then gave them a quick read, his brow furrowed, before he passed them back to her.

Miriam sensed skepticism on Thorpe's part, but brushed that off without judgment. He would see her work, her professional approach, and his doubts would wane. They almost always did.

Toby had been born in this village, had grown up here, but he had left years earlier for university, so he, too, was considered a stranger in many ways. As for Daniel and Miriam, she could only hope that they could do their work without too much interference, especially by those who saw them not as mere strangers, but as invaders.

With all formalities accomplished, they were taken to a room at the back of the station, separated from the main area by a long hallway. This was to serve as the location for the autopsy. Miriam glanced around it, looking to see if it had sufficient light, if there was table space for her work, and scales to weigh organs, if appropriate. She also paid attention to the air, whether it was cool and comfortable, and if the one window, high up on the wall, was sufficiently covered so no dust or insects could enter.

"Good enough for you, miss?" Officer Thorpe asked.

"Yes, thank you. And it is *doctor*," she replied with a smile she hoped was not condescending.

"What's that?" he asked, confusion marking his face.

"I'm a doctor," she explained. "But if you find it easier, you may refer to me as *missus*."

"Come again?" His frown told her he was now completely lost.

"Mrs. Pitt," she told him. "But when I'm working, I'm Dr. fford Croft."

"Yes, ma'am," he replied, taking a breath and holding it for quite some time.

Miriam nearly laughed. The poor man had no idea what she was saying. A woman doctor who cut into bodies without fainting? And a woman with two surnames?

She was certain he had decided not to add whatever he had been about to say. She felt disapproval emanating from him, like heat from a stove, but it was nothing she hadn't felt before.

Within the hour, she was introduced to Dr. Jolls, the village's general practitioner. He appeared to be in his sixties, rotund in what Miriam determined was a most unhealthy way, and impeccably dressed, as if his practice belonged on London's tony Harley Street and not in this little village. Dr. Jolls had a halo of hair with a very large bald spot in the center, and the bushiest eyebrows Miriam had ever seen. His expression, lackluster as a day in December, struck her as disapproving as the policeman's, but at least he seemed to be doing all he could not to show it.

They had a short discussion, during which Dr. Jolls promised, albeit grudgingly, to assist her. She gave him a list of items she needed him to gather from his surgery. Then he excused himself and rushed out, explaining that he would collect these things and change into something more appropriate.

When he was well away from the room, Miriam smiled. "He exits wearing Savile Row, and will return in God-knows-what autopsy garb!"

"No doubt he's done an autopsy or two in his days," Daniel said, "but I'm wondering if this is his first related to a violent crime." He looked around the room. "I'm not sure what good I can do here."

"Perhaps you could take notes," she said, although it was more an instruction. "And please be sure that Toby and his family remain away from the station while we do this." In her mind this was a given, but it had to be said. Nothing could be achieved with Toby, Alberta, or Esmond hovering outside the door.

Daniel said nothing, glancing at Toby, who was standing several feet away, as if hoping that distance would protect him from whatever was to come.

"You don't agree?" she asked her husband. "Were it a close member of my family about to be examined, I would prefer that." There was sympathy in her voice. Nevertheless, the message was direct and unequivocal. She, too, glanced at Toby, painfully aware that all would be less difficult if he were not present. But what could she do, ask him to leave? That would only happen if he decided that for himself.

While they awaited the return of Dr. Jolls, they checked that the windows were completely closed and sealed, in order to prevent any contamination, and that everything from ceiling to floor was clean. This required a wipe-down with several towels retrieved from a closet tucked away across the hall from the room.

In what they were now calling *the autopsy room*, there was a sink for cold water on the inside wall, but no hot water. And there were two tables in the middle of the room, positioned alongside each other.

Less than an hour later, Dr. Jolls arrived with a bag so large it might have been considered a suitcase, and one for a very long voyage at that. From within it he retrieved the surgical tools Miriam had requested, plus at least two dozen small containers, ideal for specimen samples. Miriam was impressed by his thoroughness and silently reprimanded herself for having made a quick decision regarding his medical knowledge. She helped him arrange the containers. It was her intention to return with these samples to London and examine them in the lab, although the urgency of this procedure might necessitate that she remain in the village and conduct her examinations in this room.

After all the instruments were in place, Daniel turned to Toby. "Perhaps you prefer to wait outside?"

"I'll stay," Toby said.

Daniel nodded, then walked out of the room and returned with a man from the morgue and two officers to assist him. One of them was Officer Thorpe. With great concentration, they were carrying a lengthy canvas bag. Following Miriam's instructions, they placed it on one of the tables. Two of the men left the room; Officer Thorpe remained.

Miriam glanced in Toby's direction and saw that his face had turned ashen and he seemed about to faint. Before that could happen, she took three long steps, grasped him by the arm, and gestured for Daniel to assist her. Together, they walked him into the corridor, where a young policeman suggested they go into a nearby room and he would prepare a cup of tea.

When Toby was no longer in attendance, Miriam looked at Thorpe, now standing at attention inside the room and quite near the door. "No one is going to escape," she said to him.

Thorpe nodded, but there was discomfort clearly etched in his face. "I was told to remain," he said. "In case you need anything."

Miriam gave him a little smile. "Thank you, Officer. But I do feel obliged to tell you that I will be making incisions into Mrs. Kitteridge's body, and that includes opening her chest cavity and removing organs. And then there's the odor—"

The man's face suddenly paled and he seemed about to gag.

"If you prefer, you can wait just outside the door, and perhaps spare yourself not only the unpleasantness, but also images that might haunt you for years to come. Up to you," she told him, her voice direct and yet somehow compassionate.

For a moment, he seemed confused, looking about him as if expecting someone to instruct him. Finally, perhaps registering all that Miriam had just described, he stepped out of the room and closed the door quietly.

From the corridor she could hear the sound of a chair being scraped across the floor and then placed at the door.

"Well, that's settled, then," Miriam said. "Shall we begin?"

Under the eyes of Daniel and Dr. Jolls, she pulled on surgical gloves, waited for the doctor to do likewise, and then she opened the bag to reveal the body of Delia Kitteridge.

On the adjacent table sat a large scale, requisitioned by one of the policemen, despite the protests of the local butcher. Next to it were the sterilized instruments, several large white bowls, and the scalpels, face masks, small tweezers, and other instruments for cutting, exploring, and grasping that Miriam had brought from London.

She looked around her. It was a rough-hewn room, to be sure, but now that it was set up, it was time to begin.

Miriam removed the sheet covering Delia and began her examination slowly, very carefully, eyes only, at first not touching the body or moving anything. Daniel stood nearby, ready to write, his body turned away just enough so that he could see nothing of Delia Kitteridge's body.

Dr. Jolls watched closely. "Don't know what you expect to find, exposing her like this." There was heavy disapproval in his voice.

Miriam ignored him.

As the autopsy proceeded, she began to speak. "A well-nourished female of approximately sixty years," she said quietly, looking up to make sure Daniel was writing every word. "She appears to have no wounds, other than the disturbance to her chest, on the left side, presumed to be from a gunshot." She took a tape measure and held it above the wound. "The wound is approximately two inches from the sternum. Further examination will determine if it penetrated the heart." She stood straight, stretching her back for a moment, and then leaned close to the body again. "I am now looking for any marks, bruises, cuts, that indicate further injury."

The doctor seemed about to speak, but said nothing.

Miriam nearly asked him what he was about to say, but changed her mind. If he had questions or observations, he would voice them when he felt it was the right time.

"There are streaks of blood running in fairly straight lines from chest to abdomen."

She turned to the doctor. "Did you wash her body when you examined her?"

"No, but my nurse did, for decency's sake."

Miriam wondered what evidence had been washed away in the name of decency.

"Mrs. Kitteridge was covered in blood, all over her—it's a heart wound!" His face was pale and he nearly choked on his words. "For God's sake, woman, there's nothing you can't see. Isn't it obvious that the reverend must have lost his senses?" He stepped away from the table. "This is . . . indecent."

"There's nothing indecent about a body, Doctor, only about what is done to it. I owe it to her to examine every inch of her body. There might be other wounds, barely discernible, even pinpricks."

"For God's sake," he repeated. "Why pinpricks?" His face was crimson.

Miriam nearly asked him to leave. The last thing she needed was to have this man suffer a heart attack or stroke, which was certainly possible, given his weight. And it would not do to be interrupted at every procedure. Gathering her patience, she said, "Perhaps I should have been more precise, Doctor. I'm referring to the puncture marks left by a hypodermic needle."

"A hypodermic needle? Are you suggesting—"

"I'm not suggesting anything, Doctor."

"An addiction to drugs! How dare you?" he demanded, spittle flying from his mouth. "This woman was a minister's wife! She—"

Miriam silenced him by holding up her hand. Her glance shifted to Daniel, but he remained silent, for which she was grateful. "It's my job to look for everything, Doctor, not to interpret it. She could have been injected with a narcotic, or something deadly, either by herself or someone else."

His eyes grew wide. "Do you expect—"

"No, I do not, but neither did we expect this to happen! Or did you?" In an instant, she looked up at his white face and then back to Delia, remembering that this woman who had so recently been warm and alive was someone the doctor knew, and perhaps had cared for as a friend. She was also his vicar's wife, a woman of standing in any village. "I want to rule out everything," she said gently. "I owe that to her . . . and her family. Now, if you're finding this difficult, I suggest you step outside and let me get on with my work."

Dr. Jolls nodded, as if calm and reason had been restored. "Of course," he said.

Miriam went on, carefully describing everything she observed. She spoke of the hands, their skin smooth and unmarked. "No defense wounds," she said, and Daniel wrote. "These are the hands of a woman who sewed, as evidenced by the fine puncture wound on her right thumb, undoubtedly caused by plying a needle."

She took a tool from the nearby table and used it to remove something from under Delia Kitteridge's thumbnail. "I'm removing what I believe is soil. Most probably, the microscope will reveal this to have come from the garden."

After placing the sample in one of the glass containers, she turned back to the table. "Judging by the larger muscles in her right arm and wrist, we can assume that she was right-handed."

Miriam moved down the body, from torso to abdomen. When she began to examine Delia Kitteridge's private parts, she expected the doctor to protest, but he remained silent. Looking up, she saw that Daniel was still turned away, a sign of respect. "No damage to the genitals," she said. Out of the side of her eye, she saw that Daniel was writing it all down.

After nearly an hour, Miriam stepped away from the table and turned to Daniel. "I found no bruising, except on the right small toe, which she might have stubbed two or three days ago. Her skin is clean and clear of all violations or scars, other than an old scar on her left hip. I would say three or four years old, at least. If necessary, further examination will reveal the cause."

"What could it possibly have to do with her death!" the doctor demanded.

"Possibly nothing," Miriam answered. "But in an autopsy, you must note everything, not just the things you think might be relevant."

"Do a lot of autopsies, do you?" he asked, a trace of sarcasm in his voice.

"I'm a pathologist, Dr. Jolls. This is what I do."

He shook his head. "Hell of a job for a woman. I'm surprised your husband allows it."

Miriam turned to face him. "I was a pathologist when I met him. Does your wife oppose your spending time looking at other women's bodies?" The moment the words came out, she regretted them, but it was too late. She looked across at Daniel and met his eyes, but she could not read them.

"Is that so?" the doctor asked. "And . . . might I assume that you're finished?"

"On the contrary, Doctor, we have barely begun," Miriam told him. With that, she pulled down the sheet, took the largest scalpel available, and made a Y-shaped incision, starting along the tip of each clavicle and meeting over the sternum, or breastbone, and then continuing down the full length of the torso. Satisfied by the length and depth of the incision, she bent closer and—slowly, meticulously—peeled back first the skin, then the muscle, exposing the internal organs. "The heart has been pierced by the bullet and there is blood in the chest cavity." She probed the heart with a tiny forceps and then held it up for Daniel to see. "I have removed a bullet from the heart."

No one responded, but when Miriam glanced at Daniel, she saw his relief. Perhaps it was unnecessary, but she added, "Death would have been immediate." No one wished this woman to have suffered a long and painful death.

The examination continued. Finally, Miriam stood, stretched her back again, and pulled off the surgical gloves. "I have concluded that Delia Kitteridge died from a bullet to the chest, one that entered her heart and resulted in massive bleeding. I have found nothing to explain *why* she died, or who might be responsible."

There were no words to make this any easier to bear, but she was required to speak honestly and professionally. If something came up later, such as a challenge in the courtroom, she would have only her personal notes to refer to.

Miriam placed the bullet on a small tray, pulled on a fresh pair of surgical gloves, and then returned to the body.

"More?" the doctor asked.

Without responding, she examined the lungs, stomach, liver, spleen, kidneys, abdomen, and gave a fairly cursory glance at the colon. All organs appeared to be undamaged and healthy. She removed and weighed the separate organs, and gave Daniel the figures, which he noted.

It was nearly three hours before Miriam concluded the autopsy. It had seemed endless in some ways, and very brief in others. Her conclusion was sobering. "Delia Kitteridge had been a healthy woman, and could reasonably have been expected to reach old age."

The doctor remained silent, but he looked at Miriam, as if searching for words.

"It's a wonderful thing, the body, isn't it?" she said quietly. "Any shape or size of the human body. We can study it, sometimes heal it, take it apart, and put it together again. But what makes it alive remains one of our great mysteries, one that perhaps we will never fully understand."

The doctor nodded slowly, agreement in his face, and now respect. "But do you know anything more about this tragedy than you did before? Why did he kill her? Maybe it's his head you should be looking at?" He turned and only partially looked at the body. "You didn't cut into her skull. That's something to be grateful for, I suppose."

Miriam winced. She had thought of it, of course, but looking at that unmaimed face, the eyes that were staring, without seeing, led her to decide against it. "I don't think that's necessary," she said. "There were no behavioral changes suggesting a tumor. Did she ever complain of headaches?" she asked the doctor.

"No," he said. "And I would have known. I may not have a fancy pathology degree from Europe, but I'd have told you if she'd had anything wrong with her. Been a doctor going on forty years. I've known Delia Kitteridge for decades, I have. A good woman, she was. Gentle. Patient. Good with plants and animals. And people."

"I'm sorry," Miriam said. "It's a terrible tragedy."

"Did you think you'd find anything?" His voice was not as strong as she had expected it to be. "Answers to . . . why?"

She shook her head. "No, but I did retrieve the bullet, and that's important."

"And what good is that, may I ask? Match it with the one they dug out of the wall? Seems like he shot her, then turned the gun on himself, poor lost soul. Didn't die . . . didn't even get that right. Not that I blame him. I could never turn a gun on myself, blow my brains out!"

Daniel stepped forward, exchanging surprised looks with Miriam. "Dr. Jolls, are you saying the police dug a bullet out of the wall?"

Jolls suddenly looked less sure. "That's what I heard, but I haven't actually—" He pressed his lips together for a moment, and then added, "I'm not sure . . . maybe."

"We need to tell Toby," Miriam said, urgency in her voice. "Is he still here?" She turned to leave the room, but stopped when Officer Thorpe entered.

"Toby's down the hall, going over details with the police." Daniel held up the notebook and gave it to Miriam. "I hope I got it all; I think I did."

She smiled bleakly at him. "I'm sorry. I was hoping the autopsy would reveal something definitive."

Dr. Jolls bristled. "You can't find anything if there's nothing there. At least, nothing that means anything."

Daniel turned his attention to the policeman. "Will you take the bullet to the station, or should I?"

"Wait," said Miriam. "Officer Thorpe, is it true that you have the other bullet, from the vicar's head?"

"Word travels fast," he said. "But yes, we were able to retrieve it, but it's a bit knocked around, mangled, as you can imagine, nothing identifiable."

"Are you sure it's the one that passed through the vicar's head?" Miriam asked.

"Yes, absolutely, they dug it out of the wall. It's not in good shape. To be honest, I'm not even sure where it is."

The surprise in Miriam's face was not lost on Daniel. "How could you not know?" she asked. "It's important evidence."

Thorpe looked at her for a moment, his mouth a thin, hard line. "Being a junior officer, I'm not given the opportunity to voice my opinion." He moved a bit closer to her. "But I can tell you this: if I were running this investigation, I'd consider everything, and particularly a bullet, to be vital evidence."

"And the gun?" Daniel asked. "Are you certain it belongs to Justin?"

The question brought a frown to the young policeman's face. "His daughter, Alberta, Mrs. Walsh, she's confirmed that it's his."

Miriam was not sure why this upset the doctor, but Jolls looked very unhappy as he turned on his heel and walked out of the room.

The policeman watched him go. "It's easy to forget that Dr. Jolls was more than the family doctor for the Kitteridges; he was also a close friend."

Miriam saw that Daniel was about to respond, but held back. What could he possibly say?

CHAPTER

Seven

DANIEL AND MIRIAM stood with the young officer Thorpe, all of them appearing concerned about this new piece of evidence. How was it that a second bullet had been found and not mentioned? And where was it?

Daniel noticed the way Thorpe was smiling rather bleakly, his face decidedly pale, but at the same time his eyes were moving back and forth, as though seeking approval from these out-of-towners. Or perhaps forgiveness for what now seemed to be sloppy police work leading to what was certainly a serious oversight. Miriam had just handed him the container protecting the bullet taken from Delia Kitteridge's body, and the young man was holding it with care, as if identifying it as something of inestimable value.

Daniel turned his gaze to Miriam and recognized how tired she was. There were shadows of weariness around her eyes, giving her face a rather sallow look, in contrast to the smudges of blood where she had brushed a stray hair away from her forehead. Her hair was still covered with the net designed to stop contamination of a corpse during an autopsy.

She finally spoke. "I need that bullet," she said, a firmness in her voice that left no question as to its importance. "And then I'll take them both back to London and have them properly analyzed."

"I'll do my best to find it," Thorpe said, and then he rushed off, his face and posture announcing that he would absolutely find that second bullet and deliver both to Miriam, and he would begin that search now.

Miriam faced Daniel. "Nothing is certain until more tests are run. I hope Thorpe's superiors understand how imperative it is that I have *both* bullets for the ballistics expert. As soon as I have them, I'll go back to London."

"Good," Daniel said, and then he took Miriam's hand. "It's been a long day."

She leaned into Daniel, took a deep breath and let it out slowly. "Very. Your being here—" Her voice trailed off.

Daniel heard the relief, and also the appreciation. He wanted to tell her that there was no place he'd rather be than by her side, but it didn't seem necessary. Standing here, holding each other, was all the expression of love he needed.

"Should I visit Toby's father, do you think?" she asked, leaning back a bit and looking into Daniel's face.

He considered this for a moment.

"No, best not," she said before he could reply. "I need to get my rest; we both do."

Daniel had been hoping she would take the evening to relax and was relieved that she was intending to do just that. "How is Eve feeling?" he asked, careful to cloak the question in generalities.

He recognized that Miriam had the education and the experience to determine if Eve was declining. At her age, it would not be unusual if she felt exhausted from weeks, months, years without a rest. Certainly, that could lead anyone to lose their grip on their work.

"A bit slower," Miriam acknowledged, "but that's to be expected, yes? She's brilliant, but after more than forty years in the lab . . ."

He was concerned about Eve, yes, but also for Miriam, who seemed to be bearing the increasingly weighty burden of Eve's work. "Please tell her I'm thinking about her," he said. "And take care of yourself . . . while you're caring for her."

She looked away from his eyes. "Thank you," she whispered. "I have to remind myself that Eve Hall at her slowest is still sharper than most scientists. I find myself questioning how much I can assist her without her feeling that I don't trust her judgment." She stopped for a moment, as if weighing what she was about to say. "Daniel, I owe everything to her, and it's not easy to see her slowing down. But that's childish of me, isn't it? Because it's not about me."

"Not at all," he said. "Would you want anyone else to take your place? Would they show her the same patience and kindness? The same respect?" There was concern etched around his eyes.

"No." Her voice wavered, yet at the same time she appeared sure.

Daniel knew Miriam so well, he was certain she would never walk away from someone who relied on her. He drew her to him again and held her close.

She waited a moment and then pushed gently away, looking up at him. "I'll make my report based on your notes and give it to the coroner, and then talk to the police. Hopefully, our young Thorpe will come up with the second bullet and we can have them tested by an expert, compared."

"You've mentioned 'expert' several times, but can't you do that?" Daniel suggested.

"I can, yes, but I prefer it be done by someone who specializes in ballistics. And considering my friendship with Toby, there can't be any suggestion of bias. I'm already pushing it, considering I did that autopsy."

Daniel saw more of the tension slip away from her face.

"Right now," she said almost wistfully, "I'd like to take a hot bath, put on clean clothes, and return home."

"You're exhausted, perhaps you should stay the night," he began. But then he looked at Miriam and it was clear that her mind was racing ahead. "Please?" he added. "Don't drive when you're tired. Isn't that what you tell me?"

"Yes, Daniel, but—"

"Miriam, please!" he said, insistence now in his voice. "You can get up early, have breakfast, and then leave . . . rested."

She leaned against him and he held her closer still. "You've convinced me," she said, her words muffled against his chest.

THEY SOUGHT OUT Toby and found him outside the building, leaning against the wall, eyes closed, as if he were sleeping standing up.

Daniel saw how the sound of the door being opened caused his friend's body to tense.

Pushing away from the wall, Toby looked first at Daniel and then Miriam. Daniel could not decide if there was hope or despair in his friend's eyes, they were so red from exhaustion and grief.

"We have news," said Daniel.

Toby did not speak, but the expression on his face shifted from blank to something resembling curiosity . . . or was it hope?

"There's a second bullet," Miriam said. "The one that struck your father. They dug it out of the wall."

Toby seemed confused. "But then, why didn't . . ."

Daniel shook his head. "For some reason—and believe me, Toby, I cannot explain this—for some reason, no one thought it was important. Not even the doctor. But I'm hoping they're all wrong. Officer Thorpe said it was mangled and set aside. He now understands the urgency and is looking for it."

Toby gave a little nod. Daniel saw a barely discernible light flickering in his eyes.

Early the next morning, Miriam and Daniel awoke and had breakfast in the dining room. Mrs. Prestor had prepared a full meal of bacon, eggs, fried bread, and then toast and marmalade, and hot, fragrant tea. They thanked her for the meal, and again for the sandwich she had already packed for Miriam.

"You might fancy it, before you tackle the bad traffic in the city. Not that I've ever been there, but I have an idea, and I've heard enough horror stories." She placed the package in Miriam's hand and looked at her with an anxious smile.

"That's very kind of you. I had thought to stop somewhere, but this will be nicer. Perhaps I'll find a quiet place before the city traffic gets heavy."

Mrs. Prestor smiled, but it was wistful. "I know you've done what you could for the vicar's wife, poor soul. We'll look after Mr. Toby as best we can. And your mister, like—well, it's all a terrible thing to face, and—" She stopped, as if stuck for words.

"You look after them," Miriam said, throwing Daniel a quick look. "Make sure they eat." It seemed the only practical thing she could think of, and Mrs. Prestor was a practical woman. "We don't always realize we're hungry, until—"

"Oh, don't I know that, love! I'll see to 'em, don't you worry!"

Miriam gave her the best smile she could muster. She returned to her room for a final check, and then went downstairs to meet Daniel in the hall.

"I just called Thorpe," he said, "and he's still searching . . . with great determination, it seems. As soon as that bullet is found, I'll get both of them to you."

They walked outside, the brisk autumn air of this morning carrying with it the promise of a comfortable day. The brick path leading to the little lot where the car was parked was covered with leaves, enough to herald the changing seasons, but also to announce that someone—probably Mrs. Prestor herself—was sweeping that walkway daily. If not, the brickwork would be buried under a thick blanket of them.

After a long embrace, Miriam climbed into her car and drove away, leaving Daniel standing there, one hand raised as a gesture of goodbye, of a reminder to drive carefully, and also that she was loved.

Later, when Daniel sat with Toby in the parlor, the atmosphere was entirely different. Toby was pale, even a little shaky. Daniel was certain it could only have been an emotional ordeal for him, painfully aware as he was that Miriam, in her role as a pathologist and not friend, had cut into the naked and defenseless body of his mother. He almost yearned with the need to assure Toby that she had performed what felt like a heartless and unforgiving procedure with respect and caring. But he said nothing, trusting his friend to come to this conclusion on his own. Toby knew Miriam, had confidence in her. That should be enough.

As happened so often between them, Daniel wished he knew what Toby was thinking and yet, because they were friends who held each other in respect, he did not ask. When Toby was ready, he would open that conversation. And then a thought struck Daniel, and he felt compelled to speak. "I was there, taking notes," he said. "But my back was always turned. I never looked at your mother, Toby, not once."

Toby nodded, as if one of his concerns had been allayed.

The subject of the second bullet presented itself as a safe alternative, certainly less emotionally charged than the tests run on Delia or the condition of Justin. As Daniel discussed the discovery of the second bullet, he realized that only the briefest explanation was required. Toby grasped at once the implications. In fact, he exhibited a surge of nervous energy, barely able to stand still. And in his agitation, Daniel recognized renewed hope. Could they match both the bullets to his father's gun? And if there was no match? Then everything would be turned upside down. The odds were against it, but hope required believing in even the smallest of possibilities.

Toby shifted his shoulders, as if trying to shake off the emotions coursing through him. "I'm sorry, Daniel," he said. "I know we have cases that need my attention, and I'm sorry about expecting you to carry the full load, but I can't leave the village now. That is, not until my father—" He gulped hard. "If . . . when . . . he wakes up, he can tell us what happened. If he dies—" He looked away. "I can't leave him alone, not like this." He stopped. "I know I'm repeating myself, but . . ." He gestured, as if to admit he could find no words adequate enough to reflect the tsunami of emotions rushing over him.

Daniel said, "I'll go back to London and explain the situation." He was hopeful that Gideon Hunter, KC, would have returned from his brief holiday and be more than prepared to take Peter Ward's case himself. "If Gideon cannot take on the case, of course he'll assign someone to it. Have you anything in particular you would like me to tell him?" Daniel hesitated, uncertain if he should push Toby for the insight he had shared before the news of the tragedies in Suffolk. What was Toby about to tell him that might affect the outcome of Peter Ward's case?

Toby stared at him, as if waiting for words he could grasp. But he looked blank, as though he had no idea what Daniel was talking about.

"Toby, before the news of your parents, you were excited about something. Perhaps something you had just learned?"

Toby shook his head and then closed his eyes slowly.

"It made me think," Daniel said, "that you had just seen a link to something, a kind of thread to follow—an inconsistency you hoped might reveal—" He stopped, aware that he was speaking to a blank wall.

Toby frowned; his eyes remained closed. After a moment, he said, "Did I? See a thread, that is. A connection? If I knew something, I can't remember."

Daniel wanted to reassure him, but Toby seemed disturbed by this lapse of memory. "No reason to be upset or feel guilty," said Daniel. "Given what you've been through."

"Forgive me, Daniel. I just . . ." His voice trailed off yet again, his expression one of abject misery.

"You had an idea," said Daniel. "Might you have made a note of it?"

"I'm sorry," he repeated. "But," he added, a hint of energy returning to his voice, "I do recall that an idea flashed in my mind, and it was just as you came into the courtroom. That is, I think it was. It was something that suddenly made sense. I remember thinking it might be the clue that explained it all. Something I hadn't thought of before. And that would lead to a quite different outcome—I thought."

"Can you remember even a small part of it? Because together, we could—"

Toby held up his hand. "It was such a small thing, but I thought it might . . . that I might . . . have used it to prove Peter Ward innocent. Clear him completely." He rubbed his eyes. "Forgive me, I haven't the faintest idea what it was. It was an idea, not an object found, but that's about all I can remember. I'm trying, I swear, but it's a blank."

Daniel placed his hand on Toby's shoulder. "Don't worry about it, please. If I follow all the evidence you worked from, perhaps it will come to me, too. Or if you do remember, ring me up."

Toby gave a bleak smile and nodded. "I should come back with you and—"

"No, you should not!" Daniel insisted. "You've got enough to do here. You've got fences to mend with your sister. And you need to stay in touch with Officer Thorpe. He's young, Toby, but he's smart, and he cares."

Toby shoved his hands into his pockets, his shoulders hunched forward. "What if we never find out who killed my mother?" There was a cry in his voice when he added, "Or . . . why."

Daniel nearly waved the question aside, but realized how callous that might seem to Toby. How could he respond? That the killer might never be identified? The thought was too painful to consider. He needed to stay focused on more possible conclusions. "If your father recovers—and there is a chance he will—he's going to need all your support. Both as a loving son and an astute lawyer. And if he doesn't recover," he added, and then immediately wished he had not. "Toby, your sister is going to need you very much, whether she admits to it or not. If you come back to London to save Peter Ward, when it's debatable if anyone can, and you leave your father, who is still in grave danger, then that's a fence that can't be mended. And you might never forgive yourself."

"I know," Toby said quietly. "I—" He stopped, as if again uncertain what to say, or if he could even voice the emotions that were all but overwhelming him.

"I'll study your notes, of course, but I'd like to get your feelings about the case, those things you didn't write down."

"I think he's innocent," Toby said. "But I haven't found any way to prove it. If I remember whatever it was that's now nagging at me, I'll call you or Hunter straightaway."

Daniel thought about this for a long moment. "Why? What I mean to say is . . . why do you think Ward's innocent? Give me something to start with. I've only met him that once, and I'm not certain what evidence there is against him. And, well, please don't worry. If Gideon can't step in for you, then I will." When Toby didn't respond, Daniel asked, "How can I fight for him? And if it isn't Ward, who are the likely suspects? Do we know who his friends are? And were they with him at the party? And perhaps the most important question of all, Toby: In whose interest would it be to see him hang for this?"

Toby winced. "If I knew any of this, I'd have gone for them. Peter Ward seems a very ordinary young man. Not socially top drawer. His father is a professor of English at Oxford. So, yes, our young Ward is bright enough, but in a quiet way, nothing splashy. And until now, he's been seen as a decent fellow, good. Never pokes for a fight, at least not that I know of. These charges have shaken him up, as they would anyone. But you're going to have to work at getting him to believe in himself, and persuading him that he can win."

Daniel looked at his friend and saw the deep lines of worry and fatigue etched into his face.

"I really do think he's innocent," Toby said. "If he's found guilty, and—" He stopped short of saying the word that logically followed—hanged—but it was in the air. "If we lose, then either we have lost a case we should have won, or I'm the worst judge of character possible." He drew in a deep breath and released it slowly. "I'm feeling empty at the moment. I don't know what I believe . . . about anything. My—" He stopped again, as if unable to speak the words, and that if, by speaking them, they might be indelibly inscribed in the air.

"I understand," Daniel said quickly. "When my mother was kidnapped, I couldn't think of anything else. And then Miriam's life was in danger—"

Toby smiled very slightly. "I remember."

Of course he did, but both Charlotte and Miriam had been rescued; Delia Kitteridge was dead. And Reverend Justin Kitteridge, if he lived, might hang for his wife's murder. Daniel wished profusely that he had not mentioned it. It was intended to show Toby his understanding. Instead, he had shown his powerful lack of it.

"I'll get Ward off," he promised, standing as if to leave. "Or Gideon will. And we'll find the truth of what happened to your parents, and prove your father innocent, too. So, if you don't hear from me, it'll be because I'm submerged in the case and couldn't find time, or I was hunting for something—evidence, a witness. Impney will stay in touch with you, keep you informed. Even if there is nothing new to say."

"Thank you," Toby said quietly. "I'm sorry, Daniel, I—"

"You don't need to explain," Daniel said. "And you certainly don't need to apologize. I'm leaving you here because I have to.

The judge went far beyond the weekend, giving us time to manage. I'll drive back to London, so you'll have to come home on the train."

"It won't be for a while," Toby replied. He began to speak again, but stopped abruptly.

Daniel looked at Toby's face, his eyes, and knew that there was more he needed to say, he just did not know how to begin.

Daniel sat down again. "Do you know something?" That was not actually what he meant, but he could not ask blatantly what else was crowding Toby's mind. Whatever it was, his friend needed time to frame it, give it shape . . . or perhaps decide if he wanted to say it at all.

"No." This time, Toby did not attempt to hide his confusion, or his pain. "I don't know anything, and that's wrong. I haven't been here enough to listen, and to hear the things that weren't said. I know what I mean, but I can't find words that don't sound idiotic! Alberta thinks I don't care, but I do!" He looked down at the floor. "I loved—love—my father very much." He looked away, as if seeing his father standing before him. "He taught me honesty, starting with myself. That if I lie to myself, it probably means I'm going to lie to everybody else . . . at some time or other. And he taught me the difference between lying by silence and speaking the lie."

Daniel sat quietly and let his friend continue, relieved that Toby was finally speaking his pain.

Toby looked at Daniel, his eyes pleading for understanding. "Daniel, I'm afraid I'm going to lose him."

"I know," Daniel said.

"Mother was a pillar for my father." His face shifted so quickly that it appeared to collapse into itself. "Oh God, Daniel, he's going to miss her! He had trusted her as a friend, sometimes protected her as he would a child . . . that is, protected her from his darkest moments." He fell quiet, and then spoke again. "I was well into my adult years when I finally understood: He thought Mother needed him to be, expected him to be, perfect. But it wasn't so, not at all.

She loved him and admired him as he was, flaws and all." A deep crease appeared across his brow.

"Toby," Daniel said, but was stopped by Toby's upheld hand. His friend had more to say, and Daniel would not be an encumbrance to his need to speak.

"Perfect people don't need anyone else, but Father wasn't perfect, nor did I want him to be. Still, when he desperately needed me, I wasn't there. And I wonder about the clergy. Father's heart was in my joining him at the pulpit, in the rectory, sharing his love for the church."

"Your father was proud of you." Daniel felt Toby's pain, like a coat so heavy that it was difficult to wear. "Lots of men want their sons to walk the same path. And if we all did, we'd end up doing the same things. There'd be nothing new, ever." That was an exaggeration, and he hoped Toby would understand. He leaned forward a little, and felt Toby's eyes on him, waiting. "I believe that what your father wanted more than anything was that you do something good, something that helps. Can you see that? And he wanted you to choose something that you could be good at, that you could believe in. A country can't run without laws, and the people who enforce and uphold them. In fact, we can't run anything in this world without order. The earth is full of laws. If you think about it, you work with one set of laws, and your father works with another. And, well, they aren't so very different, are they?"

Toby did not move, but Daniel could see that he was thinking, weighing what was being said. He felt a deep responsibility to say the right thing and give his friend some solace. "What I am telling you is that your father believes the path he followed, believes it desperately, and so do you. The law is not perfect, and perhaps religion isn't either, but to some degree they are what we make them to be, and try so hard, each in our own way, to improve upon them."

Toby searched Daniel's face. "Maybe you're right. I'd like to think so." His shoulders slowly relaxed. "That's the most important challenge for me, to restore Father's good name. And I also can't leave Alberta alone with this, it's too much for her. If Hunter throws me out, takes me off the case, well—" He shook his head, but it was acceptance he was conveying, not doubt, not at all.

"He won't do that," Daniel said with absolute certainty. "And neither would any of the rest of us." He gave his friend the shadow of a smile. "And if you were removed, then Impney would leave. And if he left, the whole company would fall to pieces, more so than a house of cards." Daniel's smile broadened a bit. "We might think we run the show, but it's Impney who does that. He's the director; we're just the actors on the stage."

"I know, yes, Impney," said Toby. "A good man who lets us think we matter."

Daniel could see that Toby was trying to bring a lightness into this conversation, but his voice gave him away. It was still thick, heavy with unshed tears.

"One more thing," Toby said. "Watch your back."

"My—"

"Alexandra Stanton's father, Daniel. The man is consumed by grief and lashes out. Don't be surprised if he makes a scene. Not that it's a mystery why: he lost his only child. Still, he can go off the rails, and whoever is defending the man he's sure is guilty, well—just promise you'll be careful."

Daniel sensed that this was a good time to leave. He stood up. "I'll go and say goodbye to Alberta," he said. "You and I will keep in close touch. I want to follow your father's progress . . . and ask for your advice and guidance. And yes," he added, his voice warm and caring, "I will be careful; you have my word."

Toby offered a smile that was closer to a grimace.

Daniel saw such emotion in his friend's eyes that he tried to imagine what he was feeling, and then immediately chastised himself. He could never truly understand. That is, not unless it had been his parents, and not Toby's, who were the victims. The very idea filled him with such dread that he had to close his eyes for a moment to shut out this frightening thought.

CHAPTER

Eight

THE SKY WAS darkening and the air was turning cold when Miriam finally reached home, but it did not feel like the home she had left. She told herself that this was nonsense, and it was simply that she was exhausted and Daniel was still in Suffolk.

She stood at the door, key in hand, struck by a thought, an emotion she had not expected. She was a scientist, respected in her field, an independent woman who made decisions about her life. So why was she feeling that something was missing?

It was cold inside, but the kitchen stove was still warm. The heat lasted a long time if banked with coal and coke, and left on as low as possible. *At least there will be hot water.* The thought of tea directed her to the kettle, which she filled and placed on the hob, along with a slice of bread. Seated at the table, the missing piece fell into place. This independent, successful woman was feeling incomplete, and it was because Daniel was not there. *So much for the modern woman!* She felt like a charlatan, a traitor to the feminist cause. Into this thought tumbled another: Did Daniel feel incomplete when he was away from her? She doubted that very much!

The tea was comforting, as she needed it to be, giving her time to reconsider this disparaging thought about her husband. Perhaps he only appeared to separate easily from her. What if he, too, felt the pain of distance? She took little bites of toast, hardly aware of doing so.

Miriam hated the silence, and that she would not hear Daniel's footsteps, or his voice, not tonight, and maybe not tomorrow, or even the day after. She walked to the foyer to pick up the telephone and call him, let him know she was safely home, but then she hesitated. Not that he would worry overly much; it was mainly for her, and the need to hear his voice.

Miriam ached with grief for Toby. Was an expert's examination of the bullets—that is, if they found the second one—the beginning of the answers they so desperately sought? There was no guarantee that they would learn something from it, especially if it was as damaged as Officer Thorpe had described.

MIRIAM WOKE EARLY the next morning and got out of bed straightaway. It was Sunday, but she was tense, worrying about all that remained unresolved, both in the evidence needed to exonerate Peter Ward and to uncover the truth about the attack on Toby's parents.

She still had eggs in the pantry, and reasonably edible bread, so there was plenty to eat for breakfast. However, the moment she entered the kitchen, she realized that she had no appetite. As she filled the kettle, she considered the possibility that she was wrong in her concerns about Eve. The doctors had declared her healed, after that attack in the lab months ago, and there had been several evaluations to confirm this. It was almost easier, and less painful, for Miriam to attribute the changes to injury rather than age. In fact, considering age as the culprit, Eve's condition made it more painful, because she was seeing these changes in her father as well.

These were the times when she thought of Daniel, and how, in less than forty years, he would be only sixty-five when she was in her eighties. Would he have to care for her? Bring in a nurse? Or worse, put her in a home?

"Just stop," she told herself, placing the kettle on the hob. The messages running through her head reminded her of a scratched record, repeating itself over and over until someone had the good sense to turn the damn thing off.

As unappetizing as breakfast seemed, she knew she had to eat. One egg, one slice of toast with butter and a dab of marmalade, partnered with an unusually large mug of tea should suffice. She cracked an egg and slipped it into an overly large pan, and then placed the bread alongside it. Standing there, she ran the day's projects through her mind. Simply thinking about all she had to do was making her tired. There was no room for errors, whether in judgment or the interpretation of facts. Eve had taught her the right way and the wrong way when it came to procedure, and why each step in the correct order would minimize, if not eliminate, concerns about the conclusions. Miriam smiled, recalling how, at the beginning of her career, she had been terrified to take the stand as an expert in her field.

"Never be afraid of the truth," Eve had insisted. "It is all we have."

And now, all these years later, Miriam was still concerned about this. The truth, that is.

She would sit down and eat, if only for the energy required to perform her duties through a long day, and then go to the morgue. It was time to get back to work.

MIRIAM ARRIVED HALF an hour later than usual, but she did not expect anyone to be perturbed. She had reached home too late yesterday evening to tell them she was back, and Eve was not one to watch the clock.

She went inside, hung up her coat, and was ready to work. As the door clicked closed behind her, she saw Joe turn from the bench where he was taking notes. At first, his face registered no recognition, then he raised his eyeglasses, perched them atop his head, and smiled.

"Good morning, Joe. How are you?"

"Fine, Doctor, glad to see you back," he replied.

She expected him to add a *but*, sensing this was the word he had left out. "Is Dr. Hall in?"

"Er, not yet, miss." He had been Eve's assistant long before Miriam had been here and the *miss* was not meant derogatively, simply his way of acknowledging her youth. When a conversation turned serious, professional, he addressed both women as *Doctor*. "Expect she'll be in soon."

"She's been in every day?" She moved a bit closer. "Joe, is she all right?" When she said this, she hoped it sounded as if she were asking about Eve's general health, but the look on his face said that he knew she meant much more. It conveyed the questions she needed answered: Was Eve forgetting things, misplacing them, or even losing them? Miriam and Joe had not discussed this outright, but each was aware that the other understood. One day, perhaps soon, they would have to acknowledge these concerns in words.

"Ah, yes, miss. Did an autopsy just yesterday. Poor gentleman's still in the cold room. Need to finish up my notes for Dr. Eve, then she'll check on them and we can call the interment folks to take him—that is, Mr. Leahy—and give him a decent burial."

Miriam felt as if she were standing on a beach, close to the water's edge, and waiting for the seventh wave to come in. Now she saw it. If it reached her, its power would suck her in. But a retreat would gain her nothing. "Something's worrying you, Joe." It was a statement, not a question. "Shall we look at the notes again?"

He hesitated so long, she was about to draw her own conclusion that he was afraid to answer, when he spoke. "Do you mind? Taking a look, that is. I'll say my notes were illegible, if she comes before we finish, and if she asks."

There was a wealth of information in his words. He, too, was protective of Eve.

For Miriam, nothing mattered more than accuracy. She sometimes rued the results, especially if they proved someone who seemed so obviously guilty to be innocent, but Eve had drummed into her the need to remain neutral, and how personal feelings could not only color the results, but possibly skew them one way or another. There were people in the legal field who even questioned how much it mattered if an error was made when determining the cause of death. Not if it was an illness, an accident, or suicide versus an intentional attack, but whether that attack included a weapon. It mattered greatly, especially if the possibility of foul play was accidentally overlooked, or if the evidence was misinterpreted and an innocent person accused. Thank goodness this attitude was changing, as science was evolving and more precise conclusions could be reached. This made her work not only more demanding, but far more compelling. She had chosen the right profession; she told herself that every day.

Miriam moved toward the cold room, where bodies were kept, with Joe on her heels.

They worked quickly, exchanging conversation only when it was necessary. The body before them was that of an elderly man who had died in what looked like an accidental fall. Not a surprise, considering his advanced age. The doctor had asked for an autopsy, but only because Mr. Leahy had been found in the bathroom, on the floor, yet he did not appear to have tripped on anything. Miriam's task was to determine if he had suffered a heart attack or a stroke, after which he had fallen and hit his head, or if the fall itself had killed him. According to the doctor, the old man had become increasingly ill-tempered of late, and the inheritance he left behind was considerable.

All of this was explained by Joe as they were examining the body and he was reading Eve's notes aloud. They had concluded that a heart attack had killed him, and the fall was the result of this, and not the other way around.

"There are bruises on his head," Miriam said, her voice low as she explored them as best she could through his thick white hair. A patch of it had been cut away, revealing a partial wound, but still it was difficult to see it clearly.

"Is that where he fell and struck the edge of the bath?" Joe looked anxious, his face uncertain. It was a question, not a conclusion.

"Not sure yet," Miriam replied, still peering into what seemed like quite a large and deep abrasion. "Any other bruises on him, anywhere? Recent bruises, perhaps inflicted immediately prior to his death?" As she asked, she straightened her back to have a fuller view of the body.

"Didn't find any, except one near the left shin. Looks as if he gave that a good crack on something." Joe pointed to a recent bruise on the leg.

"Is that the only one?" she asked, bending closer again to examine the discolored patch of skin.

"Yes." Joe looked down at the leg, then up at her, anxiety evident in his eyes. "Do you need me to cut his hair off, so we can see all of that injury to his head?"

"I think so, thank you. Unless you can tell me why Dr. Hall didn't do that?"

"I can't really say, miss. I know she thought he'd had a heart attack as he was getting out of the bath, so then he fell awkwardly. Possibly he was unconscious before he reached the floor?"

"We'll have to look," she answered, her voice scratchy in her throat. Were they looking at a possible murder? Now that there was evidence capable of more than one interpretation, she could not ignore it.

Joe took a scissors and cut away a large circle of hair surrounding the wound. It was not an easy task, because close to the scalp the hair was matted with dried blood. Miriam watched as he used a long-handled razor and shaved away the remaining hair, careful not to let the blade touch any part of the injury.

"We've cut the hair surrounding the laceration," she said to Joe, watching as he picked up his pen and jotted this down. "The hair away from the wound has been washed clean."

He took a closer look. "Perhaps someone in his home did it for decency's sake? Or maybe to stop the blood marking whatever he was laying on? Why ruin good bed linen? Or to make him look as peaceful as possible?" He shrugged and then looked to Miriam for her thoughts.

"Or to hide the severity of the injury," she mumbled, speaking more to herself than to Joe.

She took a magnifying glass and peered even more closely. "Who found him?"

Joe shuffled through a few pages of notes. "His daughter."

The other marks on his body were negligible, possibly incurred in the fall when he collapsed with the heart attack, which was certainly major enough to have been the cause of death.

Again, Miriam stepped away from the body. Did the head injury matter? Eve had thought not. She had dictated her thoughts to Joe, who wrote that Mr. Leahy's injury had occurred as a result of a fall.

Miriam was concerned. Unless there was some other evidence to prove this, it was an unwarranted conclusion. Did he have a heart attack and then fall, or was the heart attack the result of the trauma of the fall? And if the fall didn't precipitate the heart attack, what did? The crux of their work was to determine the cause of death. No one—not the police nor the family nor Eve—seemed prepared to acknowledge that someone might have struck the man with a weapon of some kind. Of course, it was more likely that he had experienced a heart attack, but it had to be proven. If he had died from a head injury caused by an attacker, it was up to the police to examine the scene and question the evidence, and then any witnesses, if they existed.

She looked again at the injury. Now that Joe had removed much more hair, she was able to touch the wound. The tissue yielded under her fingers. As she gently probed, she felt along the skull and found it broken in several places, and not long breaks, but the kind of break caused by a single blow leaving a deep dent. Possibly a lethal one. "We need to start at the beginning."

He nodded, his expression grave.

They did the autopsy again, carefully, with Joe taking notes as Miriam dictated. They had just finished and it was after eleven o'clock in the morning when Eve finally arrived. She had taken off her coat and hung it on the stand before either Joe or Miriam had noticed her. Her rubber-soled shoes were silent. It was her movement throwing a shadow across the floor that caught Joe's attention.

He stopped writing and looked up, and then Miriam saw his face and she, too, turned and looked.

No one spoke.

Eve's face moved from shock to anger, and then almost immediately to consternation. "What are you doing?" Her voice was flat, without emotion, and under such tight control it sounded artificial.

It was a long, frozen moment, although perhaps no more than a few seconds

Joe started to speak, but Miriam silenced him with a look.

"Joe," she began, and then stopped. That was the coward's way out, to suggest that Joe might not have confidence in Eve's report. And Eve certainly deserved better than some weak equivocation. She drew breath and began again. "Joe did not finish his notes yesterday, so we had to take out the body to complete them. It's all there, except the cause of death. I can't tell whether it was the heart attack or the blow to the head, which was very hard, and cracked the skull. It caused a lot of bleeding. I don't know who washed away much of the blood. Perhaps the relations who reported the death? Or even the doctor, although he should have known better." She hesitated. "Joe did not note down your conclusion. Or perhaps you hadn't reached one yet?"

The silence in the room was like the hesitation between a lightning strike and the sound of thunder.

Joe turned and left the room. Miriam knew it was not cowardice or any kind of scorn, it was tact. And perhaps a touch of sadness.

"I missed it," Eve said slowly. "The head wound. That is, I saw it, but determined it was the result of a fall. I thought it was the shock of falling that caused the heart attack. He was old, and had a history of heart episodes." Her eyes searched Miriam's face and she must have seen the understanding in it because her face relaxed. Even so, the tension between them remained.

"I couldn't leave it," Miriam said gently. "You taught me that. It may have been a heart attack, but also a blow to the head."

"It might be hard to tell," Eve said, leaning closer and peering at the wound. "But, of course, we must try."

"If it was the rim of the bath, it could easily have been an accident," Miriam said, "but it feels like the shape of something round. Possibly something on or near the bathtub."

"Unlikely," Eve replied. "But . . . if it was an object that has been removed from the bathroom, then we need to know why. By repute, he was a nasty man, mean-spoken and always complaining. So, as much as one might like to say it was an accident, it might well not have been." She straightened up, stretching her back with effort. "Miriam, why would I think he hit his head when falling?" She bit her lip hard, but did not wince at the pain. "I saw what I wished to, didn't I?"

This was a mercy Miriam could easily grant her. "I don't think so. His hair was quite thick. It hid most of the damage, and he didn't bleed for long, because he was dead soon after. A matter of seconds, maybe. Whether it was his heart or the head wound—well, yes, that might be the difference between a natural death and murder—but it could easily have been either."

"We have to find out," said Eve, determination in her voice.

Miriam nodded. "And so we will," she promised.

She looked directly at Eve, making certain her expression was positive, encouraging. "Let's go over our notes and compare each other's results, as we have always done." She spoke the words so casually that Eve gave her an almost mocking look, signaling to Miriam that she knew very well that this was not business as usual.

The tension was broken when Joe emerged from the kitchen with a pot of fresh tea and two cups. He set the tray down, gave a little nod, and went out again, closing the door behind him.

Miriam filled the cups and passed one to Eve.

They sipped for several minutes without speaking. Finally, Eve asked, "How is Toby?"

"Wretched," Miriam replied. She gave Eve a brief summary of what had happened, and what little they actually knew, including the discovery of the existence of a second bullet, and no knowledge of where it had been deposited. "When it's found, Daniel will bring both bullets to London to be examined by a ballistics expert."

"I'd think there were several qualified experts around Suffolk," Eve said.

"True, but Daniel is taking no chances."

Eve remained quiet. Finally, she said, "And what of Toby's case with his client Peter Ward?" She took a sip of her tea, and then wrapped her hands around the cup, as if seeking its warmth. "It seems to me that there are some major elements we don't know about it, and it's quite unlikely that Toby will be back in time to stand up for the defense. Even if he comes back by Sunday evening, he will be in no mental or emotional state to give the battle what it needs. I really wish we had performed Stanton's autopsy."

Miriam wished that as well, but Toby and Daniel were the barristers who represented the man accused of murdering her. How would it look if the wife of a member of the defense counsel of ffford Croft and Gibson performed the autopsy? What would happen if the prosecutor suggested a bias? Or worse, a false finding so they would exonerate a guilty man? And if she or Eve had performed the autopsy, and there was something reported based on an inadvertent error, there would be charges of coercion.

"The pathologist has a solid reputation," Eve said, without naming the man. "I've read his notes and they appear to be accurate. Stanton definitely died from knife wounds. I only wish I could have observed while he worked."

Miriam was about to ask Eve about the pathologist, but Eve spoke first.

"What if he missed something? Or omitted a finding that he considered unimportant? Don't even the best pathologists make mistakes?"

These questions only raised Miriam's determination to delve more deeply into all of the evidence.

At this point Joe returned to the room. He and Miriam stood next to Eve, both of them watching her, as if waiting for her to continue. But it was Miriam who picked up the conversation.

"We're right to be concerned about Toby," Miriam said. "It's unlikely he'll come back before this trial ends." She looked at Eve and Joe, sadness in her eyes. "I'm afraid the news from Ipswich is tragic. The local police seem almost fixated on charging his father with the crime. That is, if he lives. When I was in Suffolk, I did an autopsy on Toby's mother. And that was despite vehement objections from his sister, and significant resistance from the family physician." She repeated a few of Dr. Jolls's responses and was pleased when Joe smiled and Eve's face softened.

This small measure of levity was short-lived.

Eve swallowed hard, then looked steadily at Miriam. "I fear this is a tragedy that may only get worse." Before Miriam could respond, Eve went on. "It is up to us to give Toby and Daniel every assistance we can in finding the answer."

"The answer to . . ." Joe said, eyes wide in confusion.

Eve waved her hand, as if wishing him not to continue. "Not about Toby's parents; there's nothing we can do here. That is, until evidence is sent to us, or until Miriam is summoned to travel to Suffolk to give evidence. No, I'm referring to helping Toby and Daniel, assisting them in the defense of Peter Ward, and hopefully avoiding a conviction for the murder of Alexandra Stanton." She spoke quietly, but her voice was strong with certainty.

"And now what?" Joe asked, his voice tentative, but with a fragile thread of hope.

"We need to go over everything," Eve said. "Get our hands on the police reports, the pathologist's notes. Perhaps there was something they missed."

Miriam heard the challenge in Eve's voice, as if daring Miriam to defy her. Sadly, this was something Miriam would have to do. With the trial already underway, any errors or reevaluations needed to be dealt with now, but neither Miriam nor Eve had the authority to act. And with Daniel's firm defending Ward, any participation on this lab's part could sink the defense. That would not stop Miriam from doing her own research, including getting her hands on all the police reports, photographs from the crime scene, and even the autopsy findings. So often, it was the smallest detail, the minutiae, that provided the answers. But how would she tell Eve of her plans? She could not, and this knowledge added to her sadness.

CHAPTER

Nine

"I CAN'T LEAVE." TOBY looked embarrassed, even ashamed, but there was no wavering in his voice, or in his eyes. "Father's going to live . . . I think. And the police aren't letting up at all. They're certain he committed this crime. There has to be an explanation, but no one seems to care. Daniel, they aren't even looking for it anymore. Alberta is loyal and won't believe him guilty, but even she can't think of any other answer."

They stood together inside the inn, located not far from the police station and the home of Toby's parents. Daniel saw misery naked in his friend's face.

"There has to be something," Toby said.

"I know," Daniel replied. "I have to go back to London and start working on the Ward case." He rubbed his eyes, while trying to hold fast to thoughts of even one day devoid of drama. "But before I leave, have you any idea what it was you thought of, just before I came to interrupt you? Any clue at all? It might help me to know where I can begin to look. Anything come to mind?"

Toby closed his eyes. "It was only a glimpse, some fleeting thought about a possibility. But I do remember that it was a whole different angle, something that might have made it difficult to convict Peter." He shook his head. "He could have had an alibi? Damn!"

"Another person with the same characteristics?" Daniel asked. It was a flash of hope, glimpsed and then gone again. In its place was frustration. To be so close, perhaps within reach of a solution—an acquittal. One innocent man's life spared. "Can you recall what made you think of it? Or give me some idea of where I start looking?"

Toby shrugged, more a gesture of defeat than uncertainty. "I don't know, Daniel. I just . . . don't know. I can't even remember what made me think of it. Even more, I have no idea what *it* is! And I have tried, I swear. But I can't concentrate on anything, except who killed my mother . . . and why." He looked at Daniel intently. "The only thing I can think of is someone shared a secret with my father, and it was so shameful that this person panicked and needed to silence him, kill him. Perhaps my mother walked in, startled this person, and she, too, was shot."

Daniel thought about this for a moment, his brow creased in concentration, and then he spoke. "So, your father was the intended victim and your mother was unlucky enough to be there."

Toby nodded. "Or . . . perhaps the killer assumed that Father would have told her something secret, in confidence." The sudden glare of anger flashed and then died in his eyes, and in the place of that came tears. "He never would have betrayed the confidence of a parishioner—or of anyone, for that matter."

Daniel waited a moment before he spoke. "Perhaps the killer was so full of guilt that he lost all perspective," Daniel suggested. "In fact, this explains so much. But I'm surprised he doesn't stand out as someone with a history of losing self-control." He stopped. Judging by the slump of his friend's body, nothing more needed to be said.

"Then why the hell can't we see it?" Toby blurted out. "It's nearly a week. We see people every day, the whole village. Is everyone as blind as we are? Or are they protecting someone? Dear God! Would they let Father hang for it, knowing it was someone else?"

"I don't think so." The moment the words were out of his mouth, Daniel knew they were not enough. He reminded himself that this case was fraught with emotion, but they needed to remember the importance of logic. "Unless, of course, there was someone even closer, in your own family, who is guilty?"

"Like who?" Toby asked, as if the world he knew was suddenly crumbling around him.

"I'm sorry," Daniel said softly. "But someone did this. So, think: Is there anyone else? Anyone who resented him? Wanted something from him that he could not, or would not, provide? And had any access to where the gun was kept?" He stretched his back against the increasing tension that was working its way up and into his neck. "I wish we were closer to knowing, but nothing makes sense." Daniel had no idea what was circulating through Toby's head, what possibilities. "Someone from the past?" Daniel suggested.

"You mean someone who arrived, found the gun, shot my mother and then my father, and then walked away?" It would not have been necessary for Toby to state his disbelief; it was plain in his face. "It's someone from the village," he went on. "It must be. Yes, someone who had shared a confidence with Father, a secret we never even guessed at."

Daniel felt desperately guilty, leaving Toby to face this alone, but it was a choice between remaining here for his friend, or going back to London and doing his best to complete Toby's job of defending Peter Ward, who might well be guilty. But this would mean that Toby would have to fight for his father more or less on his own. The thought churned in Daniel's stomach. He was hoping to divert Toby from this sense of helplessness, hopelessness he was feeling about his father.

"I'm of no use to you here," Daniel said. "I don't know these people. Your sister does, and I do believe you could work together." The pitiful look on Toby's face prompted him to add, "I don't know whether you need that—working together—but I'm certain *she* does." As he said the words, he realized that they were intended to be of some comfort to Toby, but he was actually suggesting comfort for Alberta. He had met her husband, who seemed loyal and supportive, but Toby was her older brother; he had known Alberta all her life. That was a unique bond they shared. Daniel wondered if his presence was a barrier, that he was almost in the way. Perhaps Toby needed a bond of blood more than he needed a friend, if only for these dreadful days.

Toby was looking at him. He gave a small, bleak smile. "Yes," he agreed. "I do understand. Now, if I can just convince my sister to form that team with me."

"I'll take the first train tomorrow morning," Daniel said. "I'll go home and change my clothes, a clean shirt at least, then I'll go to chambers and read up on the Peter Ward case. If Gideon needs me, I'll be up to date on all the specifics. As for your sister," he added, hoping to leave Toby with even a fraction of hope, "I'm sure she'll come around."

"Come around? To what? We've already made it through the autopsy," Toby said.

"I meant that she'll be kinder to you, more accepting."

Toby hesitated. "Thank you," he said, so quietly the words seemed to float in the air.

CHAPTER

Ten

FOR THE FIRST time since her arrival at the lab, Eve smiled. Not a broad, joyful smile, but one that said *Yes, thank you, we are in this together*.

Miriam felt a lightness come over her. This was a glimpse of the old Eve, and it filled her heart to have her friend back with her again.

"I have been thinking," Eve said. "We did not do the autopsy on Miss Stanton, but the newspapers have certainly provided information. And from what I can see, there seem to be several questions as yet unanswered."

Joe nodded, as if he had never doubted this.

"Questions such as what?" Miriam asked.

"What knife was used?" Eve replied. "I don't mean what was it like. The wounds would have told us that. I mean, where did it come from? And was this a crime of opportunity? The body was found in the garden, where she was killed. So, I imagine two possibilities. One, that the killer arrived, argued with her, then grabbed a knife and followed her outside to the garden. It cannot have been a sudden crime, because he had the forethought to find a knife and follow her out. And two, he might have arrived and witnessed something in the garden, perhaps Alexandra with another man. If so, that tells us that he would then have to go into the kitchen, find the knife, and then revisit the garden after the man departed. When she was alone, he attacked her. And why? Was he in love, or lust, and couldn't bear her kissing another man?"

Before either Miriam or Joe could answer her, she raced ahead. "But what if that other man saw the attack? Why didn't the killer harm the other man? And why didn't the other man, whomever he was, defend Alexandra? What did he do, simply run away and say nothing to anyone? Unless, of course, she was alone in the garden. If so, why an unprovoked attack?"

"I think I see what you're saying," Miram told her. "If she was alone, why would Peter Ward attack her, rather than speak to her, kiss her, or whatever."

"Exactly," Eve said. "If he took the knife from the house—and that has not been proven—wherever he got the knife, either from there, or even brought it with him, that would make this, to some extent, premeditated."

"I don't think that helps us," Miriam said. "In fact, it makes it more—"

"I haven't finished yet!" Eve said sharply. "I am pointing out that we have not fully examined the evidence, and what it means!"

Miriam raised her hands, as if in surrender. "I'm sorry, please go on."

Eve nodded. "This was not a crime that took place on the spur of the moment. Let's not forget that there was a party going on inside the house. So, either something happened at that party causing someone to go outside to the garden with Alexandra, or else that person followed after her, already armed with a knife. And not a pocketknife, but something with a blade of strength, at least three or four inches in length and single-edged, from the newspapers' description of the injuries. The police are putting it as a quarrel, a rejection, and a sudden urge. That is not what the evidence indicates. No," she concluded, with a shake of her head, "there is more to it than that."

"What more?" Miriam asked. It was a question, not a challenge.

"It was planned, at least from some time before the act occurred. The killer armed himself before he went out into the garden after her. It would be interesting to know if he was armed when he arrived at the party."

"Are you saying that he went there intending to attack her?" Miriam could not keep the incredulity out of her voice, a tone that sounded much like disbelief.

"Not necessarily," Eve replied. "As I said, he might have taken the knife from the house. Has anyone thought of counting the table knives? Steak knives? Carving knives? Not to mention kitchen knives?"

"I don't know," Miriam replied, although she was thinking, *How should I know?*

"I'm not sure it will take us anywhere," Eve said, "but it is a question that should be answered. If the knife can be traced, then it might be possible to know who brought it. And if it was taken from the house, who had the opportunity? Who quarreled with her? It makes no sense," she mused, almost to herself. She turned her gaze to Miriam. "And why accuse Peter Ward? We need to know who were the poor girl's enemies, and who was out to get Ward. In fact, we need to know a hell of a lot more than we do. Why was the investigation completed so quickly? And how did they come to this conclusion, making Peter Ward the killer? This is very sloppy police work indeed." She gave Miriam a hard look, her eyes wide and forehead creased. "In whose interest is it that the case is closed as quickly as possible, before these questions are answered?"

Miriam felt herself smiling, although nothing was remotely

funny about this, or even pleasant, but she was reveling in the return of her friend's quick mind that often raced ahead of her own, with ideas and suppositions tumbling forth. Eve could think sideways, and around corners, see things that other people missed, and find new questions beyond the old ones. At this moment, it was as though someone were reaching inside her mentor's brain and untying a knot.

"Octamus Ornshaw," Eve said suddenly.

Miriam knew to whom she was referring. Ornshaw had been Miriam's most knowledgeable and supportive tutor, the only one who had believed that medicine depended on intelligence, curiosity, discipline, and nerve, and not whether you were a man or a woman. He knew better than to imagine women were more prone to fainting and squeamishness than men. "For heaven's sake, they deal with births and deaths, and all the many illnesses in between. It's only natural they have the nerve for it, and the curiosity for it, if they wish," he had said, and more than once.

Ornshaw had also cared deeply for Miriam. He had shared his knowledge, expanding greatly her background in pathology, and had allowed her to assist him in his laboratory. But he had let her go, and graciously, when her opportunity came to study under Eve Hall.

This was not the first time it had crossed her mind just how much she owed him.

"I've read that Ornshaw did the autopsy on Alexandra," Eve replied, almost as if reading Miriam's thoughts, "and it's doubtful he missed something. But it was his assistant who swore to his findings in court. Apparently, Octamus is not well. A young man called Anderson delivered the information." Her face was filled with concern.

Miriam was quick to see it. "You *are* up to date on the proceedings, Eve! So, you think this Anderson fellow erred when giving the results?"

"It's worth finding out," Eve replied. "Because there's certainly something missing. I don't know what it is, but let's go and see Octamus. I've never met this Anderson fellow, but someone who worked with him said he was a worm. That makes me think he's one of those *Yes sir, no My Lord, just as you say, Your Lordship* types. A real dandiprat, if you ask me! Witnesses like that are useless. They add nothing. They take the stand and say what someone has told them to say. I've faced my share of witnesses who try to disparage my findings because some prosecutor has convinced him that he'll be rewarded in some manner."

"We have no way of knowing what has happened . . . or hasn't happened. Without Toby here, we can only guess," Miriam said.

Eve straightened her back, as if to begin a lengthy walk. "A few minutes with Octamus and we'll learn much."

"But you said he's ill," Joe interjected.

"Yes, but I know him," said Miriam. "He would not want this to stand. And he might be able to help, especially if he recalls the autopsy and his findings. With any luck, he'll be in possession of his documents."

Eve frowned in concentration. "Yes," she said finally, but slowly, as though reawakening the full weight of memory in her mind. "This could be bigger, much bigger. You're right, Miriam, we need to do this now." With that, she turned toward the door.

Miriam met Joe's eyes.

He smiled.

She returned the smile and followed Eve.

After a short taxi ride, they found Ornshaw in his laboratory, as they had expected, and he was delighted to see them. Miriam immediately noticed how he had changed, the rosy complexion he called his Irish Ruddiness now pale. She watched the way Eve approached him, with the respect given a professional superior, although it was quite the opposite. Miriam knew that most people in the profession of pathology not only regarded Eve Hall as their superior, but their superior who had all the answers.

Miriam knew that Ornshaw and Eve had never worked together directly, whereas Miriam had received so much from him, his tutoring and guidance, from the time she had first been seriously interested in pathology. That was going back fifteen years or more, yet she had never forgotten him. She was sorry that they had lost touch since she had married.

The moment he saw his former student enter the room, his face lit with pleasure. "Miriam! Or should I say *Dr. Pitt*?"

Miriam smiled warmly. "Dr. fford Croft," she said.

"Pitt, fford Croft, you're still Miriam, and what a pleasure to see you!" He turned to Eve. "And Dr. Hall. We've met before, you might not remember, it was a long time ago. How are you?" For a moment his face was shadowed, perhaps by the realization that she was not the robust, forceful woman he had seen only a year or two ago. But then, the elderly often looked at an old friend with sadness, seeing the white hair and creased skin, while thinking of themselves as still youthful.

"Please come in." He pushed the door wide open, and both women entered the large, comfortable laboratory, quite obviously a working space that was at once casually untidy and yet immaculately clean.

As was characteristic of the Ornshaw Miriam knew, he came straight to the point. "What can I do for you?" He gestured to a small table with two chairs and a stool beside it. He sat on the stool and nodded toward the chairs.

Eve sat and replied, "Daniel Pitt has the task of defending Peter Ward, a young man accused of murder." She stopped abruptly, studying his face, and as if seeing that he understood the gravity and urgency of the situation, she continued, explaining their current position. "The victim is Alexandra Stanton . . . I realize that you are aware of the case."

"Of course," he replied. "And before you go any further, I must say that I believe not all the forensic evidence was given in court. I was ill, and I had my assistant speak on my behalf. Now that my gallbladder is behaving, I'm feeling better, thank goodness. It wasn't until later that I learned how vital elements were withheld out of respect for the dead, and the feelings of her family."

Eve frowned. "Do you realize that your man Anderson stated as fact that the rape did not actually occur?"

Ornshaw leaned forward. "I beg your pardon?"

"The newspaper reports were very clear on that point. Are you saying that was erroneous?" pressed Eve. "For heaven's sake, that is taking modesty to absurd lengths! Did your man not understand that, being under oath, he was committing perjury?"

Ornshaw shook his head. "I've read those proceedings and he answered what he was asked."

"In the name of heaven!" Eve said furiously. "Did the prosecution not ask if she was raped? What's the matter with the man?"

"Yes, he did ask, and an expert answer was given. Dr. Hall, please trust my findings. There was no evidence of penetration. The girl was still a virgin. When I say that evidence was withheld to protect her family, I'm referring to something quite different." His face darkened. "The killer cut away a patch of her skin that had pubic hair, and since it was not found with or near the body, we presume he took it as a souvenir. We—"

"How dreadful! And was it found?" Miriam interrupted. "In Peter Ward's possession?"

"No, not so far as I know. But if it had been, I'm sure the police would have mentioned it, whether the family opposed it or not. But you could ask them, to be certain."

"So where is it?" Miriam persisted.

"A good question," Ornshaw answered. "To which there are several possible answers: thrown away, hidden somewhere in Ward's belongings, or in the keeping of whomever really killed her."

Eve looked directly at him and asked the question Miriam believed had been on her mind since they arrived. "Dr. Ornshaw, have you heard of anything similar to this, in relation to any other crimes? It seems like a compulsive sort of criminal act to me. Is this his first offense, do you suppose?"

"No, of course not," Ornshaw replied. "You know as well as I do, this is not someone who blithely decided to attack a young woman. There will have been others, possibly less serious, or perhaps he is new to the area and they occurred somewhere else, far enough from here for us not to know about."

Eve nodded slowly. "That leaves us no choice, don't you agree, Miriam? We have to find out if there were other crimes where skin was taken. And if so, whether any of them are at all related to this one. Is this a copycat? Or is it all some passion run amok?"

Miriam recognized that they could not afford to look away. But what questions could they ask? They had no authority, just scientific curiosity and a tangential link to the case.

"We need to know how many of them there are," Eve said. "And exactly when and where they were attacked, and how many of them had that part cut away. The defense needs more information."

Miriam realized that they were moving toward a place from which there was no return. "If there are others, and it can be proven that the attacker is the same person, only then can Peter Ward's conviction be stopped. But if they convict him before all the evidence has been found, it will be far more difficult, or even impossible, to reopen the case and get the police to admit their error. There are too many in the police force who believe it is dangerous to the law itself if mistakes are exposed."

"Answers," Eve announced, her voice like a stone breaking glass. "Someone needs to find these answers! We must get involved, find out exactly how many of these crimes follow exactly the same pattern, including the souvenir patch of hair, which I know that none of the newspapers have reported, as they would have if it were known. We must ask all registered pathologists. They shouldn't be hard to find."

"Then we had better begin," Miriam said, her voice strained. "We're in a good position to take this on, Eve." She had a stark choice. If she exposed pathologists who had ignored the evidence, even if only by silence, they would be ostracized. Or would *she*? But then, who would dismiss the evidence, knowing that to conceal it would lead a man to be hanged for a crime he almost certainly did not commit, leaving the real killer free to continue slashing and murdering more women? For Miriam, that was the worst thing. The police might fumble along, but her responsibility was to act now, before more women died.

She turned to Eve. "How do you suggest we get started?"

"We need a list of all the major pathologists," Eve replied. She hesitated a moment, turning to Ornshaw. "Would you be kind enough to make a list of those you think we should speak to?"

Miriam wondered what she could say if Ornshaw did not agree. It might take just one pathologist who recognized the pattern of murder in another young woman to free Peter Ward.

There was a moment's silence before he spoke. "Of course, and I'm sure there will be a way of looking them up and providing their addresses. It is an excellent idea. Let me know if there is any other way I can be of help. This is very serious. Eve, Miriam, if I hear anything more, I shall get in touch with you at once."

MIRIAM HAD CONVINCED Eve that they should walk back to the lab. "The weather is balmy," she said. "How often do we have this opportunity?"

"Fine with me," Eve said. "But if I wear out, will you put me on your back and carry me?"

"I'll wave down a taxi," Miriam promised.

Fifteen minutes later, they were comfortably seated and on their way.

They arrived at the lab and headed to their own work areas. Miriam knew she needed far more information about these deaths in order to help Daniel. He was facing a painful reality. The trial of Peter Ward was due to resume on Wednesday morning, and by now it was obvious that it would not be handled by Toby. It would feel like a betrayal for Daniel to leave him, but someone had to return for the trial. When she argued that Gideon, as the senior member of chambers, was more than qualified, Daniel told her that he was deeply overworked in another case. Therefore, it was logical that the task would fall to Daniel. It was Daniel who had given his word to Peter Ward. And it was also Daniel, next to Toby himself, who knew most about the case. Which meant that Miriam was determined to find all she could to help.

"How far back should we go?" Miriam asked Eve. "If there are others, when did the attacks start?"

"We'll begin within the last five years," Eve replied decisively. "We want recent history if we are to track him down. I don't think we'll find much in the earlier years, or we would have seen this pattern before."

Miriam nodded in agreement, her lips tight with tension. It was a big decision to question other pathologists. No one would like it; but equally, they could not refuse to do it. That would be tantamount to riding with the tide, which had already turned an unknown number of times. It was the coward's way, and unacceptable to her. She took a deep breath. "Yes, get that list, and perhaps it will be faster if we divide it between us."

For a moment, Eve's face was blank, as if she was assessing their options. "No, better I stay here and Joe will help me." The skin around her mouth was white with tension. "Take your car, go to those pathologists whose names and addresses Octamus will give us."

Miriam would have been grateful for her help, but she had to honor Eve's decision. Her mentor might be slowing down a bit, but she was still the head of this lab, fully in charge. She placed her hand on Eve's arm and the two women stood quietly together, their bond of trust and friendship never stronger.

MIRIAM WEIGHED THE likelihood of heavy traffic and decided to travel by taxi to the nearest pathologist. It wasn't exactly Harley Street, but the building was quite new and its façade impressive. Someone had taken the time to install planters leading from the sidewalk up to the entrance, and they were brimming with autumn foliage.

She arrived to be told that Dr. Bobbitt was performing an autopsy, and she would have to wait at least a half an hour before he was free to speak to her. The time, otherwise wasted, was well spent putting her questions in order and settling her mind on how she wanted to approach the subject with him. When his assistant came to the waiting room to inform her that he was ready for her, and added that he had only a very short time, she was prepared. "Thank you," she said gravely. "I doubt I will require more than a few minutes."

He gave her a brief smile, as if not believing her for a moment. It was clear in his face that he thought she was there seeking assistance. Why else would a woman barge in like this?

Miriam smothered her irritation and followed him through to the morgue.

Dr. Bobbitt had just finished washing his hands. Turning toward her, he approached her with a halted stride while wiping his hands dry. "Good morning, Dr. fford Croft. What is the problem, and how can I be of assistance? Forgive me for being abrupt, but I have very little time." He was a comparatively young man, perhaps forty, with a keen but agreeable expression.

"Good morning, Dr. Bobbitt. I will come straight to the point. You are no doubt familiar with the case of Alexandra Stanton? She died in the course of an attempted rape and—"

"I have heard of it, of course," he interrupted. "But I know nothing other than what was reported in the newspapers." He frowned, appearing not at all curious as to why she would even raise the subject.

Miriam sensed a narrow window of opportunity, in terms of keeping his attention before he begged off to return to his important work. "My husband is defending the man accused, which explains my interest in the case. But I think it is in the greatest public interest for it to be known if this is a unique case, or if there have been others so similar as to suggest it is one of several." She saw from the change in his face that she now had his attention.

"Purely for the purpose of defense?" he asked, his expression suddenly more alert. "Or do you seem to think it might be part of a pattern?"

She felt her heart quicken. "There are aspects of it that indicate a compulsion," she replied. "I do not wish to suggest an answer to you."

"Weapon used? Pattern of injuries? Or have you some other aspect in mind?"

"A souvenir taken," she replied, recognizing that he was now fully engaged.

"Oh, I see. Yes, that certainly suggests something very ugly indeed." He ran his hand across his chin. "What was it?"

"Roughly, a square inch of skin with pubic hair, cut out presumably with a very sharp knife, and taken away," she answered, and then saw, even before he responded, both comprehension and disgust in his face.

"No," he said, "I haven't had a case like that. But I heard mention of one. It was gossip, I thought. I didn't take it seriously. I don't know where it originated. And honestly, I thought discussing it was in very bad taste. But if I recall who said it, I shall let you know."

"Please do," she said, aware of how quickly his acknowledgment raised her hopes, and then his lack of memory dashed them.

She thanked him, and left for the next doctor on the list, a Dr. Marshenk.

═

Miriam tried for nearly a quarter hour to flag down a taxi, and then girded herself for a ride on the underground. She descended into the Marleybone station and was relieved to see that the Bakerloo Line would take her directly to Oxford Circus. She had no problems taking the Tube, but there were often delays, usually due to the ongoing construction of new stations, resulting in temporarily redrawn routes.

She arrived at the building, far smaller and more modest than where Dr. Bobbitt worked. But there was one thing they had in common: this pathologist also kept her waiting. When he finally met with her, it was evident that he was not taking her questions seriously. He was older than Bobbitt, meaning that he was of that generation that believed his field of science was unsuitable for a young woman. Miriam guessed that he thought her younger than her age, and had no way of knowing that she possessed far more common sense and scientific knowledge than he would allow.

"Very busy," he said, immediately giving her the feeling of being dismissed.

"My questions are not fruitless, Dr. Marshenk. I have far too much to do to waste your time, or my own, or to simply be chasing information for curiosity's sake. I am looking for a pattern in a particularly nasty murder, primarily to prevent an innocent man from being hanged for a crime he did not commit. And secondly, because of the great urgency, to find who is guilty and prevent that person from doing this again and again!" That was an overstatement, she knew, and yet there was truth at the core of it. She could not say for certain that there was a pattern, but it did exist as a dark fear in her mind. The taking of this souvenir seemed more like a compulsive crime than having a single victim and never harming another. She said as much to Dr. Marshenk.

For a brief moment, he appeared confused. "Really? And how many instances of this rather bizarre behavior have you observed? How do you know this woman did not do it herself, for whatever reason? Perhaps you don't know as much about the behavior of young women as you imagine? Dare I say you are a little naïve. Miss Pitt, did you say?"

"Doctor," she snapped. "I practice under my maiden name of fford Croft. I work with Dr. Evelyn Hall. Possibly you have heard of her?" she asked sarcastically. All of England's scientific community knew Eve Hall.

Marshenk was temporarily taken aback. "Oh, you did not say so."

"My error," Miriam replied. "I did not think it necessary. I thought the subject was serious enough not to require a personal recommendation."

"I have," he said, his voice now lower, all accusation gone. "That is, I have seen such a thing."

Miriam moved a bit closer. "And?"

"It was a little while ago. I thought at the time she had done it herself. The . . . removal."

"Did she die a natural death?" Miriam felt her anger swell to such a degree that she could barely keep the emotion out of her voice.

He shook his head in a forceful manner. "No, she was stabbed to death. After leaving a somewhat unfortunate party, where many of the people were drinking far more than was good for them. Still, nothing she would have drunk justified such a vile crime. Her gown was soaked in alcohol, and she had clearly been in something of a fight. Her dress was torn. The whole thing was an unmistakable tragedy—doubly so as she came from a respectable family."

Miriam saw how his face was blank now, as if, in spite of himself, he felt no pity for the victim. But if not for her, then for her parents?

"I did not want to add unnecessarily to their grief by running needless tests," he said. "Surely you can understand that?"

"Yes, and I'm sure you can understand the importance of my following the facts of the case I'm asking about, because there may be other women who were victims of the same man." She said it more gently than the words would suggest. "When did it happen, the case you are referring to?"

"Just about two years ago. I don't recall the exact date. I can have my office look it up for you."

"Thank you." The words caught in her throat. "I imagine there are others still, over the last few years."

"So do I," he agreed, looking decidedly unhappy.

"The woman you examined. Do you have any ideas about who killed her?"

"No, but I'm now deducing that it is extremely unlikely to have two unrelated violent assaults and murders with such an unusual souvenir, as you put it." He looked at Miriam, his eyes imploring. "If we turn our backs to what you have pointed out as a pattern, then we are complicit."

"I know that," she said. "And I agree."

"Good luck, Dr. fford Croft. But be careful, will you?"

His warning put her own fear into words. "I will, yes."

As she left him, she knew what she must do. But could she find the energy to return home, pack a bag, climb into her car, and make the drive to Suffolk? Energy or not, she needed to speak with Daniel face-to-face. She checked the time. She would leave in the morning.

CHAPTER

Eleven

Daniel took a cab to the train station in Ipswich at six o'clock the next morning, where he caught an early train to London. He was home by half past eight, walking into the kitchen to find Miriam eating breakfast and preparing to leave.

Her face lit with delight. She put her piece of toast and marmalade on the plate, stood up, and threw her arms around him. "I was about to join you in Ipswich!"

He hugged her hard, then moved away just far enough to kiss her lips gently. "A good thing I got here so early, I'd say." And then he kissed her again.

"How are you?" she asked, concern in her eyes. "And how is Toby? Why didn't you tell me you were coming?"

"I called last night, but you weren't in," he replied. "And then I went to bed quite early, because I had to get up at five."

"Oh, yes, I was at the lab late, conferring with Eve. Are you all right? How is Toby?" she asked again. "Are you closer to learning what really happened?"

He heard the apprehension in her voice. "He's doing the best possible, considering the worry and all the unknowns. His father is still alive, which seems to be a source of surprise to the doctors." He'd been living with these emotions for a few days now, but he still felt overwhelmed by them.

"I have some information about the Peter Ward case." She went to the stove and removed the kettle, adding hot water to her half-empty tea cup. She held up the kettle and he nodded.

With two cups soon steaming, they sat down at the table. Miriam took a cautious sip and leaned closer to Daniel, as if about to share something confidential and there were others in the kitchen who might overhear. "Daniel, much has transpired in your absence. We've discovered, with the help of several pathologists, that there are other cases similar to this one."

As she spoke, Daniel had the cup to his lips. He returned it to its saucer so firmly that it sounded as though the porcelain might break. He felt his heart quicken. "Similar in what way?"

Her face was pinched with distaste. "They have the same . . . souvenir. A patch of pubic hair attached to about an inch or two of skin, and taken from the right side of the groin."

He sat back hard in his chair. "My God! How many other cases?" He was startled, but at the same time horrified, and then, in the lengthy silence, he began to feel hopeful.

"I don't know for certain," she said. "So far, two that look very much alike. The same memento, if you can call it that, but both crimes committed more than eighteen months ago, and geographically far apart, and also far from where Alexandra Stanton was killed. It was Eve's idea to question other pathologists, hoping to find a pattern. And we're very close to identifying one. Now that there's no need to travel to Ipswich, I can meet with several more pathologists. If we can establish an irrefutable pattern, then why did the killer stop for a year and a half? And what suddenly started him again? Is he a stranger we know nothing about, or someone who is often invisible? Like a servant, a caterer, or a taxi driver? Or is he someone we know, but who seems perfectly normal?"

Daniel was reminded how vulnerable Miriam might be feeling, what with Eve's questionable health and the increasing concerns about her father, and how much closer she had become to this investigation than he was. Even though she hadn't seen the bodies of the previous victims, she could imagine that these women were not so unlike herself. A few years younger, but not by much.

"I can't help you today," he told her, his voice echoing apology. "I have to go to chambers and catch up on all the details of the case. The trial is opening again on Wednesday, which gives me the rest of today and all day tomorrow. I asked Toby what it was he had found that made him believe in Peter Ward's innocence, and makes it provable, but his mind won't give up that information. At least, not yet." He took a sip of the tea. "The poor man is traumatized."

She gave a tiny nod, but the understanding in her face was complete. "Would you like breakfast? I just ate, but—"

"There's no time. I'll pick up something when I get to—"

She gave him a small smile as she reached her hand out to him. "I love you, and I missed you terribly, but don't argue with me. You'll just eat rubbish all morning, like tea and ginger biscuits. That's not breakfast. I'll make you eggs and bacon, and some toast."

"Are you saying you learned to cook while I was away? I'm very impressed!"

"It's a one-time thing, so don't get used to it." She forced her voice to sound stern, but she was laughing. In fact, Daniel could see that she was glowing with happiness.

A sense of great joy enveloped him, momentary as it was, catching his breath in his throat.

Before leaving home, Daniel telephoned the police station where Ian Frobisher worked. They had been friends since school days.

Both had gone to university to study law, but Ian had branched off and joined the police, while Daniel had graduated in law. His first position had been with fford Croft and Gibson, where he remained. Meanwhile, Ian had risen rapidly. A natural skill, coupled with a university degree, meant that he was now Detective Chief Inspector Frobisher.

As soon as Daniel heard Ian's voice, he began to state his case. "I'm calling about Alexandra Stanton. Toby was defending Peter Ward, but a ghastly family tragedy has put him out of it, so I'm picking it up."

"I know a bit about that," Ian replied. "I'm sorry. I like Toby. The man's awkward as a three-legged cow, but a really decent chap. How can I help? With your case here, that is."

Daniel felt relief pass through him. "I realize this case isn't on your pitch, but the situation with Toby is tragic." He then took a few minutes to give Ian a summary of the details. "So, you can see why Toby is remaining with his family."

"Yes, of course," Ian said softly. He had lost his own wife while she was giving birth to their only child, a little girl now about three, being cared for by Ian's butler and his wife. He knew tragedy too well. "I wasn't aware of the details. So, his parents live in—"

"Suffolk," Daniel offered. "Near Ipswich. There's an investigation, but it's unsatisfactory. The local constabulary has decided that it's a murder-suicide situation, but I find that idea outrageous. With so little support, however, we're struggling to uncover evidence that will prove Reverend Kitteridge innocent. But that's not what I need your help with. The Peter Ward trial resumes on Wednesday."

"I don't know anything about that case—Peter Ward, that is—except for what I've read in the papers. As you said, it's outside my jurisdiction."

"I understand," Daniel said. "But I've got a theory, at least part of one. May I come to the station and discuss it with you? Have you an hour or so to spare?"

"A theory?"

Daniel smiled to himself. Ian was not one to jump into the fray without careful study and consideration. "I need your help in sorting out my ideas. I haven't time to play around; a man's life is at stake."

"I suppose you know what you're talking about," Ian responded. "Do you want to meet here, at my station, or at a coffee shop? Or perhaps at my place, off all our beaten paths? It's damn cold outside, and it's likely to rain, so let's not include one of your interminable walks along the river!"

"I'll come to your place now," Daniel said, and then reconsidered. "No, let's meet at the station. No need for both of us to uproot, especially with this weather."

"Should I have Bremner join us? He's developing into a respectable detective. Might even surpass me one day!"

Daniel knew that Ian was referring to his right-hand man, Billy Bremner, a policeman with a wit so dry that it was often misconstrued as coming from a chip on his shoulder. Daniel had dealt with Bremner on previous cases, and he knew the man to be an acute observer of human nature. At the same time, no two men—that is, Ian Frobisher and Billy Bremner—could have been more different in both personality and physical description. Where Sergeant Bremner was quite short and stocky, with hair nearly the color of carrots, Ian was tall and slender, almost stately, and with lighter hair. A well-educated man, Ian had a voice and mannerisms that set him apart from his sergeant, who came from coal mining and hard labor, evident in his rougher language and aggressive stance. Bremner had been a scholarship boy, an up-from-the-bootstraps lad who found his way into the police force. And, as luck would have it, into a challenging and satisfying relationship with his mentor, DCI Ian Frobisher.

"Right," said Ian. "I'll put on the kettle. Have you any ginger biscuits?"

That was something of a standing joke between them, and Daniel was sometimes embarrassed by how deeply this idea affected him. Tea and ginger biscuits were familiar, something that stayed the same in a world that was subject to violent and tragic change. He thought of Toby, at the moment so lost, completely out of his depth in emotional loss, wanting to comfort his sister, with no idea how to. "I'll bring some, but not a word to Miriam!"

He forced his attention on preparations for his meeting with Ian, yet he could not fully shake the thought that tea and a biscuit could be so comforting, so . . . known.

Ian and bremner were waiting for Daniel when he arrived. Ian stood up behind his desk, which was covered with papers, while his sergeant rose from one of the two straight-back wooden chairs facing his boss to shake Daniel's hand.

Before Daniel had time to sit, he noticed how Ian suddenly straightened to full height and pushed a handful of floppy hair off his brow, a gesture that almost always heralded him saying something important. "You've found something," Daniel said. Not a question, a statement of fact. He should not have been surprised, knowing how Ian, like himself, could move rapidly from a curious listener to a bloodhound searching for answers.

"A few cases that might interest you," Ian said gravely. "The reference to tokens, mementos taken, is a bit vague, but I'm guessing this is due to some officer who found it offensive to describe it accurately."

"Sir?" Sergeant Bremner inquired.

"Skin with pubic hair, Sergeant. Taken from the victim."

Daniel glanced in Bremner's direction and saw the normally pale-skinned man turn decidedly red. Bremner nearly spoke, but seemed at a loss for words.

"I spoke to one of the inspectors in charge," Ian continued, "because I found this particular report vague." He tapped his finger against a folder on his desk. "The crime in question was quite a distance from yours, at least fifteen miles and with a tangle of city roads between them, as well as several years earlier. The murder itself was abominable, based on what I've read. Some part of the victim was removed, but only alluded to here. Was it the same man? It's possible, yes, but there's insufficient evidence. Without having a clear description of what you call the *souvenir*, there is no way to prove a link. The prosecution could have the judge throw it out and you'd be looking worse than if you hadn't mentioned it."

"What else?" Daniel asked, trying to keep the frustration and anger out of his voice. Desperation was soaring inside of him. It was far more than his customary drive to win: it was what the case meant to Toby and Peter Ward. And what about Miriam? Would she make enemies and put her professional reputation in jeopardy if she exposed even a single pathologist who, for whatever reason, had not included the most important element . . . removal of skin?

"Daniel?"

He almost jerked to attention. "Sorry, I was thinking about Miriam and the price she might be forced to pay for being so professional and . . ."

"Decent?" suggested Ian.

Daniel nodded. "I find it difficult to understand why the autopsies failed to mention this. One autopsy I could understand, but there were . . ." His voice trailed off. "To be honest, I don't know how many. That's what Miriam and Eve are exploring." He looked from Ian to Bremner. "Even if the autopsies excluded that piece of information, why isn't it in the police files? They can't all have missed that!"

Ian ran his fingers through his hair. "We don't report to each other. That is, different precincts. And a thing like this . . . well, we don't tell the press, in case they make a front-page spread out of it and botch up the investigations. If it were your wife or daughter, God forbid, would you want the whole world to know? Can you imagine what that family would suffer? It's natural to want to protect your dead child from being remembered like that."

Daniel nodded. "Yes, I see what you're saying. Added to which," he said, leaning forward in the chair, his face glum, "printing this information invites a copycat, sometimes vicious comments and accusations. The victim suddenly becomes someone who asked for it."

Sergeant Bremner, who had remained silent to this point, spoke up. "Apart from the indecency of making these facts public, there is always the danger of vulgar journalists writing what they guess is truth, but isn't based in fact. This can only add to the grief of the family. It's nasty business."

"It is certainly that," Daniel agreed. Not for the first time he asked himself how a pathologist could forget, much less omit, such a graphic feature. And if it was a failure to report it, even if doing so was intended to protect the memory of the murdered young woman, would they now admit to having seen it, if pressed?

Daniel reminded himself that Miriam was going from one pathologist to another, asking difficult and perhaps incriminating questions. Would they tell her the truth? How would she persuade them to speak, possibly in court? And even if she found as many as four or five, what were the chances even one of them would come forward with the specific details, date, place, and time of day the crime occurred? He believed it unlikely, perhaps even impossible, that a respected scientist would sit before a judge and admit that he had seen this abhorrent removal of skin and pubic hair, yet had omitted it intentionally from his testimony. How could this be excused? And if, under oath, he denied it, who could prove that he was lying? The law would hardly allow bodies to be dug up, simply to find if a patch of a woman's private anatomy had been excised.

As if reading his thoughts, Ian said, "We can get an order to exhume one or more bodies, but after time . . . the evidence might not be so easy to identify."

"We need to prove that Peter Ward, on trial for his life, is not guilty," Daniel said. "Could anything be as important as that? And yes," he quickly added, "we need to find out who's responsible.

This will save more young women from being murdered." The tension in his neck was increasing, and it seemed as though every time he straightened and felt the bands around his neck loosen a little, they tightened somewhere else. "I also worry about what the newspapers will make of this, if they get hold of the story. As you said, a graphic description could have the victims seem more like the criminal. Young women's reputations could be sullied, ruined. Dead young women. And, along with them, their families."

"I'm reluctant to admit this," said Ian, "but I can see why the pathologists left out this detail in their reports to the police." When he saw that both Daniel and Bremner were about to object, he rushed to interrupt. "Not that it's right, mind you, but isn't that human nature? We could go around to all the police, doctors, and pathologists involved in similar cases and ask if they had noticed such an unusual element . . . and what would they say? That they had, and failed to report it? Or would they lie and say they never noted it? No one could prove them wrong. Or right!"

Daniel felt queasy, hearing Ian put into words his own most troubling concerns, thoughts of malfeasance running through his body like a bad meal. "Can you get me the specifics of any death that might fit into this pattern, without raising suspicions? The more I can get . . ."

"What about Miriam?" Ian asked. "If she's pursuing this, will it jeopardize her position at the lab, or her reputation?"

It unnerved Daniel to hear his friend echoing his own worries, but he said nothing.

Ian looked at him steadily. As if picking up the meaning of Daniel's silence, he said, "Are you happy to lump them all together, if there are several, and prove your man innocent that way?"

"I don't see any other choice, do you?"

"The prosecution will do their damnedest to argue you out of that. They'll say your chap Ward was a copycat," Ian pointed out.

"What did he copy? That a square of her skin was cut away? It wasn't in any of the papers and I doubt it will be in any police reports. Eve Hall is certain this was a pattern, which is why exhumation is necessary."

A look of distress crossed Ian's face. "Can you put her on the stand, Daniel? The last time I saw her, she was quite fragile. I'm afraid the prosecutor would tear her apart, no matter how keen her mind, and at the same time cast doubt on all the evidence. It will only take one slip on her part, one uncertainty, an extra ten seconds before she responds, and then anything she says would lose credibility."

"I'm not thinking of putting Eve in the witness box," Daniel nearly snapped. "And that's a loss for our side. She may be elderly, but she can think circles around nearly everyone I know. I'd put Miriam there, if I'm sure we're on solid ground. With her testimony, we could reveal multiple cases like this—if we can find them—and prove beyond doubt that Peter Ward was innocent of any of them. And there's your grounds for appeal, if they are so blind as to convict him. We argue that he could not have committed any of these attacks, and the case falls to bits."

Bremner cleared his throat, drawing the attention of both Ian and Daniel. "If you take to task the pathologists who did those autopsies, you're going to have to prove that their forensic evidence is unreliable. If any of them who omitted this information told no one, how do we prove it?"

"Good question, Sergeant," Daniel said. "I'll only have to prove that this happened with more than one victim, whether the pathologist described it or not. Think of Alexandra Stanton as Victim A. If this deviant act was the same with Victim B, then there is certainly reasonable doubt. Especially if we can prove that Peter was far away from the Victim B crime when it was committed. After we prove that, then all similar cases become suspect and must be reexamined."

"Right," Ian said reluctantly. "It would be impossible to convict Peter Ward, but it wouldn't put anyone in his place. I know that.

And it certainly wouldn't make me any friends, were I to become involved in this case. Or you either. Does that bother you?"

"Of course not," Daniel replied. "It's not about me. The day I forget that, and imagine it to be all about winning a case, right or wrong, I should quit. That is, before I'm thrown out."

The men sat in silence for some time, each lost in his thoughts, as if wondering how to proceed. It was finally Ian who spoke.

"A sad business, Toby's. Damnable thing about his parents."

"That's another case we haven't solved," Daniel pointed out gloomily. "Looks as if the doctors are going to save him. And for what? So he can be tried and hanged? We might never know what really happened, or why. Another reminder that we're not nearly as clever as we like to think."

"Then we had better try harder." Ian looked down at the piece of paper in front of him. "Going back to Peter Ward, there are a couple of chaps we could see. It will take up a good deal of the day. They're—"

"Who are they?" asked Daniel, his mind still on Toby.

"Inspectors in different stations. I believe they'll help, if they can."

For the first time in several days, Daniel felt some of the tension ease up, and he did not hesitate. "Right!" he declared. And then, his voice lower, softer, he looked first at Ian and then at Bremner and said, "Thank you."

CHAPTER

Twelve

WITH BREMNER REMAINING at the station running through the list of calls he needed to make, Daniel and Ian left in Ian's car. Had they taken a train, they would have had to look for taxis at every stop, and they expected to have to travel to more than one place before they found the men they were seeking.

"Any word from Miriam?" Ian asked, his eyes forward, watching a horse-drawn carriage moving slowly in front of them.

With more cars on the road every day, Daniel imagined anything not driven by a motor would soon be banned as a danger to the public.

"Daniel?"

Ian's voice pulled him back. "Sorry, no, nothing more than I've already told you. She's following those leads, also meeting with pathologists. I can only hope these interviews will uncover some answers. God knows we have enough questions."

"But you must not let her travel too far afield," Ian said, his voice conveying concern. "She could be in grave danger. This killer—"

"For now, she's speaking only to pathologists," Daniel said, interrupting his friend. "They may not like her questions, but they're not dangerous."

THE DRIVE OUT of London was smoother than Daniel expected. There were an increasing number of automobiles being purchased by Londoners, and also by those men living in the nearby countryside who preferred to drive, rather than rely on the underground or taxis. It gave Daniel a sense of pride that his wife had not only purchased her vehicle, but drove it with great joy and expertise.

They pulled up in front of a charming cottage that struck Daniel as so very English: the white picket fence, arched gate, and a brick pathway leading to a front door that was elegantly painted in black enamel, the knocker a polished brass lion's head.

Ian knocked, with Daniel standing slightly to one side of him.

"Willoughby was a demanding officer," Ian said. "But he was fair. I learned so much from him. Fifteen years, it was. Good years. Tough, but always fair. And patient with me—not always a small feat."

Daniel already knew that the now-retired Chief Inspector Willoughby had left the force less than six months ago, so there was a good chance he could help them with this investigation. In his position, he was kept updated on homicides in and around London.

If the chief inspector was surprised to see them arriving at his doorstep, he gave no indication. He stared at Ian for a long moment, and then a recognition was in his eyes. "Frobisher, isn't it?" he asked politely, then turned to Daniel, his eyebrows raised in inquiry.

"Daniel Pitt, sir," Daniel replied. Taking the offered hand, he was rather surprised by the strength of the answering grip. Willoughby struck Daniel as a studious-looking man; not quite as tall as Daniel, and far thinner. In fact, he had the appearance of a librarian, or a schoolmaster of a class focused on the classics, such as Latin or ancient Greek. "I'm a lawyer representing Peter Ward. I assume you know about this case, a young man—"

"Anyone who reads the papers knows about this," Willoughby said.

Daniel nodded. "I've come at rather short notice, for which I apologize."

"Pitt, you say. Any relationship to Thomas?"

Daniel smiled. "Yes, sir, he's my father."

"Fine man. Solid, always dependable." He took a step back into the foyer. "Come in." He turned and crossed into the hall, stepping carefully around the handsome black-spotted Dalmatian standing at his side.

Daniel said nothing, nor did he move, allowing the dog—the very large dog—to inspect him. When she had apparently found him acceptable, Willoughby led the way into a pleasant sitting room. Through the French doors there was a generous garden, still bright here and there with late asters.

Willoughby indicated for them to sit down at a little table with four matching chairs, and did so himself. Then the dog sat also, leaning against her master's legs. Daniel wondered briefly whether that was for the dog's need for safety, or to protect her master. There was a fireplace very close to the table and he was tempted to ask Willoughby to get it burning.

Once settled, Willoughby turned to Daniel. "I'm only vaguely aware of the Ward case, what I read."

Daniel briefly explained the death in Toby's family and his own need to step in and take over. He made no mention of his relative ignorance of the case.

"So, what can I do for you?" Willoughby asked, looking from one to the other of them.

Daniel took the lead. "I'm trying to see if there were other crimes with a particular type of souvenir taken, one that was not reported either in the police report or the autopsy."

"How do you know that it even existed, this souvenir, if it's reported nowhere?" Willoughby asked quietly.

"My wife is a forensic pathologist," Daniel began, then looked at the man's face. "Dr. Miriam fford Croft. Perhaps you have met her?"

"Indeed, I have," Willoughby responded, his face illuminated with pleasure. "A brave and delightful woman. How is she involved?"

Daniel took a moment to briefly explain Miriam's involvement as well as the basics of the case, but when he described the souvenir taken from the victim's body, he saw the shift in Willoughby's expression from curious to distasteful. "We had assumed that this may be the only time this suspect has killed, but now we're learning that this . . . souvenir . . . has been taken before, from two other murdered woman, and we're hoping—"

"I see," said Willoughby. "Well, your suspicions make sense. In fact, I had a case a little over a year ago. Young woman, raped and then killed. Almost a square inch or so of skin with pubic hair was taken, using a sharp knife, or perhaps an open razor. It wasn't made public—or included in the police or pathology reports—for the sake of her family, and for a certain amount of decency. I suppose we seek areas to offer comfort, or attempts at it. There are often very good reasons not to expose such a shameful thing." He raised both hands, as if warding off an attack. "It wasn't my decision to omit that piece of evidence, but I think that if I'd had to choose, I might have done the same."

Reluctantly, Daniel nodded in agreement. He didn't really agree, but he did at least understand.

"But it is often the exchange of information, the things that others can go on, that help to solve a case," said Ian. "If we delete anything, then it makes it hard to catch the perpetrator because we don't see the pattern."

"There's always the risk of someone copying a pattern, if the papers describe it," Willoughby added. "But I agree with you, there should be some cooperation. This last poor woman might still be alive if the information had been exposed."

"It's too late for that," Daniel said quietly, and with as much respect as he could, though feeling no small measure of anger. "But we need this information not for next time, but for now. I have to go into court and defend this man. I have nothing to present. Unfortunately, I can't ask Toby to come back. His mother is dead and his father faces being tried for her murder."

Willoughby looked down, his face pale. "That's appalling, I'm sorry, Pitt. It's a fearful situation. The best I can do is point you in the right direction, according to what I know, or can find out. There is at least one case I will discuss with a few associates and I'll let you know, and as immediately as I can."

"Thank you, sir," Daniel said with gratitude. For the first time, it felt as if somebody had introduced a glimmer of hope.

THEY RETURNED TO the police station and the quiet of Ian's office. Despite fragments of that hope, both men appeared downcast.

Bremner arrived with sandwiches, and then rushed away to prepare hot tea.

"I'm feeling empty," Daniel said. "I've never entered a courtroom so poorly prepared. This man could hang, thanks to me." He glanced at the food and felt his stomach turn over. He thought of his father, a former homicide detective, now retired as head of Special Branch, a man who refused to ignore even the smallest bit of information, convinced that everything both seen and unseen constituted evidence.

Ian offered Daniel a rather benign smile. "You've been put in an almost untenable situation. If you walked into that courtroom fully armed, you'd be more than a genius, you'd be a hero. Step away from the self-recrimination. Don't focus on what you can't do, focus on what you can."

For a brief moment, Daniel's mind went to his early breakfast with Miriam, and the pleasure he felt merely sitting across the table from her and sharing the calm. Her presence in his life gave him confidence, the feeling that he could achieve anything.

The silence in the room was broken when Bremner came through the door. "Mr. Pitt, you have a call from Dr. ffo rd Croft. It seems she's been trying to reach you for several hours. She says it's of the greatest importance."

Daniel stood at once, turning to leave Ian's office. If he knew one thing about Miriam, it was that she avoided hyperbole. "I saw her only this morning," he said to no one in particular.

"Use my phone," insisted Ian, taking up the receiver and instructing that the call be put through. He gave a signal to Bremner, who left the office.

Daniel felt a deep relief when he heard Miriam's voice. "What is it?" he asked.

"Daniel, I'm back in Suffolk."

"What? Suffolk? But I just saw you!" He glanced at Ian, his forehead creased in confusion.

"I received a call from Officer Thorpe and decided to drive there."

"Toby's father. Oh, God, don't tell me—"

"His father is still alive," she said. "Daniel, listen to me! Officer Thorpe has taken it upon himself to do what his superiors refused to. He tracked down the second bullet, the one that injured Toby's father, the one they dug out of the wall. And then he called me."

As she was speaking, Bremner returned with two steaming mugs of tea. When he saw that Daniel was still on the phone, he placed them on Ian's desk and leaned against the wall.

"Daniel," Miriam said, "I've just inspected the bullets. The mangled bullet taken out of the wall after it passed through Reverend Kitteridge's head . . . it was not fired from his gun."

Daniel heard a rattling sound, like a bullet being placed in a container. "Are you saying—" He was holding the phone in such a tight grip that his hand began to hurt.

"The bullet that was fired into his head is somewhat like the one that killed his wife, but it isn't the same. If I were in court right now, I couldn't swear to it," she said. "But give me an hour in the lab and you'll have all the proof you need." After a pause, she added, "The one taken from the wall is damaged, unlike the one that penetrated soft flesh. But the differences are obvious."

Daniel repeated this information to Ian and Bremner. The expressions on their faces—was it shock or jubilation, he couldn't tell—nearly made him laugh. Any possibility of levity was interrupted when he heard Miriam's voice.

"It's unlikely—dare I say impossible—for someone to shoot Delia, pull out a second gun, and shoot Justin. We're looking at two guns."

"So there were two shooters?" He spoke the words slowly, deliberately, as if reluctant to speak them at all. He felt his heartbeat pounding against his chest. He knew he must be professional, accept this information and process it using his legal knowledge, but he was so close to this case now. Even more, he was close to the people affected by it. "I wish you were here with me," he said into the phone.

"So do I, my darling."

In that moment, Daniel felt something shift inside him, as if he had been harboring a terrible darkness that was now seeking, and then finding, the light.

He ran a hand across his brow. When he spoke again, his words were stronger, more resolute, each one tinged with hope. "Miriam, you must reach Toby. This changes everything."

CHAPTER

Thirteen

DANIEL COULD DO no more than hope for kindness, perhaps clemency, his heart racing as he sat in Judge Lambert's chambers and waited for the man to render his decision.

When the judge finally spoke, his voice was firm, resolute. "I believe the court has shown compassion for Mr. Kitteridge," he said.

Daniel had no need to hear more; the ruling would not be in his favor. There would be no room for dispute. Sure of this, he paused before replying, again carefully noting the presence of the man seated before him. There was nothing refined or elegant about this judge. He appeared to be around sixty, and with a complexion Daniel thought of as coarse: closely shaven, but despite the early hour, already showing signs of bristle. His appearance brought to mind a stevedore, and not a leading member of London's judicial elite.

"You have, yes, My Lord," Daniel finally replied. "And we are very grateful."

The judge lowered his head and peered over his pince-nez. "And yet you push for a continuance." He was seated behind a desk of rich mahogany, its surface empty, save for a small crystal vase holding a fountain pen, and the wig he would slip on before entering the courtroom.

Daniel said nothing for a long moment, struggling to avoid locking eyes with a man he found so intimidating that it brought to mind his family's visit to the Brighton Aquarium for his tenth birthday, and how the sharks slowly circled their next meal. He preferred to remember the day his father, at the time a police officer rising in the ranks, took his children, Daniel and Jemima, to see the inside of a courtroom and how, when the judge entered, little Jemima pointed to the man's wig and announced in a high-pitched voice, "Oh, look Daniel, he's wearing a squirrel on his head!"

Daniel sat before this austere judge and did his best not to smile, while at the same time finding it difficult to push that old memory aside.

He focused on the wig before him. Today, as a young attorney, that ornate object represented all that was meaningful to him: the rule of law, the impartiality of a system that possessed the power to determine the life or death of every citizen accused of a serious crime. And it spoke of the men wearing it, men with great influence, often unpredictable, fallible men who made those decisions . . . and sometimes got them wrong.

Daniel took a deep breath, released it slowly, and then turned his focus to the judge, noting how his black robe added to his air of austerity and authority. "My Lord," Daniel began, but fell silent when he realized that the man was standing up. There was no need to speak: the decision had been made.

Daniel recognized that his only recourse was to accept defeat, and it was imperative that he do so with humility and respect. But how could he, when the stakes were so high? Resting against his leg was his briefcase filled with files and notebooks, every piece of information related to the charges of murder leveled against his client, Peter Ward. It wasn't a particularly large briefcase, but the weight of it felt like a boulder's weight of responsibility. "My Lord," he repeated, while at the same time standing up. "The situation with Mr. Kitteridge is far more complicated than first believed."

The expression on the judge's face, the raised eyebrows and pursed lips, felt like a warning Daniel could not ignore. This man held the life of Peter Ward in his hands, and it would serve no good purpose to annoy him. Even more, to anger him.

"More complicated . . . how?" he asked, taking up his wig.

Daniel reminded himself to show the deference a man of this prominence would expect. "What everyone, including the local police, assumed was a murder-suicide is now being viewed as a possible murder committed by more than one person."

"A terrible tragedy, losing your parents like that," the judge said, while inspecting his wig's white curls.

"His father has survived, My Lord, and it seems that he might recover," Daniel said, careful to keep impatience out of his voice.

The judge picked a piece of lint from the wig. "That may be so, young Mr. Pitt, and I don't mean to sound heartless, but none of this has any bearing on the case." Before Daniel could respond, the man pulled himself to full height, which was several inches taller than Daniel. "And I certainly hope you're not using this as some shoddy tactic to slow down the proceedings. I will not allow it. Any further attempts will signal a serious lack of preparation, a failure not permitted in my court."

"But, My Lord," Daniel began, and then was silenced by the wave of a judicial hand.

"Nothing happening in . . . what was it, Suffolk? . . . should have any bearing on this trial. Now," he added, pulling on his wig and shifting it into place as he moved toward the door, "shall we begin?" Almost as an afterthought, he added, "You are more than qualified to defend Mr. Ward."

Daniel followed as the judge entered the front of the courtroom, and then waited as the man proceeded up the steps leading to the bench, where he stood and faced the room of spectators. His clerk, an elderly man as nondescript as the chair on which he sat—both man and chair longtime fixtures in this chamber—immediately rose to his feet and called out, "All rise!" The clerk watched that everyone in the chamber stood and remained standing until the judge sat down and gave a nod.

Daniel paused at the threshold. The chamber was alive, buzzing with excitement and expectation, spectators chattering and moving about, elbowing each other as they jockeyed for the best seats, everyone preparing for the kind of drama surrounding a trial, and particularly when the charge was murder.

On so many occasions, Daniel had been thrilled upon entering this room. It was a reminder of the exciting challenge ahead, and with it came a resurgence of confidence engendered by the hard work he always put into preparing the defense's arguments. For Daniel, the chamber represented all that was good and fair. Today, however, a chill ran through him. For the first time, he saw this as a place devoid of challenges, offering only uncertainty, perhaps injustice. And the possibility of failure.

He kept his head down as he walked to his table, while telling himself not to glance over to where the prosecution team sat. They would see the fear in his eyes and use it against him.

Standing at the defense table, Daniel was struck by a penetrating emotion: loneliness. Where was Toby Kitteridge? He was always here, seated and waiting for Daniel to get settled. Or Gideon Hunter, KC, who might offer Daniel the wisdom of his years of experience in the courts? How Daniel would love to have someone of Kings Counsel stature here to advise him! He knew the answers to these questions. Toby was living with his tragedy, trying to make sense of it while doing what he could as the loving son. And Gideon? Trusting Daniel to take the lead. He took his seat, aware of the undercurrent of shuffling feet and low murmuring. Leaning to the side, he opened his briefcase, and in what felt to him like moving in slow motion, he removed the half-dozen files, one by one, each carefully labeled, as was his practice. Everything in its place and ready to be produced when needed.

He had learned this the hard way. During his very first appearance before the court, he had been shuffling through papers to find the one needed and was chastised by the judge for wasting the court's time. Not only had Daniel been humiliated by his failure to consider this before entering the courtroom, but he also understood how it left this inexperienced young lawyer subject to glances of silent ridicule from the opposing side, as well as disapproval from the jury.

He placed the files neatly on the table and finally looked around the courtroom. It was not so long ago that his parents had been seated in the visitors' gallery, watching with pride as their son argued his first case. And later it was Miriam, often there to offer an encouraging smile that told him he belonged in that historic place, the Old Bailey, and would leave the building victorious. Today, there would be no Toby, no parents or wife, no Kings Counsel to advise. Today, he was the solitary figure about to fight for the acquittal, and the very life, of Peter Ward, accused of raping and then murdering Alexandra Stanton.

Daniel needed more time to find the evidence and evoke the testimony that would clear his client. He'd been at this game long enough to know that even the most iron-clad prosecution cases had weaknesses. Evidence can be called into question, doubts sown against a witness. There were objections he could raise . . . and so could Prosecutor Cornell, far more experienced than Daniel. And then there was Judge Lambert, who was already impatient. Daniel had very little room for error.

He scanned the list Toby had made of everyone already called to the witness box, as well as a few notations describing their responses to his questions. Daniel had studied these notes while in Suffolk, when he could ask Toby questions, but his friend had had difficulty keeping focused.

Daniel had reviewed everything again and again when he returned to London. He knew that, under less stressful circumstances, every witness and testimony would have been memorized by him, but not this time. There was so much emotion around Ward's trial, so much uncertainty and apprehension, and so little time for preparation, that each glimpse at the outline felt as if he were seeing it for the first time.

The strike of the gavel brought the noise level down a bit, but it was the second strike, louder and made with far greater force, and accompanied by a most ominous expression on the judge's face, that silenced every voice. There remained a few ambient sounds—the rustling of a newspaper, the shifting of a body—and then utter silence.

The judge gave those seated in the gallery a long and meaningful look, and then announced, "Bring in the defendant."

Peter Ward was escorted into the room and seated in the dock. The man's eyes were wide, almost unblinking, as though unable to register the scene before him. He turned his gaze to Daniel, looking desperate. Daniel wondered if Ward recognized him—the look on the man's face suggested he did not—although they had spoken at length the day before, and again this morning, less than an hour earlier. And then finally, as if remembering, Ward nodded at Daniel, nothing more.

Into the silence came the judge's stentorian voice. "Mr. Pitt, when court was adjourned, your colleague was questioning Mr. Martin Flynt. Have you further questions of this witness?"

Daniel stood. "I have, My Lord."

The judge nodded, the extensions on his wig hanging over his ears bouncing with the movement.

Martin Flynt entered the room and stepped into the witness box. He seemed perfectly relaxed, exuding the confidence that questions would be neither difficult nor challenging. And that as soon as he responded, he would be on his merry way, returning to his life of wealth and comfort.

Daniel knew about Martin Flynt. Not only what he had read in Toby's notes, but by reputation as well. A handsome young man, he was the son of Sir Anthony Flynt, a man of great influence in both industry and government.

He glanced around the chamber and saw that Martin's father was in the gallery, as he had been a week earlier, when Daniel had interrupted the proceedings to deliver the terrible news to Toby. Again, he was struck by the resemblance of father and son, handsome men, angular faces, the father's radiating power, control. He wondered why such an influential man was taking time to watch these proceedings. Surely, he had far more compelling events on his calendar.

Daniel turned back to face the younger Flynt, who was not so much smiling at Daniel as smirking, as if harboring information that mattered, and would make sure was never revealed. Two words that entered Daniel's mind were *privileged* and *smug*. Martin Flynt struck him as both. Daniel wondered how confident he must be feeling, knowing that his father wielded such power as one of the country's leading industrialists, with factories in England and Wales fulfilling much of the nation's electrical needs, including the modernized electric streetlamps being erected throughout the United Kingdom . . . and beyond. And yet, in a way, Daniel understood the young man's confidence. Daniel's own father had directed Special Branch, the most significant security organization in the country, thus providing a certain level of protection to members of his family, Daniel included. The difference was that Thomas Pitt would never abuse that power to save the reputation of someone he loved if a crime had been committed, whereas Sir Anthony was known to pull whatever strings were necessary if someone in his sphere, business or personal, needed absolution.

Daniel took a few steps away from the defense table, not to have a clearer view of the witness, but to indicate to the judge and the prosecutors that he had no need for notes, and was more than prepared to step in for Toby. What they could not see was the trembling in his legs, and he was most grateful for that.

"Mr. Flynt, I want to thank you for returning. I realize that you have answered some of these questions, but—if you will allow—I'd like to clarify."

The young man nodded and offered a subtle smile.

"Very good," Daniel said. "To begin, you testified that you did, in fact, know Miss Stanton, the victim of this terrible crime."

"As I told your colleague, we had been introduced, but we were not friends."

"Were there occasions when you spoke to her?"

"Yes, but never what you would call a real conversation."

"I see." Daniel looked at the judge, relieved that he saw no impatience in the man's face. "Is it true that on the night of the crime, you confronted someone who was being unpleasant to Miss Stanton?"

Martin Flynt tipped his head a bit, as if trying to remember. Daniel wasn't sure if the young man was making an effort to recall what he had said in court, or what had actually happened . . . if anything at all.

"He was being rather aggressive," Flynt said. "If I recall, he gave her a little shove. I stepped in and suggested he stop. I was relieved when he left the party."

"And you didn't know his name, is that correct?"

"I'm sorry, but I have no idea. Until that night, I'm quite sure we had never met."

"Mr. Flynt," said Daniel, taking a few steps closer to the witness. "Do you see that man in this courtroom?"

The question seemed to catch the young man by surprise.

"Take your time," Daniel suggested. "Is he in the gallery? Anywhere in the courtroom? In the dock?"

He knew he was taking a big risk. Any lawyer of worth knew better than to ask a question without already knowing the answer, but he was looking for anything, positive or negative, that could become a part of his defense. If Flynt didn't recognize Ward, would that clear him of this crime? But then, if he said it was Ward who had troubled Alexandra Stanton, there were two possibilities: he was giving honest testimony, or he was throwing the guilt on Ward to protect someone else. The challenge for Daniel was to discern the truth.

Perhaps Daniel's intentions were clear, fully grasped, because Martin Flynt smiled. "No, sir, I see no one in this courtroom who resembles that man."

A murmur ran through the chamber, a low, droning sound, and then it escalated to a din. The judge restored order quickly, using his gavel and the threat of emptying the room.

Martin Flynt's testimony sent a flood of relief over Daniel: a fire had been extinguished. And then, knowing this was a risk, he jumped into the flames. "To be clear, Mr. Flynt, when you say that you can identify no one in this courtroom who confronted Miss Stanton, you are including Peter Ward . . . is this not so?"

Martin Flynt looked at Daniel for what felt like a long time, and then he said, "No, sir, Mr. Ward is not the man I saw."

Daniel tipped his head, suggesting that this response was right and good, and precisely what he had expected. "Thank you, Mr. Flynt."

"Mr. Pitt," the judge said. "Do you have further questions of this witness?"

"No, My Lord," Daniel replied, "I do not."

The judge addressed his next question to the prosecution table. "Cross-examination?"

The prosecutor, Harold Cornell, stood with energy and confidence, making no effort to step away from his table. He appeared absolutely composed, a man wanting everyone in the courtroom to know that he wielded not only power, but mastery over these proceedings. No matter what this young Flynt had just said, Cornell knew that Ward was guilty, he would prove it, and the young man would hang.

Daniel had never appeared in court opposite Cornell, but he knew of his reputation. Word had it that the prosecutor kept a leather strap in his office, and every case won resulted in a notch carved into it. If the rumor was correct—and Daniel had no reason to believe otherwise—there had to have been dozens of them, perhaps scores. He had no idea how many trials Cornell had lost, but he guessed there were few. Very few.

Cornell approached the witness box.

Daniel almost felt pity for young Flynt, having to face questioning by someone who considered himself unequaled in his profession, and even more so in the Old Bailey.

"Thank you for returning," Cornell began. "And the court apologizes for this unforeseeable outburst. I realize it's an imposition, asking this of you, and especially after such a lengthy recess of the court. These rarely happen, unless there are . . . circumstances."

Flynt did not respond, but a brief change of expression crossed his face. Daniel was watching him, trying to determine if this was confusion he was seeing or something else. Perhaps the young man had been taught well to mask his thoughts and feelings. But he was not alone in his reaction. Daniel, too, felt something shift. Was Cornell intending to expand upon his mention of *circumstances*? If he was heading in a new direction with this comment, Daniel needed to know. As for a changing tide, one had to be prepared for what followed or risk being caught in the undertow.

And this was Cornell, who entered every courtroom accompanied by his reputation for brutal cross-examinations that often included groundless accusations with a convincing ring of truth to them, the man who had a knack for pulling cats out of bags and eliciting testimony that could set a courtroom into a frenzy. Perhaps this time would be different . . . perhaps not. Dare he hope that Cornell would say or do something brash, use a gesture or tone of voice that came across as overconfident, and offend members of the jury? Or might this be a slip on the prosecutor's part, opening the door for Daniel, an entrée into the crucial lines of attack Cornell was planning to use? One small intention made visible, and Daniel could plan his own attack.

Daniel nearly stood to demand what circumstances were suddenly in play, but then considered that Cornell might be baiting him to make a protest, so he said nothing.

The young Flynt glanced toward his father, who was seated in the downstairs visitors' section. He stood a bit straighter and said, his voice now strong and certain, "I understand, sir."

"Then please explain to the court why, if you cannot identify the defendant, Peter Ward, as the man who confronted the victim, you are standing in that witness box?"

Flynt shifted a bit, as if he had been in the box for hours, not minutes. "Sir, I would help you if I could, but I am called as a witness only because my name was on the guest list. And yes, I do go to a lot of these parties, all held by the society set I know. But I couldn't tell you the name of the young man. As I've said, he was nobody I had seen before."

"Mr. Flynt, you testified that you recognize no one in this gallery resembling the man who accosted Miss Stanton, is that so?"

"Yes, sir, it is."

"How can you be so sure?"

The witness reached out and took hold of the railing around the box. "What do you mean, sir?"

"Well, it was nighttime, yes? And this happened . . . this confrontation between the man and Miss Stanton . . . it took place in the garden, yes?"

"I suppose . . . yes, in the garden."

"And was the garden illuminated? That is, were there lights out there?"

"I—I don't recall."

"But there must have been, if you saw him clearly enough to know he's nowhere in this courtroom," insisted Cornell.

Daniel watched Flynt's face, saw all signs of youthful confidence, even cockiness, slip away.

Before the witness could respond, Cornell looked up at the judge. "No further questions, My Lord."

Daniel saw the young man's expression turn from confused to something resembling disbelief, as if this walk in the park, easy and quite a lark, perhaps even giving him a bit of short-lived fame among his friends, had been turned into something threatening. As he stepped down from the witness box, he looked into the gallery.

Daniel glanced over to where Sir Anthony Flynt was staring first at his son and then turning to look directly at the prosecutor, his face almost passive. And yet Daniel sensed something under the surface, some emotion contained, controlled.

There was a pause as Martin Flynt returned to his seat next to his father. As soon as he was settled, Sir Anthony turned to his son, his face now imprinted with what struck Daniel as rage. The elder Flynt leaned close to Martin and spoke in undertones, his jaws clenched. There was no need to hear his words to know that he was angry.

Before Daniel could sort through his mind and come up with any reason why this important and influential man was livid, he heard the judge speaking.

"Mr. Pitt, your next witness."

Daniel eyed his files. He knew what he must do. The question was, could he do it? Could he lead a pathologist into a viper's nest, force the truth, and do so without throwing a shadow over a respected scientist's reputation? He imagined Miriam standing there, hands on hips, and admonishing, *You can do this, and you will!*

"My Lord," Daniel said, "I call Dr. Octamus Ornshaw."

Daniel looked into the gallery and recognized . . . what was it . . . glee? That, and the public's thirst for blood? He could see that the crowd was expecting drama and fireworks, and Daniel had been at this long enough to know that getting the public and the newspapers behind him was an important step leading to an acquittal. As much as it repulsed him, it was a game that needed to be played.

He watched Dr. Ornshaw move toward the witness box, his steps cautious, suggesting he feared losing his balance and falling. Miriam had told Daniel that Octamus had been ill, and Daniel could see this now. He felt a surge of guilt, calling him as a witness when he might be better served to remain at home, or in his lab, without the stress and demands of a courtroom confrontation. Daniel dared not imagine what Cornell would do to him in the cross-examination.

Dr. Ornshaw stepped into the witness box and immediately gripped the railing, making no pretense regarding his frail state.

"Dr. Ornshaw," Daniel said, "thank you for agreeing to testify today."

Ornshaw nodded, and Daniel saw humor in his eyes. *Did I have a choice?* could have been on his lips.

"Doctor, you were the pathologist who performed the autopsy on Alexandra Stanton, is this so?"

"I was, yes," Ornshaw said.

"Can you please describe to the court your findings?"

Ornshaw reached into an inner pocket of his jacket and removed a pair of glasses, looping one wire temple behind each ear. From another pocket he drew out a sheet of folded paper and held it up. "May I? I want to be sure the information I give is accurate."

"Yes, of course," Daniel told him. "We all understand the gravity of this case and the importance of such accuracy."

He unfolded the paper and read from it, listing a comprehensive description of the knife wounds and various abrasions.

"Doctor, is there anything in your findings that would point to Peter Ward's guilt?"

Ornshaw seemed puzzled by the question. "Could you please repeat that question?"

Daniel ran through several alternate phrases, but nothing came to mind. "What I'm asking, sir, is this: Was any evidence left behind by the assailant? And if so, can you testify that it was left by the defendant, Peter Ward?"

"No . . . to both questions. Nothing was left by the attacker. So, no, there was no indication that it was anyone identifiable."

"Identifiable . . . or anyone at all?" Daniel pressed.

Ornshaw inhaled deeply, held that breath for a long beat, and then exhaled. "No one at all."

Daniel took a folder from the table and held it up. "Sir, these are the notes, the conclusions, from the autopsy performed on Miss Stanton. I'd like to take you through them."

Before Ornshaw could reply, Cornell stood and called out, "Objection!"

"You object to what?" the judge replied, clearly annoyed.

"My Lord," Cornell said, "the poor young woman is dead, yes, but her family . . . her reputation . . . must every sordid detail be publicized yet again? You saw the agony of her father. Is his daughter granted no respect, no decency?"

The judge turned to Daniel. "Mr. Pitt, what say you to Mr. Cornell's argument?"

Daniel had prepared for this. In fact, it was sometime in the middle of the night, while his mind was running through his questioning of Ornshaw, that he'd anticipated such a protest from the prosecutor.

"My Lord, we have new information that bears heavily on these proceedings, information that will clear my client of all charges."

Cornell threw up his hands. "And you've discovered this now? During your little vacation from the trial?"

Daniel was so taken aback by this sarcasm, a low shot even from someone as arrogant as Cornell, that he said nothing.

The judge said it for him.

"Mr. Cornell, you will curb your comments relating to Mr. Kitteridge's absence. You know very well that he has suffered a tragedy in his family. One more comment like that and—"

"My apologies to the court," said Cornell, cutting across the judge. He returned to his chair, sat, and appeared, in Daniel's eyes, theatrically contrite.

"Mr. Pitt," the judge instructed, "please continue."

Daniel stepped away from the table and approached the witness box. "Dr. Ornshaw, we have established that you performed the autopsy on Alexandra Stanton. Did you do this alone?"

"I did not," Ornshaw said.

"And who worked with you?"

"My assistant, Mr. Anderson."

"Is he also a pathologist?"

"No, he's my laboratory aide. While I perform an autopsy, he stands nearby and takes notes, based upon my findings and my comments."

"And did you testify to these findings earlier in this trial, when Mr. Kitteridge was still defense counsel?"

"I did not."

"Please explain to the court why not."

"I was ill and for several weeks was unable to perform my duties . . . including giving testimony."

"And Dr. Ornshaw, please remind us who testified on your behalf."

"My assistant, Mr. Anderson."

"Sir, have you had occasion to read what Mr. Anderson told the court?"

Ornshaw shifted again, only this time, judging by the way he winced, he did so with what Daniel recognized as discomfort, even pain.

"Dr. Ornshaw?" Daniel hated himself for pressing a man who was clearly in pain, but there was another man fighting for his life.

"Yes, I read Mr. Anderson's testimony."

"And, in your estimation, was it all accurate."

"Absolutely, yes." His voice conveyed certainty, but also a hint that he knew something was about to happen.

Daniel recognized the man's unhappiness. Nevertheless, he forged ahead. "Dr. Ornshaw, you say that everything in Mr. Anderson's testimony was true."

Before he could go further, Cornell was on his feet. "My Lord, how many times must the good doctor answer the same questions? Mr. Pitt is badgering him!"

The judge opened his mouth to speak, but was stopped when Daniel blurted out, "Truth is truth, Doctor, but what about omission?"

"Mr. Pitt!" declared the judge.

"My Lord," Daniel replied. "I'm sure everything Mr. Anderson said in court was true, but I also know that he left out information that could very well determine my client's fate."

"I'm not certain I approve of where this is going, Mr. Pitt," said the judge, "but I will allow it . . . to a point."

Daniel nodded his thanks and turned back to Ornshaw. "Again, sir, was there anything you discovered during the autopsy on Alexandra Stanton, and that was in your notes, that your assistant, Mr. Anderson, did not share during his testimony?"

Ornshaw closed his eyes for a moment, and then said, "Yes. Regrettably, yes."

Voices in the gallery rose again, before Daniel could pose the obvious question. A murder trial was titillating enough, but this? Daniel was grateful when the judge demanded order and succeeded in establishing it.

"Sir," Daniel said, "please tell the court what was omitted."

Ornshaw looked at the judge, the prosecutor, and then did a slow study of faces in the room. "There was something taken from Miss Stanton. It was in my report, but Mr. Anderson chose not to mention it, out of respect for her good name . . . and for the sake of decency."

Daniel waited a long moment before asking the question that everyone in that cavernous room was straining forward to hear. "Please tell us, Doctor: What did you find in your autopsy of Alexandra Stanton that your assistant omitted from his sworn testimony?"

"It was—" He paused, clearly struggling with what he was obliged to say. "It was a small patch of skin. That is, a patch that had been removed from her body."

There were whispers throughout the room, but they quickly abated.

"I know this is uncomfortable for you, Doctor, as it is for all of us, but I must ask you to be more specific."

"Yes, I understand," he said. "The killer removed a small patch of skin from the pubic area."

A gasp ran through the room, followed by protests from men in the gallery.

"Vile!" shouted one.

"How dare you!" said another.

The hush that had been hanging over the courtroom was shattered by the eruption of voices, some of them shouting, as though a current of unharnessed electricity had been released. It took several loud strikes of the judge's gavel before a semblance of quiet was produced. Even then, words like *indecent* and *shameful* rang out, until everyone was silenced yet again by the judge's gavel.

As if no outbursts had occurred, Daniel forged ahead. "Dr. Ornshaw, the removal of this—shall we call it a *souvenir*—is deeply disturbing. But even more disturbing is that this same souvenir has been taken from other young women murdered and sexually assaulted, isn't that true?"

Cornell leapt to his feet with such force that his chair toppled over. "Leading the witness! Leading the witness! Mr. Pitt is putting words into this witness's mouth!"

"Be seated!" demanded the judge, his eyes flashing in anger. He turned his attention to Daniel. "In my courtroom, sir, we ask the questions, we do not provide the answers. Do you understand?"

Daniel tipped his head. "I do, My Lord."

A semblance of quiet returned to the courtroom.

He turned back to Ornshaw. "Are you aware of this souvenir, as we now call it, having been taken from any other murder victims?"

"I am, sir, yes."

Those four words lit the fuse that triggered yet another explosion, not so much of spectators breaking into animated conversations, but of many journalists jumping to their feet and rushing out of the chamber, determined to be the first to get this revelation printed and on the streets. Murder trials sold papers, but they could also secure a reporter's future. And those who remained? They were the veterans, the ones who knew that there was always one thing more.

Daniel waited for the tumult to settle. He thought again of the perils of treading in dangerous waters. He could not say anything that presumed he was suggesting even the gender of the dead. "And please tell us, Doctor, who were these victims?"

"All of them were young women. And the patterns were the same: they were assaulted, murdered, and then the same patch of skin was removed."

"Doctor, I know this is a difficult question. You mentioned *assaulted.* Was Miss Stanton sexually assaulted?"

The room was so quiet that the movement of a moth could have been heard.

"If you mean was she raped, she was not."

"Again, forgive me, but can you be more precise?"

Daniel expected Cornell to scream in protest, and was surprised when he sat in silence.

"There was no penetration," said Ornshaw, "which is the medical definition of rape. Miss Stanton was a virgin." He waited a moment and then added, "But this doesn't mean there was no sexual assault, mind you. Assault doesn't always include penetration."

The quiet in the room told Daniel to pursue this no further. His point was made . . . so far. "Doctor, I've read the police report and there is no mention of any skin being removed."

"In my experience, this sometimes happens when the police are trying to protect the family, or the reputation of the victim."

Daniel took a step closer to the witness box. The silence in the chamber sent a frisson up his spine, and with it, new energy and determination. He tried to push away the image of those circling sharks, and the thought that he could soon be bait. "Dr. Ornshaw, let us say for the moment that I'm an officer of the law, a policeman investigating the death of Alexandra Stanton. And let us say I was aware that this removal of skin had happened before, to at least one other young woman. As a policeman, surely I would be required to look closely at this pattern of behavior. Do you agree?"

"Absolutely," said the pathologist. "That is why I wanted to testify today, so that the court understands that this appears to be a repeat offense. I can't say that Peter Ward did nor did not commit this crime, but whoever did this has done it before, perhaps quite a few times. This kind of behavior is what we call obsessive."

Daniel waited a long moment, hoping this revelation would sink in. And not only with the jurors, but with the prosecutor, judge, and everyone seated in the gallery. "Obsessive," he repeated. "So, what you're saying, Dr. Ornshaw, and based on your many years of experience and the evidence before you, is that Alexandra Stanton may have died at the hands of a serial murderer."

He heard the gasps and outcries, but his mind was too busy to register whether his comment was met with agreement or absolute condemnation. Damnation, in fact. He only needed to keep this going and focus on timing, how to lay out his case, bit by bit, like a spider's web, until the jurors were ensnared.

"Can you explain why, if this was indeed a repeat offense, and patterns were consistent—that is, the removal of skin—nothing was mentioned in the police report describing Alexandra Stanton's death? Or, I might add, during the testimony of your Mr. Anderson? Please tell us, Doctor, is it true that this vital piece of evidence is nowhere to be found?"

"My Lord," Cornell said, pushing himself into a standing position, his voice suggesting that this young attorney was so out of his depth that he barely merited a place at the table. "Please remind, or perhaps instruct, our Mr. Pitt, new as he is to our profession, that this is not for a pathologist to know, but the police."

Daniel made a half turn toward the prosecutor and smiled. "Thank you for clarifying this, Mr. Cornell. And please be assured that I'll get to the police soon enough."

He turned away from his red-faced adversary and looked at the judge. Daniel was not prepared to place any bets, but he was quite certain the jurist was working hard to suppress a smile.

He turned back to Ornshaw. "One last question, Doctor. I am not asking your opinion, but your response based on thirty years of experience in your field."

"Forty," Ornshaw corrected.

"Forty," repeated Daniel. "I stand corrected. In your forty years as a scientist, and equally important as a man called to testify by various departments in our police community, can you think of any reason why—other than protecting a woman's reputation—such a vital piece of evidence would not appear in . . ." He tapped one of the folders on the table. "In one of the twenty-three meticulously prepared pages that constitute the police report?"

Daniel girded himself, half expecting Cornell to leap to his feet, cross the aisle, and grab the folder. Instead, the prosecutor was fully focused on Octamus Ornshaw, now holding himself upright with visible effort.

"Doctor?" Daniel said, hoping his voice conveyed respect, patience, and perhaps a bit of hope. "Might you be more comfortable if you were seated?"

Ornshaw shook his head. "Thank you, no." After a moment, he continued. "In my experience, Mr. Pitt, this oversight most often happens due to two possibilities."

"Could you please share them with the court?" Daniel asked,

knowing full well what was coming. These were the moments that justified pretrial meetings with witnesses.

"There's the situation when someone intentionally deletes the report to protect the dignity of the victim. We've already looked at this."

"And the second?"

Ornshaw closed his eyes, as if wishing all of this would go away.

"Doctor," Daniel said, his voice gentle but urging. "The second?"

It seemed that everyone in that cavernous room was tilting forward, hardly breathing, awaiting the dramatic moment.

"Dr. Ornshaw?"

The witness looked around the room before he spoke. "In my experience, I have seen the mention of important evidence omitted because someone is being threatened, blackmailed, and feels he has no choice." Before Daniel could respond, he quickly added, "Or someone inside the police force has been paid to delete it."

The hush in the room was profound, what Daniel thought of as the clichéd *stunned silence*. Even Cornell remained still, his eyes wide. Daniel expected both the judge and the prosecutor to accuse this neophyte, this upstart attorney, of daring to soil the reputation of London's finest, but before any recriminations could be voiced, the room suddenly erupted as the remaining newspaper reporters raced from the balcony and slammed through the heavy wood doors. This was the scandal they had been waiting for.

CHAPTER

Fourteen

NOTHING POSITIVE COMES from a telephone ringing before the sun shows even the faintest signs of light on the horizon. Daniel wanted to ignore it, but knew it could be important.

Miriam stirred beside him. "Stay," he said, reaching out and touching her hand. "I'll get it."

In nearly total darkness, he crossed the bedroom, made his way down the stairs, and then stepped into the foyer, its cold tiles sending a jolt through him, a marked contrast to the warmth of Miriam's body against his.

The phone sat on the oak pedestal brought from the home of his parents. His mother had insisted he take it. "In case you forget us," Charlotte Pitt had said with a laugh that reminded him of wind chimes. Behind that laugh, Daniel heard the anxiety of a mother sending her child into a world of uncertainties.

"Pitt residence," he said, holding the phone to his ear.

"Sorry, Daniel, but it's important."

Daniel tried to shake off the residual fatigue that was lingering after too many difficult days, as well as consecutive nights of interrupted sleep. Between Toby's family tragedy and the pressure to find the well-concealed path leading to acquittal for Peter Ward, there were too few moments when he could rest, clear his mind, come up for air. But he also understood that Ian would never call at this ungodly hour were it not urgent. "What has happened?"

"Not on the phone. You need to meet me at the station . . . post-haste."

Daniel was now fully alert. "Tell me now . . . please."

"Our man Cornell, no doubt considering himself a contender for the Victoria Cross for prosecutorial excellence, sent a police team into Peter Ward's rooms late last night."

"For what?"

"Another search."

"Another . . . But why? And to no benefit, I'm guessing," said Daniel, but the very moment the words were spoken, it struck him that had there been no benefit for the case against Ward, nothing found to incriminate him, Ian Frobisher would not be calling at this hour.

"I'm afraid it was frightfully beneficial, Daniel . . . and not for our side. This time, they removed the grill over a floor vent and found a small box. Inside was a piece of skin, a square of skin with hair still attached."

For a brief moment, no more than two seconds, Daniel felt as if he might fall. He knew that knees could buckle, but he had no memory of ever having experienced this, except perhaps the time he had learned that Miriam was being held hostage. Brief as that sensation was, it nevertheless gave him a feeling of utter helplessness.

He wasn't aware that Miriam had joined him until he felt her hand gripping his elbow.

"What is it?" she asked, her voice filled with concern, although the question came across almost as a demand.

He recognized alarm in her face. "It's about the Ward case."

She closed her eyes, pressed her forehead against his shoulder, and exhaled. "For a moment, I thought . . ."

"It's not your father," he said, who had suffered several heart attacks recently, "and not Toby's either. Go back to bed." He kissed the top of her head.

When she remained, he continued, "They raided Ward's rooms again, last night, and they found a patch of skin hidden in an air duct."

Miriam shook her head slowly. "No," she said. "Not possible."

Daniel felt his fingers cramp from gripping the receiver. He was about to say more, but that look—whether it was concern or sadness, he could not decide—informed him that silence might be preferred.

She raised her eyebrows, shook her head again, and then turned and padded into the kitchen. One of the many qualities he loved about his wife was how she knew to hold back questions until he had been given all the information. Perhaps this was due to her training as a scientist, a field that demanded all tests be run and results carefully analyzed before any conclusions could be reached. In both law and science, interpreting evidence before all the facts were in could lead to disorder . . . or worse.

"We need to figure out what this means," Ian said.

"It can't mean anything good," Daniel replied, his mind racing with possibilities. Had the time come when he needed to consult Gideon? As their chief lawyer and a Kings Counsel, Gideon Hunter might be able to point Daniel in the most effective direction. But then, would that be seen as tantamount to Daniel waving the flag of surrender?

Daniel heard background noise coming through the receiver, men's voices and clattering typewriters. Behind him, from the kitchen, came the clank of the kettle being placed on the hob and the icebox being opened. Despite the drama emanating from this phone call, he was by turns soothed to hear Miriam moving about.

It reminded him that no matter what was happening in the world outside, here, in his home, he felt safe; he felt loved. Miriam knew him so well. Whether he was awakened at two o'clock in the morning or six, the moment his mind was switched on, it would remain electrified until he fell into bed late that night. Understanding that there would be no more sleep for Daniel, she figured he might as well have something to eat.

He awaited Ian's reply, but heard only a lengthy pause accompanied by a ringing phone and a man's booming voice, the words unintelligible but the tone angry.

"Are you there?" Daniel asked, his anxiety growing.

"Still here, yes. Sorry about the shouting. A regular visitor being escorted to the drunk cell." There was another pause accompanied by background shouting, peppered with profanities, most of it alluding to someone's mother and body parts.

Daniel leaned into the phone, pressing the earpiece more firmly against his ear. "What they found, Ian—we have to be certain the jury understands that the first search covered every inch of Ward's living space and revealed nothing."

"I agree, yes."

"From what you've been told, does anyone seem surprised or suspicious that it wasn't found during the first search? That it suddenly appears, just like that?"

"From what they're saying, they were surprised, but there it was . . . yes, just like that."

Daniel thought about this for a moment. "I can see how that could happen."

"You can?" responded Ian. "I defy you to give me one logical explanation for the sudden appearance of the very piece of evidence that will seal Peter Ward's fate."

"Magic."

"I beg your pardon?"

"Magic," Daniel repeated.

"So, let me make sure I understand you," Ian said. "They arrive in his room and, thanks to the waving of a wand, or because God decreed it and they found his words etched in stone, the evidence is discovered . . . magically."

"That's right," Daniel said. "Now, if you'll excuse me, I'm going to have a cup of tea, perhaps a slice of toast, and then go back to bed."

He knew that Ian would not let that pathetic attempt at light humor go unchallenged.

"Since we've put aside all things absurd," Ian replied, "could we please—"

"I'll dress and be at your desk very soon," Daniel said, interrupting what he knew was Ian's request that he do just that.

"Not until you eat," Miriam said, suddenly appearing at his side.

Daniel held the phone away from his ear, so she could be part of the full conversation.

"I heard that," said Ian with a little laugh.

Daniel smiled and took Miriam's hand. "We'll get to the bottom of this," he said. "But Ian, whatever they're playing at, it's trouble."

"Methinks that something is rotten in the state of Denmark," Ian announced, bringing a smile to Daniel's face and memories of their youth shared at university.

Miriam shook her head, rolled her eyes, and headed to the kitchen.

"We just lost our audience," Daniel said.

"Indeed," Ian replied, and then the phone went dead.

He watched Miriam disappear into the kitchen and then he turned toward a noise outside the front door. There were vertical glass panes on either side of it and running its full height. One of them offered a view of two gray squirrels scuffling over what appeared to be a very large acorn. With so many oak trees on his street, this was not a rare occurrence. The fleeting thought, *I wish I were that carefree* ran through his mind. But with the stress and intense emotions stirred up around Toby's family and the Ward case, *carefree* seemed out of reach.

AFTER A QUICK breakfast, Daniel went upstairs to dress, Miriam following close behind.

She pulled open the middle drawer of the dresser and removed a clean shirt. As she waited for him to take it from her hands, the chime of the grandfather clock in the foyer announced that it was five o'clock.

"Thank you," Daniel said, taking the shirt.

"There is one very important element," she said, watching him slip it on. "Ian said they found a patch of skin—one patch. But what about all those others taken from the victims? Wouldn't the killer keep these as well? And if so," she added, turning him a bit so she could adjust his collar, "where are they?"

Daniel studied his image in the looking glass, ran his fingers through his hair. He was due to visit the barber, but when would he find the time? "That's the question we need answered." He was comforted, knowing that Miriam shared his quest for results. She was a scientist dedicated to the truth, not happenstance.

He followed Miriam downstairs. The squirrels were still there, but they scampered off when he opened the door. He turned and kissed her. "Go back to sleep," he said, and then nearly laughed. They shared many habits, and one they had in common was the inability to return to sleep after being awakened, especially when working on a challenging case. For both of them, an early rising most often resulted in their dressing and going to work when the sky was still black. He kissed her again, pulled on his woolen coat and hat, and stepped outside.

"When you learn more," she said, "please call. You know where to find me." A wind was kicking up and she pulled her robe tightly around her.

"Miriam, go inside before you catch your death."

She stepped back a bit further into the foyer. "It sounds suspicious, Daniel. Someone is either trying to destroy Peter Ward as a personal vendetta, or will be satisfied to throw guilt over no-matter-who, pulling the focus away from himself."

Daniel started to descend the steps, and then turned back. "I wish I had the answer," he said. "I'll call you as soon as I know more. Ian's waiting for me."

"I'll be at the lab within the hour."

He threw a warm smile in her direction. "As if I didn't know," he said, and then he bounded down the steps.

Before he could reach the corner, a taxi appeared. There were mornings when it took at least ten minutes before he found one. Perhaps this was a good omen.

WHEN PRESIDING JUDGE Lambert arrived at his chambers later that morning, at a time when London was awake and street lamps were being extinguished throughout the city, he found Daniel waiting at his door. "Mr. Pitt," he said, his voice giving no indication of any pleasure at having discovered this eager young lawyer. "I take it this is not a social call." He unlocked the door to his chambers and stepped inside.

When he neither gestured for Daniel to enter nor made any movement to block his way, Daniel crossed the threshold and closed the door behind him.

"This had better have merit," said the judge, slipping out of his winter coat and hanging it in an armoire standing majestically in the corner. From its interior he removed the black robe he would wear in the courtroom and draped it over one of the two empty chairs facing his desk. He gestured toward the other one and Daniel settled into it.

Daniel held back for a moment, fearful that the judge might respond with anger. Had the man just mentioned merit? If what he had come to say had no merit, why was he putting himself before this sometimes unpleasant man? "My Lord," he said, presenting a countenance that he hoped was both sincere and professional.

"There has been an unexpected event. During the night, the police entered my client's rooms and discovered new evidence against him." Having said *discovered* with a modicum of sarcasm, he girded himself for what he feared could be an unpleasant rejoinder.

The jurist's response was far worse than Daniel was expecting. It was a stony silence, coupled with a clenched jaw and narrowed eyes. When he finally spoke, the words were measured, each one given equal weight. "And why are you telling me this?"

A voice in Daniel's head warned him to remain calm. Would he ever get used to one man, one judge, wielding such power over the lives of so many? He thought not, yet here he was, warning himself to face Judge Lambert, despite the fact that, until now, the man had proven himself to be fair, impartial . . . judicial. He reminded himself that either he learn to play this game or explore another profession. "My witness list, My Lord. I'm asking to add the name of Sergeant Reginald Gorman, the senior officer who led the search." He wanted to call it a raid, but could ill afford to incur more of this judge's wrath.

"For what purpose?"

Daniel silently acknowledged himself for having anticipated that question and practicing his response while riding in the taxi between Ian's office and the Old Bailey. "A thorough search was conducted last month, My Lord, and nothing was found. Mr. Ward doesn't live in a five-room home; he has two small rooms. During the initial search, they were pulled apart, floor to ceiling. And then last night, there was a second search and a vital piece of evidence is discovered, something mentioned only yesterday in court. That is, mentioned for the first time. I owe it to my client to explore this. Sergeant Gorman is best qualified to explain to the court his reasons for this second search." Daniel bit back the words he so wanted to add, the suggestion that evidence might have been planted to cast an even greater shadow over Peter Ward, a discovery that would push him one step closer to the noose.

Daniel expected the judge to send him away and instruct that he return for his decision shortly before the trial resumed. Instead, he leaned back into his ornate leather chair, placed his fingertips together as if in great concentration, and nodded. "Granted. Call this Sergeant . . ." He paused.

"Gorman, My Lord."

"Yes, fine, Gorman," he said testily. "Call him as your first witness this morning. Let's clear this up now."

Daniel thanked him and left at once, anxious to get Gorman on the stand before the prosecution had ample time to communicate with, and in some way influence, this witness.

He stood in the hallway and smiled at the thought of how that bastard Cornell would react if Daniel could get the policeman to admit flaws in the search. Flaws . . . or worse. Nothing energized a defense attorney more than the element of surprise.

THE MOMENT THE court was called to order, Judge Lambert directed Daniel to begin his questioning of the police sergeant. It was almost comical. Before Gorman had even entered the vast chamber, before he could stand in the witness box and share with the jury information that Daniel was certain would change the course of these proceedings, prosecutor Cornell was leaping to his feet with such energy that Daniel imagined him as a massive beast about to eviscerate its prey.

"Your Honor, My Lord!" Cornell began. "It is most—"

"Be seated, Mr. Cornell," demanded the judge, his voice rolling like thunder through the courtroom. "I will allow this witness to speak."

"But, My Lord," Cornell sputtered. And then, as if realizing the futility of his pleas, he dropped back into his chair.

Daniel stood and approached Sergeant Gorman, acting as though Cornell were nowhere in the room. "Sergeant, could you please state your name and rank?"

"Reginald Gorman," the man said, his voice strong with what sounded to Daniel like pride. "Police sergeant."

"My Lord!" declared Cornell, now beseeching.

Daniel was tempted to tell Cornell that he was doing a poor job of expressing righteousness, but thought it wiser not to press his luck.

"This is highly irregular!" Cornell continued. "The court has given us no notice that this man would be testifying. We've had no time to prepare our questions for him."

The judge seemed unmoved by Cornell's histrionics. "Mr. Pitt asked only a short time ago for the court's approval to call this witness, and his request was granted."

As much as Daniel was enjoying Cornell's petulance, he reminded himself that this was a worthy adversary and things could quickly take a turn for the worse. One glance toward the jury confirmed this. These men were attentive, to be sure, but why were their eyes riveted on the prosecutor?

He turned back to the witness, warning himself to form his questions with care. This man and his team had found the most incriminating evidence possible, and Daniel wanted the jury to understand how.

"Sergeant Gorman, I want to thank you for coming on such short notice," Daniel began. He recognized what he believed was a guardedness on the policeman's part, indicated by the way he stood, back erect, chin up, and his head tilted slightly, as if he were expecting something that was likely to be unpleasant. Daniel awaited Gorman's response and reminded himself that this witness was no newcomer to courtroom procedure.

"It's my duty to appear," he told Daniel, his words accompanied by a small twitch at the corner of his mouth. "Although why I'm here, I have no idea."

"None?" Daniel asked. "But did you not lead the raid into my client's rooms late last night?"

Cornell moved as if to speak, but the policeman was two steps ahead. "It was not a raid, sir," he said.

Daniel felt himself too close to a precipice. He had asked the question, but recognized that it sounded less like a question than a provocation. He warned himself to go slowly, cautiously. "I stand corrected." He gestured for Gorman to continue.

"It was a legal search, carried out by some of my squad."

"With you at the lead."

"Yes, with me at the lead."

"Sergeant, would you please take us through your movements, from the time you entered Mr. Ward's rooms?"

Before Gorman could respond, Daniel held up his hand. "My apologies, Sergeant, I'll come back to that in a moment. My first question is this: What prompted the police to return to Mr. Ward's rooms for this search? After all, a very thorough search had been performed some time ago and nothing was found."

"I believe it was suggested that the first search hadn't been as thorough as it could've been."

"Suggested by . . . whom?"

Daniel Pitt was a well-educated man, someone who avoided clichés or any bastardization of the English language, but when he glanced over to see Cornell's face, all that came to mind was *champing at the bit*. Had the judge allowed it, the prosecutor would have dragged Daniel from the courtroom and locked him in a closet.

"Beggin' your pardon?" the sergeant said.

"You said it was suggested by someone. Do you mean a call to the station? A note slipped under the door? Sergeant, who suggested that a second search would prove fruitful?"

Gorman stared at Daniel for a long beat and then shifted his gaze to Cornell, as if hoping the prosecutor would somehow stop this. "I'm not sure," he said. "I was called into the station last night, given the address, and told to go there and search the place, top to bottom."

"And were you told specifically what to search for?"

Gorman looked up, as if having found something fascinating on the vaulted ceiling, and then his face took on a reddish hue. The shift was so dramatic that Daniel almost felt sorry for him.

"Sergeant?"

"Skin," he said, his voice low.

"Skin," Daniel repeated.

"A patch of skin . . . or several."

"Did anyone describe that patch of skin?"

This time, Cornell stood. "My Lord!"

"Let the witness speak, sir!"

Daniel took a few steps closer to Gorman, while warning himself not to appear in any way menacing. "I'll repeat my question, Sergeant. Did anyone describe that patch of skin?"

"Yes . . . sir."

"Would you kindly tell the court how it was described, this patch of skin that you were instructed to look for?"

Gorman turned slightly so he could see the judge. The expression on his face struck Daniel as not only one of misery, but displaying a need to be saved.

"Sergeant?"

"Skin . . . with hair."

Daniel nodded, as if hearing this for the first time. "I assume you mean a patch of skin from someone's head."

Gorman shook his head and then replied, "No, sir, that's not what I mean."

"Then please explain," Daniel said, his voice calm, with a tinge of compassion.

"Skin from the . . . nether regions," Gorman said.

Daniel was tempted to leap at that, to ask him to be more specific, but he was no fool. The jurors now knew, as did everyone seated in that grand chamber, precisely where it came from, without Daniel pressing the point.

"Sergeant, thank you for your candor," Daniel said, and then turned and walked back to his table, where he remained standing.

"Now, let's return to my previous question. You were told to look for this—shall we call it a souvenir?"

Daniel noted how Gorman again shifted his glance to Cornell. Clearly, the sergeant was not at all sure how to respond and was seeking help.

Daniel sensed that this was the time to bring this questioning to its dramatic climax. "When you were told to look for this souvenir, did anyone suggest specific places where you might find it? That is, were you told where to look?"

"I'm not sure I understand . . ."

"In the closet? The drawers? Somewhere hidden in the bed or the furniture? With only two small rooms, the hiding places had to have been limited."

"I was told to look everywhere."

"Under the floorboards?"

"Yes, anywhere that could hide a small box."

Daniel reared back, as if avoiding being struck. "Sergeant, you were told specifically to look for a small box?"

Gorman shifted from one foot to the other, making no effort to conceal his displeasure. "Maybe they didn't say a small box. Maybe I'm thinking that because it's what we found."

Daniel let that pass. If he pounded on this man with too much force, he could lose any sympathy the jurors might have for Ward. "Yes, perhaps that's why. I sometimes confuse who has told me what."

Gorman nodded, as if having won a small victory.

"So, please explain how this small box was discovered."

From his pocket, Gorman took a notebook no larger than his hand and held it up. "I took notes."

Daniel nodded. "I'm also a notetaker, Sergeant, so I understand how helpful they can be." When he saw Gorman's shoulders relaxing, he sensed that he had established enough trust to go for the jugular. Delicately, of course.

Gorman opened the notebook and read the list of places his

team explored. It was a long list, considering the size of Ward's rooms.

"I must admit, Sergeant, I am very impressed," Daniel said. "I can see that you indeed looked into every nook and cranny. Please tell the court, where did you finally discover that little box holding the patch of skin and hair?"

Gorman closed the notebook and slipped it back into his pocket. "One of my men thought to pry off a grate covering a floor vent. It didn't come up easily."

"How did he manage to remove it?"

"With a screwdriver." Gorman gave Daniel a look suggesting that a man of Daniel's social status would never have occasion to use one.

"A handy tool," Daniel said.

"Any search, we always take tools, sir."

"Sergeant, you were there, watching, leading the search, yes?" Gorman nodded and Daniel rushed forward. "Can you please tell me—and I realize I'm asking you to guess—can you please tell me how a team of seasoned policemen went to Mr. Ward's rooms some time ago and found nothing?" He picked up a folder from the table, opened it and glanced at a document. "Wait, forgive me, this report tells me that you also led the first search. Is that so?"

Gorman looked at the large doors leading to the hallway, as if hoping to make his escape. "Yes . . . sir."

"And would you say that the first one was also a thorough search?"

"Yes, of course!"

"And yet here you are, Sergeant, testifying that while nothing was found during that first search—a comprehensive search that you led—the second search produced this dramatic evidence."

Gorman closed his eyes for a moment, as if deciding how to best answer. "Before the first search, I wasn't told about the patch, so I didn't look for it."

Daniel felt a little chill run up his back. He was almost there. He had set a trap and this witness was about to step into it.

"Sergeant Gorman, I've looked at your record with the police department and it is clear that you are both respected and trusted."

Gorman gave a little nod. In the man's eyes, Daniel sensed the return of distrust.

"Furthermore, you are most often the man sent into a delicate situation." Daniel saw the man's eyes narrow and he warned himself to ease up on the compliments. If you give someone too much honey, it begins to feel sticky; too much vinegar and it's acidic. He needed to find the balance between the two.

Daniel walked away from the table and approached the witness box, standing as close to Gorman as the layout of the room allowed. "Sergeant," he said, hoping to all the gods he could muster that this next question would not explode in his face. "I realize that you are not aware of previous testimony given by a leading pathologist, and therefore have no knowledge of the enormity of your discovery." He waited a moment, although briefly, and then took one step closer to the precipice. "What would you say if I told you that there might have been other victims, other young women, and that they, too, had a square of skin removed?"

He expected Cornell to scream his protest, but the man seemed stunned by the question. As for Gorman, he opened his mouth but no words came forth. Perhaps the prosecutor was holding back because this questioning was so damaging to his case. And then another thought nudged its way into Daniel's mind. What if Cornell was remaining silent because Daniel was digging a deep hole into which he might soon fall? How could he know if he was in trouble? And what could he do to salvage this? He thought of one of his Criminal Law courses and what the instructor had told his students were tricks of the trade. *Never ask a question that leaves your witness free to decimate you. Because when you fall from grace, you take your client with you.*

He looked directly into Gorman's eyes, as if he and his adversary were the only two people in that room. "Let me answer a question for you, Sergeant. In fact, let me answer several. Question: Why didn't you find this evidence during your first search? Answer: Because it wasn't there. Question: If that's so, then how is it you found this damning evidence during your second search? Answer: Someone planted it there. Someone intent on Peter Ward hanging for a crime he didn't commit. Question: Who is that someone? Answer: I have no idea, but I intend to find out."

There was an eerie silence hanging over the room. The men comprising the jury seemed frozen in place. Made of stone, Daniel thought, and then reminded himself that they were more like soldiers on a battlefield, artillery attacks all around them, and they had nowhere to hide.

Cornell was equally rigid. Daniel wondered if this was resentment—or was it fear?

He forced himself to look away from the prosecutor and saw that the judge was watching him. What was he seeing in that man's expression? If he didn't know better, he might have described it as cloaked respect.

"My Lord," announced Daniel. "I have no further questions of this witness." He picked up several folders and placed them in his briefcase, signifying he had made his point.

"May I remind you that we are still in session," intoned Judge Lambert. "Therefore, the gentleman will remain in the witness box. Mr. Cornell," he said, redirecting his attention, "are you prepared to cross-examine this witness?"

"I do have a few questions, My Lord, and I ask the court's permission to pose them now, and then return to this witness later in the proceedings, after I've been given time to hear other witnesses and consider Mr. Pitt's allegations."

"Granted," the judge said. "Please proceed."

Cornell remained seated at his table. "Sergeant Gorman, you've been in the police department for how many years?"

"Going on twenty-six, come November."

"Impressive, to be sure. And in those nearly twenty-six years, have you come across a crime where several people, even many, have been murdered, but one of them is the victim of a copycat?"

Daniel felt sick to his stomach. He didn't have to scan the room to know that Cornell had struck gold.

"Yes, sir," Sergeant Gorman responded. "And sometimes he's the most difficult to find, the copycat is."

"So, to be clear: other women could have been killed by someone who's identity is yet unknown, but Mr. Ward could well have taken the descriptions of those victims and repeated these vile acts on poor Alexandra Stanton. A woman, I might add, whose name was hardly mentioned today, as if her life and her death never mattered." He nodded to the judge, indicating that he had nothing more to say.

Every ounce of Daniel wanted to protest, but he recognized not only comprehension in the faces of too many in that room, including the jurors, but also acceptance.

"Mr. Pitt," asked the judge. "Have you finished with this witness?"

"I have a few more questions, Your Honor."

The judge nodded and Daniel rose slowly, running words and possibilities through his brain. And then there was a flash of light. "Sergeant, there is one aspect of this that I do not understand, and perhaps you can help me."

"I'll do my best, sir."

"According to the reports I've read—that is, concerning some of the previous murders of young women—there was never a mention of skin being removed. And yet we now know that this terrible act did, in fact, occur."

"Correct, sir."

"So, please tell me, Sergeant. Based on your many years of service, if it was never reported; if the police were never told about this unmentioned mutilation; if the newspapers never divulged this, then please explain to the jury how Peter Ward could have known? There can be no copycat if there's nothing to copy, do you agree?"

Daniel watched Gorman's face closely, but was unable to read it.

Gorman looked directly at Daniel, perhaps wishing to determine his demeanor. "Well, sir, I guess you'll have to ask Mr. Ward. It seems clear that he must've known someone, don't you think? You say you want me to help you, but why don't you ask him? He's your client! And did it ever occur to you that maybe he didn't act alone? Let's say he has an alibi for a murder that took place last January, and he can prove he was far from the crime scene. So, maybe a mate did that one."

Daniel glanced at the jurors. A few were looking pensive, possibly questioning if this policeman was making sense. Rather than feel concern, he felt that a door had blown open. "Sergeant, for the sake of argument, let us say that Mr. Ward is, as you suggest, in league with others to commit a series of copycat murders."

Gorman's face changed from wary to confident, as if he had just given this attorney from some hoity-toity law firm an important idea.

"If this is so, can you please tell the court the steps you have taken to find those others? Have you had no leads before now? After all, there have been multiple murders with some frightening similarities. Why is it that you have only just thought of this possibility now, at this moment, and in the witness box in the trial of Mr. Ward?"

Gorman appeared at first nonplussed, and then he smiled. "The answer is right there in front of you," he said, pointing to Peter Ward. "Doesn't matter how many others did the crimes . . . we all know that he killed poor Miss Stanton."

Daniel looked at the jurors again. Several of them were nodding their agreement, while a few were glaring at Ward. They were convinced; their verdict was a certainty.

Daniel had set the trap, but now he felt as if he were the one falling headfirst into it. He sat there, unsure how to proceed. His sense of failure was so great that at first he didn't notice the door opening and an elderly woman entering the chamber. Suddenly aware of the disturbance, he turned and watched as she made her way along the aisle and handed a note to the court recorder. He gave it a quick look, stood, and approached the judge.

Daniel watched the judge read the note and saw the man's expression shift from curious to annoyed.

"It seems that I'm needed on an urgent judicial matter," the judge said. He turned to the jurors. "I have no choice but to dismiss you with the court's apologies." Without awaiting a response, he announced, "The court will reconvene at nine o'clock tomorrow morning."

Cornell walked over to Daniel. The prosecutor was now the cat, Daniel the canary.

"Interesting line of argument, Pitt," the older man said. "I'm curious to see where you'll go with it."

Daniel asked himself if he had ever gone out on a limb with such dire results. Would his brilliant tactics be the death knell for Peter Ward? He saw no choice but to prostrate himself at Cornell's feet, an act of contrition he had never had to perform. If the jury found Ward guilty, Daniel would have little opportunity to produce enough evidence to overturn that verdict. He needed time. Without thinking it through, without consulting Gideon Hunter, he blurted out, "If Ward admits to what you're charging, and he gives you the names of his accomplices, will you take the death penalty off the table?"

Those were words he could never take back, and they made him feel sick. Admitting guilt when his client was innocent? But the way these proceedings were heading, a guilty verdict seemed inevitable, and this could mean only a short wait before Ward was hanged. Daniel needed time to find the evidence and win his client's freedom on appeal.

Cornell gave him a long, penetrating look. "What, and miss the opportunity to watch the judge slip that black cap onto his wig? No chance, Pitt."

"But there were many other victims," Daniel argued. "Aren't you interested in finding the person who killed them? Or stop someone from killing again?"

Cornell slipped a stack of files into his case. "If Ward committed even one of those crimes, that one is worth hanging for." And then he smiled. "Old Marcus fford Croft will rue the day he hired you. Hardly up to the challenge, Pitt. Unlike your very capable wife."

A scathing retort rushed into Daniel's head and he struggled to remain quiet. It would serve no purpose to express a vulgarity belonging in a back alley. Still, the man's words pulled at him with a force he felt unable to resist.

Daniel left the courthouse defeated. Never had he failed his client so completely, nor himself.

He stepped into the chill of the day and saw that the world was continuing as always. Men coming and going, women with children, taxis and buses carrying riders around the city.

He raised his hand and a taxi pulled to the curb. He climbed in and gave the address of his chambers. Unless he could find the real killer, he had no right to pass himself off as the defender of anyone. For the first time in his short and so far illustrious career, he felt like a fraud.

When Daniel was at his desk, he was unable to banish images of this morning's debacle. He was grateful and relieved to be out of the courtroom, away from Cornell's sneering comments. He needed this time to collect his thoughts, although he saw no logical way out of this mess. Why in the hell had he offered to bargain with Peter Ward's future?

CHAPTER

Fifteen

THE FIRST THING Daniel did upon arriving home was to walk directly into the sitting room, stack a few pieces of firewood in the hearth and set them burning. As the fire began to catch, he removed his coat and draped it over the arm of the loveseat. It was a rarity, a fire burning in early autumn, especially when it was not terribly cold. In fact, there was almost no chill to be managed, but he needed the soothing effects of the heat, the aroma of burning wood, the soft light cast around the room.

The disaster in court haunted him and he was not at all sure he could discuss it with anyone. Not Miriam, not his father, not even his mother, who was often the person he turned to when in need of bolstering. Not to say his father and Miriam had ever failed him, but it was Charlotte Pitt who was present, reachable, not working in a lab or giving occasional counsel to Special Branch. Discussing this with her would only remind him of how far he had come at such an early age and how, in a few minutes of what he regarded as utter lunacy, he had thrown it all away.

What he sought was not advice, or even a kind ear, but silence, and a place to feel utterly miserable and alone. It was a punishment he had earned.

He was rather enjoying his bout of self-pity when he heard the front door open. At any other time, the arrival of Miriam would have propelled him to the foyer, where he would greet her with an almost smothering hug and a long, stirring kiss. His sense of gratitude for having her in his life never waned. In fact, as time went on, it only became stronger. He could not, dared not, imagine life without her. Tonight, however, he remained on the loveseat, a piece of furniture well worn and normally very comfortable. At this moment, there was no comfort to be found.

Miriam entered the sitting room, her cheeks flushed from the brisk autumn air. She stopped, her expression shifting from the pleasure of seeing him to the realization that something was terribly wrong. "Daniel, what has happened?"

He knew he should rise. Was this the first time in their marriage that he did not pull her to him when one of them arrived home?

"Daniel?"

It had to be told, and better hear it from him than some other source. He could not imagine who would describe the scene to her, but it would be from their viewpoint, or even thirdhand. These things had a way of being repeated in whispers. His gaffe would no doubt serve as amusing repetition in pubs, at the dinner table. The courtroom had been filled with spectators. What were the chances that one of them had mentioned it to someone, and that someone passed it along, and like a fast-moving river, continuing on to another, and then another . . . curious listeners, some of whom reveled in the failures of others? If Miriam was to hear about it—and how could she not?—it had to come from him.

Yet, just seeing his beloved wife infused him with a fresh wave of optimism and hope. After all, there were perhaps a dozen people in all of England who gave a whit about his embarrassment. To think for even a moment that he would be shunned, ridiculed, thrown out of chambers was utter nonsense . . . paranoia. He had recently read an article about this newly described illness and he certainly did not fit the description.

"It's been a ghastly day," he finally said.

One of the burning logs shifted. Miriam picked up the poker and pushed it back into the pile, and then she joined her husband on the loveseat. She took his hand but said nothing.

"I did one of those brilliant ploys that causes a witness to reveal the perfect piece of information," he said. "In this case, it was Sergeant Gorman."

Miriam remained quiet and Daniel loved her all the more for it. She always knew when he needed a listener, as opposed to an adviser.

"I set it up perfectly, so Gorman would have to admit that it was strange to find only one souvenir in that hiding place. Instead, he announced that it wasn't strange at all, because Ward had murdered Alexandra Stanton and some unidentified accomplice had murdered the others. Or," he added, "as the sergeant so wisely pointed out, Ward was probably a copycat. The jury loved it, Cornell loved it, and I was left looking like a damn fool. And no one seemed to care that Ward had no way of knowing about that souvenir!"

Again, Miriam remained silent. Her only response was to tighten her grip ever so slightly on his hand.

"And then—" Daniel felt the words catch in his throat. "And then I did what is perhaps the most idiotic thing I could have done: I asked Cornell if we could plead guilty in exchange for prison time and no hanging."

He felt Miriam's body shift and was afraid to look at her. What if her face expressed disapproval? Or worse, contempt? But how could it not, considering these were what he was feeling about himself? His insecurities came rushing back. He could survive losing the respect of his friends and colleagues, but not his parents, and most certainly not Miriam. She was his backbone, his motivation to be a better and more compassionate man. If he lost that, what remained? And what about Ward? If he failed, would an innocent man die? He tried to push these thoughts away before he was consumed by them.

Over the next few minutes, Daniel repeated in detail his examination of Sergeant Gorman, including the policeman speaking to him as if he were a fool, an attorney who knew nothing about the law. And then he told her about Cornell, and how the man had treated him with an almost amused condescension. Cornell's voice rang through his head suggesting that Marcus was likely regretting having brought him into the firm.

After painting the full picture, he was relieved to see kindness in Miriam's eyes. Not sympathy, and definitely not pity. He would have felt crushed if it were either of those. "So," he said, forcing what he knew was a pathetic smile. "So, which do you prefer: to divorce me and salvage your reputation, or to tell me about your day?"

She smiled. "As always, much to tell."

He smiled again. Although this smile was a bit forced, it was not painted on to cover his humiliation. "I'm here; I'm listening. And I welcome a short holiday from my tale of woe."

Miriam leaned over and kissed him.

For a moment or two, Daniel got lost in that kiss, a kiss that meant so much. No contempt, no pity, only love. When their embrace ended, he felt as if he had just been given medical aid, a tonic that was good for his heart and his soul.

Miriam shifted closer until their arms were pressed together. "First and foremost," she began, all lightheartedness missing from her voice, "it's unlikely I'll be making any further trips to Suffolk." Daniel began to respond, but she continued. "You know that I'll do everything I can to help Toby and his family. Officer Thorpe is there, and from what I can see, he's very much involved, committed."

Daniel sensed that the silence she provided when he was explaining the events in court was now required of him.

Miriam stared into the fire, as Daniel had been doing when she arrived home. This made sense to him. Fire was mesmerizing, whether in a hearth or a burning building. One could easily get lost in its colors, its intensity, its allure, a magnet pulling one into its center. He watched Miriam and thought how she had changed during their short marriage. She was more relaxed, easier on herself. The fifteen-year difference between them hardly showed. And if it did, so what? Some might judge him for marrying a woman so much older, but it had made perfect sense to him. It still did. Even more, it suited him just fine. They would grow old together, and he would always be there to guarantee her comfort and security.

It was a good minute before Miriam spoke. "It's Eve." The sadness in her eyes was amplified by the fire's reflection in them. She turned to face Daniel. "Her mind is quite fine, but I think she's going to retire. You know how meticulous she is, precise, never room for even the smallest error, but I can see that she's tired. And with this, her confidence is beginning to fade. There's such conflict for her, wanting to be in the lab and doing flawless work, yet understanding that she's not as astute as she once was. If I return to Suffolk, Joe will be left with a responsibility he can't shoulder. I don't mean watching over Eve—he can do that very well. But what if he's put in the position where he has to assure her that her work is accurate? His knowledge of pathology is rudimentary. No," she added, with a shake of her head, "I have to be there."

Daniel shifted his arm and draped it over her shoulder, pulling her closer. "No one will fault you for this decision, I promise. The lab is where you need to be. And for the moment, where you're doing the most good."

"The hardest part of this," she said, "is that as much as I care about Toby and his family, I care more about Peter Ward. I'm sure he's innocent. No, I take that back. The most difficult part is our inability to prove him innocent. I share your concerns that he'll be convicted. All the more reason I must be here, close by, in case you need me."

"I don't know what I was thinking," he admitted, almost to himself. "Taking that risk and offering a guilty plea."

"You did it to give yourself time to pursue the case further, until we find out what actually happened."

He nodded and released a sigh. "Nearly impossible. No surprise why Cornell turned me down: he's convinced that Ward is guilty, and I can't prove he's not."

"Daniel, if anyone can get this man exonerated, it's you."

"I'd like to think so." The moment those words were spoken, he knew that no matter what he said or how he said it, his tone was not convincing. How could it be, when he felt so certain he was going to fail?

THEY WERE WELL into dinner. The tender roast beef with onion gravy was hardly touched, the green peas pushed around the plate, along with the miniature boiled potatoes. Even the apple cake baked earlier in the day by Mrs. Cutters offered no enticement, despite the bowl of freshly clotted cream sitting beside it. Miriam had extolled this woman's culinary virtues nearly every day since one of her friends in the scientific community had recommended her to be their cook. Such trust had grown between Miriam and the elderly chef that she was given a key to the front door so she could let herself in and leave the day's meal in the kitchen. The joke between Daniel and Miriam was that, without Mrs. Cutters, they could very well starve.

Daniel had just stood to help Miriam remove the dinner plates when there was a loud knock on the door. They looked at each other, as if neither was sure whether to be alarmed or annoyed. It was getting late and they were both extremely tired.

Daniel strode from the kitchen into the foyer, where he opened the door to find Ian standing before him.

"I seem to have a talent for calling or showing up at the most vexing times," Ian said, stepping into the foyer.

As if to emphasize his proclamation, the grandfather clock began to chime, and continued until the tenth strike was delivered.

"Come through to the kitchen," Daniel said. "Have you eaten?"

"That depends on whether you consider a bit of lemon tart and something vaguely resembling a tea biscuit to be food."

As if having a sixth sense, Miriam had already placed a slice of the roast beef on a large dinner plate, along with heaping portions of green peas and potatoes. "Let me know if you want more," she said, as the men appeared at the door.

Ian turned to Daniel. "How does she do that?"

Daniel gave him a little smile.

Ian sat at the table and Daniel joined him. Miriam placed two plates on the table, one of them in front of Daniel. Nothing was as it had been only minutes earlier, with the food in disarray. Everything on his plate was perfectly in place, as if it had never been touched. Without a word, Miriam placed her own refreshed plate on the table and sat down.

"After dinner," she said, "we are obliged to eat a good part of the apple cake. If not, Mrs. Cutters will be offended."

Ian smiled. "You're asking a lot of me, Miriam, but I'll do my best."

The three of them sat in a comfortable quiet, the only sounds being forks and knives tapping against dinner plates. When words were uttered, they came as questions put forth by Miriam regarding extra portions.

It was not until a good part of the apple cake was consumed, along with every bit of clotted cream, that a conversation ensued. By then, it was nearly eleven o'clock.

"I'm quite sure you didn't appear on our doorstep, bedraggled and hungry as you were, because you needed to be fed," Daniel said.

"If we may," replied Ian, gesturing to the plates, "could we clean all of this and then move into the sitting room?"

"You two go," Miriam insisted. "I'll get things sorted here and join you."

"I'd rather you be present," Daniel said. He rose and began clearing the table.

With the three of them working together, it took only minutes for the dishes to be washed, dried, and returned to the shelf adjacent to the sink. The cutlery went into the proper drawer and what little remained of the apple cake was returned to its dish and covered with a glass top.

"A good and efficient team," Miriam said. "And you, Ian, are always welcomed here."

He gave her a rather silly grin. "My mother taught me to behave in such a way that I'm always invited back."

"A wise woman," Daniel told him, offering his first unforced smile of the day.

They adjourned to the sitting room, where Daniel added firewood to the hearth and poked at it until it caught. It took only a few minutes for the fire to spread its warmth throughout the little room. The three of them sat together, not speaking, sharing this sense of well-being, yet each one understanding that dramas were taking place that needed their attention.

Ian shifted in the chair, crossed his legs at the ankle, and leaned back. And then, as if deciding that his information required a less casual stance, he planted his shoes on the carpet and leaned forward. "My men have been working to find links, clues, whatever might help Ward's case." He pulled a notebook from his breast pocket and flipped it open. "From what we can tell, there have been at least six other murders like this one. That is, with a patch of skin removed."

"Six?" repeated Daniel. He looked at Miriam. She appeared as startled as he was, her eyes wide and her mouth open.

"Seven, if we include Alexandra Stanton," Ian said. "And we definitely must."

"Death times seven?" repeated Miriam. "My God."

"That we know about," Ian responded. "There could be more. Our search was restricted to areas in and around London."

"But how could the police have missed this?" Miriam asked.

"Each police district acts independently," Ian explained. "They keep their own records, and there is often little exchange of information among them. And what adds to the problem, the procedures of each station are often quite different."

"Are you saying that records aren't shared?" she asked.

Ian inhaled deeply and released a heavy breath. "Not records . . . nor secrets."

Daniel could not let that go by. "Is it possible for seven different police stations to hide the same secret? Seven stations deleting the mention of a square of skin from their reports? How can that be?" The moment he asked the question, he knew that Ian had an answer.

"I read Dr. Ornshaw's testimony," Ian said. "He believes that someone is either paying off policemen in each of those stations, or blackmailing them. In any case, I'm afraid we'll never get them to testify."

"But they must!" Miriam insisted. "If they're called to the stand, they have no choice; they are legally obliged to appear and tell the truth!"

"That may be," Daniel said. "But who will stop them from lying?"

"I agree," Ian said. "Getting honest testimony when their careers are at risk? It won't happen."

"Of course it won't," Daniel said. "It would be more than the end of a career. Whether they are age twenty or fifty, they will never again see the inside of a police station . . . except if they're arrested." Not for the first time, Daniel wondered why there was so little prudence in jurisprudence, but he said nothing.

"It could also put them in danger," Miriam reminded them. "If someone very powerful is involved—and I'm guessing that's the case . . ." She left the sentence unfinished.

Daniel and Ian nodded, as if they knew what she was saying and they agreed with her.

By the time Ian left, it was coming up to two o'clock. Daniel and Miriam ascended the stairs to their bedroom. They could barely find the energy to undress, don their nightclothes, and slip under the blankets.

As she always did when struggling with a dilemma, Miriam fell into a deep sleep. And as he always did when struggling with a dilemma, Daniel lay awake for hours, his mind taking him from the debacle in the courtroom to myriad ideas and solutions. Most of them were quickly discarded.

In the morning, there was another early telephone call, this one coming when Daniel was fully dressed and seated at the kitchen table with Miriam, enjoying the meal she had prepared. The crispy fried bread was just right, a nice balance to the egg, over-easy as he liked it, and accompanied by one pork sausage and a dollop of baked beans sitting atop a slice of fried tomato. And, of course, the always-present cup of tea. After the restless night, he was certain he could not eat, but he found himself throwing off his anxieties and savoring every bite.

"Who is it this time?" he mumbled, placing the linen napkin on the table and passing through to the foyer. He was almost too tired to consider that, this time, it could be news of Marcus having another heart attack, or Justin Kitteridge taking a turn for the worse.

He removed the handset from the cradle and pressed it against his ear. "Pitt residence," he said, his voice more of a murmur.

"Daniel, it's Toby."

"Toby!" he said with enthusiasm, and then realized that this could be terrible news. "Is everything—?"

Toby cut him off. "It's good news, for a change."

"Tell me!"

"The doctors are quite certain that Father will recover."

Miriam appeared and stood very close. Daniel gave her an enthusiastic nod and then tipped the receiver away from his ear so she could listen.

"Miriam is here, sharing your good news. Go on."

"Not only is he recovering, but he's beginning to speak."

Daniel felt his heart racing. "Well enough to give you anything helpful?"

Before Toby could answer, Miriam took the phone from Daniel, giving him a stern look. "What my dear husband means to say is, this is wonderful news, we are thrilled."

Daniel kissed her cheek, feeling chagrined. What would he do without this marvelous woman?

They both heard Toby's laugh, a musical sound that flowed out of the receiver and filled the air around them.

"Wonderful news, indeed," Daniel said. "That would have been my next response. But now that we know . . ."

"He's able to give me recollections in bits and pieces. But there's one thing he remembers clearly: there was a stranger—definitely not a young man—and he is the one who shot both of them—and with different guns."

"He's certain?" asked Daniel, almost breathlessly. "Absolutely certain?" He felt Miriam's hand on his arm, the excited squeeze. For a moment, he was almost lightheaded. He might not be doing stellar work for Peter Ward, but perhaps he would see progress in identifying Delia Kitteridge's murderer.

"Without question. He remembers the man who shot them, and is positive he was a stranger. It was the same man who had been given a tour of the church and the gardens earlier that day. Father even remembered the man's name, but I'm guessing it was a false one."

Daniel felt the enormity of what he was hearing, and one glance at Miriam told him she felt it as well. "Is there anything else he remembers?"

"He was vague about a description, but remembered with clarity that the man was at least middle-aged. Dark-haired and quite attractive, he said. The way he's progressing, Daniel—much of the pain medication is being reduced, which is helping his memory—I might have more information later today."

Daniel took the next few minutes to describe what had been transpiring at the Old Bailey, and the dramatic discovery made by Ian's men regarding the other murders, each woman mutilated in the same way.

"I'm . . . astonished," said Toby, his voice low with emotion.

In the short silence that followed, Daniel was overtaken by the need for full disclosure. Toby was going to hear this one way or another, and he would rather it came from him. "There's one more thing," he said, and then he described in detail his gaffe with the prosecution the day before. "Cornell was chortling," Daniel added, feeling the shame returning.

"He can chortle till the cows come home," Toby said. "In the end, you will prove that you were right and he was wrong. That's what counts. But I know you, Daniel. Don't be too hard on yourself. And in case no one has said this, you are not perfect."

Daniel smiled, as did Miriam as she turned and headed upstairs. "No, I've never been told this," he said. "That is, not in the last few hours."

When their discussion about the case was finished, Toby shared the latest about his family.

As Toby spoke, a thought ran through Daniel's mind. "Toby, sorry, but can we go back to the Ward case for one minute? Have you managed to remember what you were thinking before you received the news of your parents?"

"Yes, right, I've been so pleased by my father's recovery that it slipped my mind to tell you. It was the flash of a thought that related to another case, something I'd read several years ago, nothing to do with any souvenir, but I think it was a young woman murdered after she had left a posh party. It made me wonder if there could be a series of murders, not just this one."

There was a pause, compelling Daniel to press him. "Can you be more specific? You've touched on something we're working on. Were there other similarities? The more I can put in my appeal, the more powerful it will be."

"I wish I could, Daniel, but does it matter now?"

"Perhaps not. Don't worry."

Toby gave a quiet laugh. "It seems that memory problems run in my family. Yours, too."

"Mine? Who's struggling in my family?"

"Well, not really your immediate family, but I know that Miriam has been concerned about Marcus and Eve."

"Fortunately, Eve seems to be doing well," Daniel said. "It's less a matter of her old head injury than it is one of age. We forget this, because her mind's so sharp, but she's well along in years."

"A remarkable woman," Toby said.

"She would love to continue working full steam, but I think she's looking at her options. It reminds me that the hardest part about our memory fading is that we're often not aware of it, but others are."

"I would not handle that well," Toby said, the tone in his voice making him sound lonely, forlorn. But when he spoke again, after a pause, his voice showed new energy. "I still have much to do up here. So, for now—and I'm truly sorry, Daniel—but I'm quite useless to you."

"You're doing what you can, we all know that."

"Perhaps there's more I can do," Toby said. "I've asked a few locals about this man, on the slim chance that they would remember."

"It's been hardly more than a week, so perhaps someone remembers the presence of a stranger."

"It's a village, Daniel, not London. Strangers aren't commonly seen here. Oh, they come to Ipswich, certainly, but not to this little enclave. In any case, there are three people who are able to describe him. Four, including Alberta. And just to be certain, I asked for as detailed a description as they could give me." A hint of excitement ran through his voice. "Daniel, their descriptions were very similar, and coincided with the one my father gave me."

"Have you told Officer Thorpe? This is central to his case."

"That's my next call. It's the first tangible clue we've had."

"You sound like Conan Doyle," Daniel teased. "The big mystery is solved!" The moment the words were spoken, Daniel heard how inappropriate they were. With Toby's mother dead and the future of his father's health still in question, there was nothing to laugh about. "Toby, I'm . . . Forgive me. That was insensitive."

"I know you, my friend," Toby replied. "You're far from insensitive. You were merely sharing my excitement in the moment."

"You're being too kind; I feel like an idiot—again."

The conversation ended on a warm note, with Daniel promising to call as soon as he received a response to the formal appeal, and Toby assuring Daniel that he would call the minute his father added more information.

Miriam walked into the foyer, her leather case in one hand and her keys in the other. "It all sounds promising," she said. "This news about the assailant's description should ease your heart."

"You heard?"

"I didn't have to, your responses made it quite clear."

"Maybe it will ease my nerves as well. And my guilty conscience."

"You have no reason to feel guilty, Daniel, not when your actions are directed at saving a man's life."

He pulled Miriam to him and embraced her. "What would I do without you?"

She took a step back. "You would be lonely, miserable, and a tyrant with everyone in chambers." Having said her mind, she opened the front door. A nippy gust of autumn blew into the foyer and she quickly closed it.

"Let me know if anything new comes to mind about those seven women," he said, while taking a wool scarf from the coat hook, wrapping it around her neck, and tucking the ends under the collar of her coat.

"Of course," she said. "And you let me know how the appeal goes."

Daniel pulled on his heavy winter coat, they kissed, and he opened the door and followed Miriam outside.

He watched her drive away in her red sports car and then hailed a taxi. The next few hours were crucial. A man's future was about to be determined.

The taxi was minutes from his office when Daniel began trying to fit together pieces of what little they knew about the attack on Toby's parents. Why would someone enter the vicarage and shoot Justin and Delia Kitteridge? There was no theft, nothing vandalized—just two people left to die. He grappled with this, attempting to see the evidence from all angles, but the result was more frustration.

The building that housed fford Croft and Gibson came into view just as another thought rushed into his head. What if Toby's parents were shot not because of their work in the village, or the confidences shared with Justin, their spiritual adviser, but because of something else, something entirely overlooked? He pushed that thought away. Justin had been clear that the man was a stranger.

The taxi pulled up to the entrance of the building and stopped. Daniel sat in the back of the car, his heart racing. He heard the driver speaking, but the words were lost. "Sorry?" he asked.

The driver repeated the fare owed and Daniel paid it, adding a bit more as a thanks for the man's patience. As he stepped onto the road, a jolt ran through him, an idea as outrageous as it was implausible; an idea that had not been mentioned by anyone involved in the attack on Toby's parents. There were so many questions that had not been answered. And how could they have been, when everyone was so quick to accept the murder-suicide explanation?

"Good day, guv," the driver said, then pulled from the curb and drove off into the busy morning traffic.

Daniel went immediately to his office and closed the door. Seated, he placed his elbows on the desk and his head in his hands. Anyone entering might have assumed he was suffering. Instead, he was considering something so improbable . . . and yet it made perfect sense.

He picked up the phone and called Ian Frobisher, grateful when he got through without too many delays.

"Daniel," Ian said, his voice registering curiosity. "Have you filed the motion to dismiss the charges against Ward?"

"I'm in my office and will prepare it soon. Court convenes in an hour, so I might have to present my arguments to the judge orally, with the formal written document to follow."

"Good. Anything else?"

Daniel took a very deep breath and let it out slowly. "Toby called this morning."

"Anything new up there?"

"Not only new, but of significance. His father is coming around and is able to describe his attacker."

"An attacker! That's progress, to be sure. God, my hands are sweating!"

Daniel felt his heart quicken. "There's more, Ian. He asked his sister, Alberta, as well as those three villagers who remembered having seen Justin with this stranger, and their descriptions correspond."

"You're right, that is significant! Any idea who this man might be?"

This was the moment when Daniel would reveal his theory and Ian would either pretend it was interesting, when in truth he found it absurd, or he would consider it.

"I've thought of a possible motive," Daniel said. "But before I share it with you, promise not to ridicule me. I've had quite enough of that from Cornell."

"You have my word."

The level of his voice told Daniel that he would listen, and would not be quick to judge. Daniel ordered himself to remain calm, and not sound like one of those crazies who swear the world is flat or that someday they would all be living on the moon. "What if Justin and Delia Kitteridge were shot because they were Toby's parents?"

There was a lengthy silence, into which Daniel felt part of his certainty deflate.

"I'm listening, but I'm not following you."

Daniel thought for a moment that this might be a good time to drop the idea and save whatever dignity remained, but there was something in his theory that felt right.

"Daniel?"

"Hear me out. And forgive me if I ramble a bit . . . I'm thinking aloud." After a moment, he said, "What if this attack had to do with the possibility of Toby proving Peter Ward's innocence? If Toby is forced to leave London and be with his family, would that increase Ward's chances of being proven guilty? Toby's an excellent lawyer, right? And if he's not here, then one of us from chambers would have to step in, being relatively unaware of the specifics."

"I'm listening, Daniel, but I'm still not sure what you're saying. Who's the connection between the murder of Alexandra Stanton and the attack on Toby's parents? Are you saying that someone knew her . . . *and* the Kitteridges?"

"I'm saying that the person who killed Alexandra might have been complicit in the shooting of Toby's parents."

Daniel waited for Ian's response. He imagined his friend shaking his head and pressing his lips firmly together, as he did whenever trying to unravel a dilemma. He had learned during their college days that Ian Frobisher was smart, very smart, and he had the gift of studying a problem from many angles, sometimes every angle, which made him the best problem solver Daniel knew. That is, with the exception of his own family, particularly his father. No one could solve a puzzle faster than Thomas Pitt.

"I don't see where this is going, but tell me what I can do. I learned long ago not to get in the way of your instincts."

That admission, coming from an old and trusted friend, nearly brought a smile to Daniel's face. Perhaps another time, not now.

"What I need you to do is work with me, go through all the autopsy reports and police files dealing with these six women, and then we'll do a cross-check of every guest list we have from all those parties the victims attended. That is, the parties they went to on the same night they were killed. Also, we need to find out if anything else was reported to the police on those nights, something like a fistfight or a loud argument. If there were any altercations, they might be related to the murders."

"When would you like me to start? I have a few cases on my desk that need my immediate attention."

Daniel thought through this, how to mesh his schedule with Ian's and Miriam's, because she would certainly want to work with them. "How do you feel about meeting later today, even if it means we have to work through the night?"

"I need time to pull these files together, along with the autopsy reports and any other information I can find. If there were parties taking place the night even a few of the women were killed, my men need to follow up, get lists of guests. Some of these took place a year ago, even three or four, so it's going to take some time. Go to court, argue for your dismissal, and I'll set my team into motion. While you're performing your legal magic, I can take everything we've learned and put it together."

"So, you might not be able to dive in until . . . when?"

"I wish I could say tonight, but it might be tomorrow morning."

"I'll let Miriam know. We don't have much time."

"I'm aware of that, but we can only do what we can do, yes? And we must be sure it's done right. If we take half-baked ideas or flawed evidence to court, the judge will have our necks."

"I understand," Daniel said. "I don't like the delay, but I do understand. I've got the paperwork in front of me, but I'm due in court in an hour. Our judge will not be happy when I throw this boulder into his serene pond."

"An understatement, I'm afraid. Hopefully, he won't intercept that boulder and heave it back to you."

The men shared a light and very short laugh.

"I'll ring Miriam now," Daniel said. "She needs to know that we've pulled her into our little circle."

Daniel called Miriam at the lab and presented the plan—that she and Ian, Joe, and Eve would search for links between the dead women, the parties, and the men who attended them. He held back his thoughts about the possible relationship between the death of Alexandra Stanton and the attack on Toby's parents. He needed more proof before taking that step. What if he was wrong? No matter how many times Miriam told him that she believed in him, he still feared looking like a fool in her eyes. He seemed to be doing that far too often.

"We'll get to it now," Miriam told him. "We'll have to harness Eve; she loves this kind of sleuthing!" Hearing Miriam's voice, knowing that she was fully committed, released some of the tightness in his neck.

"What's your next move?" she asked.

He explained that he was about to write the motion and then approach the court when he filed it. "Actually," he added, "I'll wait until you've checked on those names. So, expect a call from Ian sometime later today. At least, I hope it's today. He didn't sound terribly optimistic and thought tomorrow was more realistic. In any case, he's pulling everything together so you can begin cross-checking all the information."

When the call ended, Daniel sat in his office knowing exactly what he needed to do.

CHAPTER

Sixteen

THE FOLLOWING MORNING, Miriam arrived at the lab a few minutes before seven. It was still dark outside, her day was just beginning, and she was already tired to the bone. She was surprised to find Eve at her desk. Perhaps it was unwise, accepting this role of overseer of the assemblage and analysis of any and all information related to the charges brought against Peter Ward. But then she reminded herself that Daniel was convinced that this was their only path to acquittal, daunting as it was. They all needed to work together until it made sense. That meant dedicating every waking moment to this mission, waking moments that promised to far outnumber her hours of sleep.

At eight o'clock, Joe entered the lab, Ian close behind, the men together carrying a large cardboard box that Miriam assumed held the autopsy and police reports. Anything more, she could only guess. Photographs? Bits of evidence? As for the lists of party guests, she was quite certain they were tucked into one of Ian's pockets, too important to toss into a box. The arrival of this information should have made her happy, or at the least relieved. Instead, she experienced a downcast moment: that carton represented many more hours of work for her and Eve. As if reprimanding herself, she walked over to one of the long tables, moved several instruments out of the way, and watched the men set the box down.

"Have you heard from Daniel?" Ian asked her. "It will be interesting to hear how Cornell is behaving this morning. That is, if Daniel submitted that motion. I think he's waiting for the results of our work."

"I wish I knew," Miriam said. "He was preparing it and concerned about how the judge would respond to even the suggestion of a delay."

Ian's face clouded over. "Based on what Daniel told me, Cornell has become a vulture, with poor Daniel his prey." As he spoke, he shifted the box that was on the examination table. Opening it, he removed what appeared to be a dozen files and spread them on the table, end-to-end, like stepping-stones in a garden. There were, however, no trees to provide shade, nor were there flowers for color. Instead, only the harshly lit sterility of a pathology lab, and the ominous aura of purpose and tension suspended over it.

Miriam leaned closer to read the labels on the files. "It seems that Cornell is so confident he's ready to push for a ruling today."

Joe stepped up to the table and began to rearrange the laid-out files, making sure they were lined up in chronological order. He glanced at Miriam and gave a little shrug. They both knew that precision was always his aim.

"A ruling?" Eve repeated. "Today?"

"So, we don't have time on our side," Ian said, urgency in his voice. "If Daniel has to rest his case today, that leaves the door open for Cornell to rest his as well. And then . . ." His pause was short, but fraught with worry, evident by the pulsing muscle Miriam detected in his jaw. "And then the jury would take over."

"All very good to wonder about the judge and the prosecutor, and even the jury," Eve said, her back against the large oak cabinet holding files from twenty years of autopsies. "But what about Peter Ward? How does *he* feel about any of this? I assume he knows that Daniel will be filing this motion."

Ian removed folded papers from his jacket and handed them to Miriam. "The lists." When she slipped them into the pocket of her lab coat, he added, "I'm not certain Daniel will go ahead with his motion to dismiss. I can see he's feeling defeated, but the Daniel Pitt I know will pull the rabbit from the hat. It's not like him to err and then accept defeat."

Miriam gave him a warm smile, reminding herself that he was right, her husband was no quitter. She wouldn't be at all surprised to learn that, at this very minute, in the cavernous courtroom of the Old Bailey, Daniel was conceiving a plan to capitalize on what he considered to be the unforgivable error of offering a guilty plea. If Cornell had been chortling over this plea in exchange for waiving the death penalty, his glee could very well be short-lived. But that depended solely on finding the real killer, who she was certain existed somewhere in these lists.

She watched as Eve opened more files and spread documents across the table, and noticed that Ian was watching, too. When he redirected his attention to Miriam, they exchanged smiles, which Miriam read as their tacit agreement that the work needed to be done, and Eve would make it go that much faster and smoother.

Joe crossed to where Miriam was standing and did a quick glance at the box. And then, as if knowing by instinct where he was most needed, he moved to Eve's side. "So, what do you have for me?"

Eve gave him a look that nearly made Miriam laugh. It was tantamount to witnessing the evil eye!

"What I have is a gentle yet firm suggestion that you not hover over me," Eve said, the warmth in her voice not lost on anyone in the room.

"Under penalty of death?" he asked.

She laughed. "Yes, something like that. I'm thinking guillotine."

"Then I shall proceed with caution," Joe said, holding up both hands and backing away.

Ian asked Miriam for the lists, which she produced. He took them, unfolded each one, and placed them on the specimen table. He gazed at the papers covered with columns of names and places. "Some of these parties were quite small, with only a handful of guests, while there were others with dozens."

Miriam took up one of the sheets and scanned it. "How do we differentiate between those who were invited, those who dropped in on the spur of the moment, and those who came with someone as a couple, but who had not been invited?" Ian had explained to her that the names of the uninvited guests had been added to the evidence files, following the police investigation, to complete the lists, but she was wary of anything the police had pulled together so quickly.

"We do the best we can," Ian said. "It's the same with the geography. That is, most of these parties were in London, but there were a few in nearby towns."

"How far back did you go?" Eve asked. "Did all of these parties take place in the last year or two?"

Ian explained that the lists covered every party they could identify that took place around the time of the sexual assault and murder of a female victim, and then they had to determine if any of those victims had actually attended one of those parties. "A few happened in the last two or three years, and there's at least one from nearly five years ago. So, this was painstaking work. My men have been working nonstop to get this information."

Eve held up a small stack of files. "The autopsy reports," she said. "We've taken a closer look and we're quite sure we'll identify a few common threads. They were all young. Did they have the same patch of skin removed? You won't find that mentioned in these," she said, indicating the police reports, "nor in any of these autopsy reports." Almost as if speaking to herself, she added, "How in the hell did a pathologist leave out that detail? So," she continued, turning back to Joe, "while you're working on those lists of guests, I'll do another thorough study of them . . . and you'll help me. We're looking to catch discrepancies, perhaps even outright and intentional errors."

He smiled. "Of course, Doctor, that's why I'm here!"

The last bit of tension running through the lab now dissolved. Miriam felt the tightness in her shoulders release. The team was ready for battle.

A FEW HOURS LATER, there was a quiet hanging over the lab. Not that it was often noisy, but this was different. This was a silence heavy with purpose. Miriam, Eve, Joe, and Ian stood together, with Eve and Joe leaning against one of the tall specimen tables normally holding clean ampules and glass tubes, and now dedicated to open files.

"We're doing what we can," Eve said. "But this task of comparing guest lists to victims . . ."

Miriam wanted everyone to understand the cross-checking procedure they were using and the urgency that it be done quickly and faultlessly. With a man's life on the line, there was no room for error. She nearly announced this, but there was no reason to. They all understood what was at stake.

"My team is on the road questioning the friends and families of the six young women," Ian explained.

He picked up the sheet of paper near Eve's elbow and gave it a quick look. "I see you've already moved a few things around."

Eve read over the document. There were circles drawn around specific dates. "These are the parties attended by the victims that took place around the time of a death. Most of them," she added, pointing to several entries, "fall on the very same date—or within hours, if the death came after midnight."

"That's good," Ian said. "My officers interviewed some of those hosts, most of whom were not happy with us, not at all."

"I can imagine," Eve said. "From the looks of the addresses, more than a few parties were held in posh homes."

"That might narrow our search," Joe said. "Limit it to the wealthy?"

"Tempting," Ian said, "but putting limits on this search means we could miss something. In any case," he added, "my men knew to keep the search wide-ranging until a thorough list was made. And as you can see," he said, gesturing to the paper, "there are scores of names."

Miriam turned to Eve. "I know it's tiring work, but putting together the names of victims who attended one of the parties, and then identifying the one man who was there at all of them, will give us the name of our killer. We have to keep going and—"

Ian interrupted her. "My team has been working tirelessly day and night."

"You rule with an iron hand," teased Eve. "They must obey."

Ian smiled, but quickly became serious. "The truth is, they know that mistakes were made and evidence might have been falsified. This infuriates them. They're working around the clock to make this right." He released a cough before speaking again, then took a handkerchief from his pocket and blew his nose. "Top brass will not be happy when they learn that some of the interviews took place in the middle of the night, and more than a small amount of information was extracted after, shall we say, unwavering persistence? Daniel needs incontrovertible evidence, and my team means to provide it."

Miriam saw Eve's face come alive with a mischievous grin.

"Extracted information?" Eve said. "Like a rotten tooth being pulled?"

"For some of these party hosts, it was probably more painful," Ian responded with a chuckle. "No one wants to be awakened by a policeman at three in the morning, demanding to know about a party that took place last year."

Miriam watched this interchange with such pleasure, being able to push aside what now seemed like unwarranted concerns about her friend.

As if reading her mind, Eve tapped Miriam's hand and said, "Worry not, my dear, I'm not dead yet."

"No," Miriam said, "you most certainly are not!"

"There's something I need to do," Ian said, interrupting their conversation. He turned to Eve. "I'll need to close myself in your office and use your phone."

Eve gestured for him to take his leave. As if on cue, the phone began to ring. Miriam rushed into the office, picked up the receiver, and announced the name of the lab.

"Thank heaven it's you," Daniel told her. "I've only a few minutes and wanted to catch you up."

Miriam realized she had been holding her breath. She let it out slowly. "I'm listening."

"Cornell is gloating. I've been trying to act humbled by my gaffe, this plea offer nonsense, and he's buying it. He's now so certain that the jury will find Peter guilty that he's slowing things down a bit, as if wanting to savor his certain victory."

"True to form, I would say. So, where does it stand now?"

"I'll delay as much as I can, until I hear from you or Ian. The minute you've placed the same man at several of those parties, we'll drop the bomb. But until then . . ."

"We're working as fast as we can, Daniel. Ian was up all night with his men, collecting names of guests—invited and uninvited—from some very unhappy hosts. We're already comparing to see whose name appears on multiple guest lists. As soon as we have a name, we'll get it to you immediately."

"Is Ian nearby?"

"I'll call him to the phone."

She put the receiver on the desk, stepped out of the office, and gestured for Ian to join her.

He crossed the lab and entered the office. "It's Daniel?"

She handed him the receiver and stood quietly as the two men brought each other up to date. Before the call ended, Ian held the phone so Miriam could hear.

"I'm about to contact certain policemen and pressure them to inform me—or inform on their men—who altered those reports and why," Ian said.

The men agreed to talk as soon as either of them had news, and then Ian immediately placed another call. Miriam left the room, closing the door behind her. She had taken only a few steps when she heard Ian speaking, his voice firm and authoritative, giving her a sense that something significant was about to happen.

It was nearly an hour before Ian emerged from the office, his face grim. "I've been speaking to policemen in several of the precincts where the parties and killings took place. What I've uncovered is not only unsettling. If it's true, it will end the careers of men who were considered very good and dependable."

Miriam took a few steps until she was facing him. "What did you find?" she asked, the words thick in her throat.

It took Ian several moments to compose himself. Miriam could not determine if his emotions were anger or sadness . . . perhaps both.

"In each of those stations, someone altered the reports, removing information about the patch of skin, under the threat of losing his job. And," he added, holding up his hand to stop any comments, "a few of them had the safety of their families, their wives and children, held over their head."

Miriam and Eve said nothing. Their faces first registered disbelief and then, as the possibility became more evident, concern.

"You do know what this means," Ian said. Not a question, a statement.

"I do," Miriam said. "Somewhere, one person is responsible. One person with great influence is pulling the strings."

"More than that," Eve said. "One person with great influence . . . doing what's needed to point the finger of guilt at Peter Ward."

Ian walked over to where the lists were displayed. "Is it possible?" he murmured, almost under his breath. He picked up the sheets of paper and ran his finger down the first page, then did the same with the second and third.

"We have all the pathology reports, guest lists, and assorted files we need to make a good show of it," Miriam said.

"Daniel needs more than a show of it," Eve said. "He needs that final piece of irrefutable evidence. I think I can find it."

Miriam nearly jumped when Eve reached out and wrapped her fingers around her arm.

"I know what you're thinking," Eve said.

Miriam began to speak, but Eve cut her off.

"You're worried that this is too taxing for me, that I'm not of sound mind—or sound enough mind—to stay focused. Let me do my work," she added, her eyes imploring. "Old doesn't mean incapable."

"Eve," Miriam said, her voice low and barely audible.

"I'll study all of the autopsy reports, looking for anything they might have in common. Now that we know what most of the pathologists actually found, I'll have a more solid base to make comparisons." She stopped for a moment, her face almost serene. "And if I feel I can't handle the work, I'll step away. Agreed?" Her grasp on Miriam's arm tightened ever so slightly.

Miriam nearly winced. Instead, she covered Eve's hand with her own. "Agreed."

Joe left and returned a few minutes later dragging a large chalkboard. Ian helped him set it up, while Miriam fetched a handful of white chalk. Over the next few hours, they carefully reexamined the guest list of every party one of the victims had attended, with Joe writing on the board the names of all the attendees. After all the names were listed, Ian read each one aloud and Miriam circled every name that was repeated, adding a number next to each name to indicate the number of times that person was present.

While the final list was being revised, Eve and Joe disappeared into the office to call all of the attending pathologists in order to confirm, yet again, what they had written in their reports . . . and encouraging them to admit to what they had failed to include.

It took nearly an hour to compile the final list, because Miriam wanted a second pass to be certain no errors were made, no name repetitions missed. After the last name was read aloud, she erased every name that appeared only once. She stood back and studied the chalkboard.

"How many do we have?" Ian asked, looking over her shoulder.

She did a quick count. "Eight," she said. "All of them were at several of the parties where a young woman ended up dead."

"We can cross off these," Ian said, pointing to two names. "Unlikely a woman is the criminal."

"I agree," Miriam said, erasing them with a rag. "And that leaves six." She stared at the list for a long moment. "And here we have it."

A moment later, her face turned pale, as if a brush with white powder had been drawn down it, from forehead to chin. "I think I know who it is."

As if on cue, Ian moved closer.

"Look," Miriam said, pointing to one name.

He stared at the new list and his eyes grew wide. "He was at every party."

Miriam drew a circle around the name. "We have our murderer," she whispered. "We . . . do." And then she stepped away from the blackboard. A small step, but one that created distance from the drama of this discovery.

The air in the room changed, as if someone had opened the door to let in a brutal draft.

"I need to call Daniel," she said, her voice breathy. "He must keep this case open, so we can—" She turned to Ian. "How can I reach him?"

Ian strode to the lab phone, his footsteps echoing through the room. He picked up the receiver, waited for the operator to come on the line, and announced, "The Old Bailey. Police business. It's urgent."

Miriam arrived at his side, soon joined by Eve and Joe. She watched Ian's face, how he pressed his lips together, the skin around his mouth white with tension.

It took nearly five minutes for Daniel to get the message and come to the nearest phone in the courthouse.

"Ian, what is it?" he asked, his voice so loud that Miriam could hear each word. Ian facilitated this by holding the receiver away from his ear.

"We have our man," Ian announced. "Stall as long as you can, we're on our way."

"I need to let the judge know there's a new witness," Daniel said. "Which of you will take the stand?"

Miriam looked at the faces around her: Joe, Ian, Eve. "Who does he suggest?" she asked Ian.

"It has to be someone who can respond to questions about the autopsies and the police reports," Daniel responded. "Or, if I must, I can call two of you to testify. Ian, you can tell us about the police reports and the lists; Miriam, I'll call you to testify about the autopsies."

The moment he spoke, Miriam looked at Eve, whose face revealed no emotion. Miriam had known her long enough to understand that she was containing her anger.

Ian handed Miriam the phone.

She took it and pressed it to her ear so firmly that no one nearby would be able to hear Daniel.

"Are you there?" he asked.

"I am."

"We can't put Eve on the stand," he said, his voice almost pleading. "Cornell will tear her to shreds, capitalize on her age."

"I know," she said. "I know."

She hung up the phone and walked into the lab, with Eve close behind.

"I can do this," Eve said. "I'll have no problem giving expert testimony. You do know that, yes?"

"I do," Miriam said. "There's no question about that, Eve."

"Then what?"

"Cornell is a nasty man and he won't hesitate to do everything possible to impugn your testimony. He'll make your age a point of concern, try to convince the jury that you're incompetent. It's not right, and it's ugly, but it's how he plays."

Eve nodded, her eyes dark. "You're right."

Miriam reached out and took her friend's hand. She saw understanding in Eve's eyes, but also sadness.

It wasn't until Miriam was in the taxi and nearly in front of the Old Bailey that she realized something. All of them had shared this dramatic revelation, but Daniel never asked who had committed the murders. This told her one thing only: he already knew.

CHAPTER

Seventeen

DANIEL ENTERED THE courtroom feeling hopeful. He was quite sure he had succeeded in lulling Cornell into the belief that Peter Ward's own defense attorney was doubting his client's innocence. If Daniel played it carefully, he might be able to capitalize on that. His strategy was actually quite simple: give this prosecutor such confidence that he would feel no need to call more witnesses. Including Peter Ward. As for the appeal, it was on hold until he had solid proof of Ward's innocence.

It took less than thirty minutes for Daniel to question the next two witnesses, upstanding and socially prominent young men, both of them having attended parties after which one of the guests was murdered. They denied having seen Peter Ward at the party, or at any other time. He was, according to them, a stranger.

While the next man was moving toward the witness box, Daniel gave Ward a quick glance. The young man should have been relieved to hear this testimony, but he was grinding his teeth. Daniel would have liked to know why, but he had established a certain rhythm in these questionings and did not want to risk breaking the pace.

After Daniel felt there was nothing more to be learned from this witness, he made a pretense of checking his papers.

"Mr. Pitt?" said the judge.

Looking up, he said, "I recall Martin Flynt to the stand, My Lord."

"Is your intention to waste the court's time?" the judge said. "Because if it is, you're succeeding."

Daniel tipped his head, hoping the judge would see this as a sign of respect. "I believe Mr. Flynt can provide information previously not given in testimony." He was aware of the risk. After all, young Flynt had already testified that Peter Ward was not the man he had seen arguing with Alexandra Stanton the night of her death. If the jurors could hear it one more time, perhaps they would be convinced that a young man of such pedigree and whose father, Sir Anthony Flynt, was highly respected in England and known for his strong ties to leaders, both political and industrial, would tell only the truth.

The judge leaned back in his chair—one that reminded Daniel of a throne—and made a little steeple with his fingers. "And your belief is based on what, Mr. Pitt?" The man's voice was flat, as if his patience had come to an end. Before Daniel could defend his decision, the judge leaned forward, his hands now clasped together, as if he were about to pray. "Mr. Pitt, do you intend to call everyone who attended these parties? If so, we could be here for days, weeks."

"No, My Lord," Daniel replied. He understood the challenge facing him, and that was to keep the questions moving along, and to make those questions so relevant that neither Cornell nor the judge would reprimand him, and certainly not recognize that he was stalling as he waited for Ian and Miriam to arrive. Until they could be called to testify, the case against Ward, in the eyes of the jurors, would continue to seem airtight.

Reluctant to anger the judge with further delay tactics, Daniel tried not to dwell on the concern that was causing his mouth to go dry: he had run out of options. Other than Martin Flynt's testimony, everything pointed to his client as the killer. "Your honor, I will put aside my renewed questioning of Martin Flynt. Instead, I call Peter Ward." When he saw the judge react with a nod, rather than a rebuke, he felt the pressure in his chest subside.

Ward stood and faced the courtroom. If there was ever a classic countenance suggesting guilt, he was presenting it. As much as Daniel had advised the young man about his appearance, Ward was disheveled, with one corner of his shirt collar curled up and his hair seemingly uncombed. Certainly not the image of a young man innocent of a heinous crime, perhaps many.

After Ward was sworn in, Daniel took a few steps closer to his client. "You have stated that you have no idea how this . . . souvenir . . . found its way into your flat."

"Yes, sir," Ward replied.

"You now swear this, under oath?"

"I do, sir."

"And you testify under oath that you were not familiar with Alexandra Stanton."

"That is correct."

"Mr. Ward, are you aware of anyone who might want you to be punished for a crime you did not commit?"

Cornell leaned forward as if to stand, and then stopped.

Daniel looked over at the prosecutor and saw something in his face that unsettled him. With someone as clever as Cornell, there was no guessing what might be coming, but he would swear on all that was precious to him that this man had something planned. For what was not the first time in the course of this trial, Daniel saw Cornell as a dangerous predator, only this time it was not only Peter Ward, but Daniel as well, who was his intended prey.

"Mr. Ward?" Daniel prompted, and then waited for the young man to reply.

"No!" he declared, the word delivered almost as a cry, a plea for help. "But whoever is doing this is destroying my life," he added, his voice now so low that Daniel had to strain to hear each word.

Daniel picked up a paper from the desk. "Mr. Ward, I have here the dates when other young women were murdered."

"Objection!" Cornell said, his voice booming. "Mr. Ward is on trial for the murder of Alexandra Stanton, no one else. Any questions related to these other unfortunate deaths have no place in this courtroom."

Daniel shifted his gaze to the judge, expecting him to rule in Cornell's favor.

"Your objection is sustained," the judge announced. "Mr. Pitt, please move on and restrict your inquiries to the charge at hand."

Daniel responded with a curt nod, biting back words that, if not restrained, he would later regret. He glanced toward the door. Where in the hell were Ian and Miriam? "Mr. Ward, I have one final question. Please think carefully before responding."

Ward nodded, the solemnity on his face heightened by his pallor, as well as the beads of perspiration now catching the overhead lights and glistening on his forehead and upper lip.

"Mr. Ward," Daniel said, his voice ringing with emotion, "did you murder Alexandra Stanton?"

"No, sir, I did not, I swear!" Ward declared with a violent shake of his head.

"Thank you," Daniel said. Turning to the judge, he added, "I have no more questions of the defendant, My Lord."

The judge turned to Cornell. "Do you wish to question Mr. Ward?"

Cornell's mouth turned up ever so slightly, nearly a smile. "Most definitely, My Lord."

Daniel suddenly wished he had omitted breakfast from his morning routine.

Cornell stood and approached the accused. "Mr. Ward, do you understand the importance of honesty in the courtroom?"

Before another word was spoken, Daniel felt his stomach lurch yet again. Cornell would never lead with this. That is, not unless he knew something that would sink the defense. He had no choice but to wait, and hope that what was coming was not lethal.

"I do, sir," Ward replied.

"And do you understand that there are penalties for lying under oath?"

Daniel felt his mouth go dry.

"Yes," Ward said. "Yes, sir."

"But you have lied," Cornell said, his eyebrows raised. "Have you not?"

Daniel saw how Peter Ward squirmed, gripped and released the railing surrounding him in the witness box. Daniel imagined a chasm opening in the floor beneath them and swallowing everyone in the courtroom. For a moment, he wished it would.

Before Ward could respond, Cornell went in for the kill. "Mr. Ward, I have witnesses prepared to testify that, in fact, you knew Alexandra Stanton. And you not only knew her, but you were in love with her."

Daniel's last meal rose to his throat.

Ward appeared stunned. He opened his mouth, but said nothing.

"And even more," continued Cornell, "she rejected you . . . and you were angry. What say you?"

Daniel stood. "My Lord, I request a few minutes to confer with my client."

Any attempts Cornell had been making to suppress his smirk fell away. He turned to Daniel and shook his head, as if to say, *Oh, you poor boy, didn't I warn you?*

"No, Mr. Pitt, you may not," the judge said.

Cornell took his time, clearly savoring the moment, and then he said, his voice almost goading, "Mr. Ward, were you in love with Alexandra Stanton?"

When Cornell took a few steps closer to Ward, the young man closed his eyes and nodded.

"Is the court to take that as a *yes*?" Cornell asked.

Ward shifted, as if wishing to flee, and then whispered, "It is, yes."

Daniel saw satisfaction in the prosecutor's face. Even more, he saw victory.

"My Lord," said Cornell, "I have no further questions for Mr. Ward . . . at this time." He took his seat, picked up several files, and placed them in his briefcase, as if these proceedings were already over and it was time to send Peter Ward to the gallows.

Daniel was working to pull himself together, while his mind raced with strategies designed to counter this devastating revelation. He saw no choice but to attack the allegations head-on.

"Mr. Pitt," the judge said, "do you wish to question your client further?"

There were sounds behind Daniel, spectators leaning forward, whispering to each other, certain they were witnessing exactly what they had hoped: the dramatic climax to a grisly case and the fall of a young man who had murdered at least one poor young woman and probably many more. He saw the Flynts, father and son, the elder Flynt appearing almost bemused, while his son kept his eyes down.

Daniel turned to question Peter Ward, but was interrupted by a loud noise behind him, the stomping of feet against the floorboards of the chamber. Turning to determine the source of this noise, he saw a man rushing down the aisle, screaming, "Monster! Hanging is too good for you!"

Daniel recognized him as Alexandra Stanton's father.

Spectators were pointing, shock registered on their faces. Or was that a kind of wicked glee?

As Stanton neared the witness box, Daniel stepped forward and grabbed his arm.

"Murderer!" the man shouted, gesticulating wildly at Ward, seemingly unaware that he was being held. "You'll not get away with this! So, you paid your rich friend here to lie for you, did you?

Birds of a feather, I say!" While he ranted, he was squirming to release his arm from Daniel's grasp.

The judge called for the guards with an urgency that rang through the chamber.

Stanton turned away from Ward with such force that his momentum drove him directly into Daniel, who was knocked off balance and fell against the table. As he tried to right himself, he felt a sharp pain in his wrist.

"And you," Stanton said, directing his vitriol at Daniel. "You are a pathetic excuse for a man of the law. For shame!"

The guards arrived at Stanton's side. He looked directly at the judge. In a voice so hushed that Daniel strained to hear it, he said, "I hope all of you rot in hell."

"Take him away," ordered the judge.

As two guards were dragging Stanton out of the chamber, he turned to one of them and sobbed, "She was my child, my girl. They'll pay, all of them."

It was several minutes before the judge was able to restore calm to the chamber. "Mr. Pitt, I believe you were about to question your client."

Daniel rubbed his wrist, wondering what the hell had just happened. He moved closer to Peter Ward and looked at the young man's face, expecting to see terror. Instead, he saw grief.

"Mr. Ward, is it true that you were acquainted with Alexandra Stanton?"

"Yes, I was," he said, his words almost a cry.

"And is it also true that you were in love with her?"

Ward looked to the side, as if unable to meet Daniel's gaze. "I—I was."

"And was Miss Stanton in love with you?"

The courtroom was so quiet, the room could have been empty.

"Mr. Ward?"

"No, sir, she was not."

"And did she express this to you?"

Ward now looked at Daniel, his eyes pleading. "She said I was very nice, but that she had no feelings for me. Romantic feelings, that is."

"And how did you respond?"

"Not by killing her, I swear!"

The silence around Daniel disappeared, as voices called out, "Villain!" and "Killer!" Several men stood so they could see Ward more easily.

Daniel knew the question that needed to be asked, but he was taking a terrible risk, not certain of Ward's answer. It was too late to turn back. He knew it, Cornell knew it, and perhaps half the people in the gallery knew it. He needed to inch in the direction of that question, give his client an extra moment to compose himself.

Daniel took a deep breath, let it out slowly, and then asked, "Mr. Ward, did you ever tell me that you knew Alexandra Stanton?"

Ward pressed his lips together, perhaps hoping this would suppress any response that might damage his case. Finally, he said, "No, sir, I did not."

"And did I ask you this, during at least one of our meetings?"

"Yes, sir, you did."

Daniel nodded, while preparing himself for what could possibly be the most important question posed to Ward. "Could you please tell the court why you withheld this information . . . and lied about something of such importance?"

The question hung over the room, a dark cloud descending. For the first time during these proceedings, Daniel heard the large wall clock ticking. It made him think of some ominous prop in a West End play.

"Kindly answer the question," the judge instructed.

Ward looked at Daniel, and then shifted his gaze to all the people seated downstairs, and then to those leaning forward in the balcony, everyone awaiting something, anything, that might determine his fate. Daniel recognized that the way Ward's body was slouched forward gave him the appearance of a guilty man.

"From the day I was arrested," Ward said, "nobody believed me. Mr. Cornell has treated me like a murderer, his mind already made up." He suddenly stood straighter and raised his chin. "I lied because I knew that by telling the truth . . ." He paused and tears came to his eyes. "I would hang."

At that very moment, as if in answer to his prayers, Daniel caught movement nearby and turned to see Ian and Miriam enter the courtroom. They crossed immediately to the spectators' area and each took a seat. He locked eyes with Ian, who gave him a nod sufficiently reassuring that he felt a sudden surge of hope.

Daniel gave Ward a moment to contain himself, and then excused him from the stand.

"Have you concluded your questioning of Mr. Ward?" the judge asked, directing his question to both Daniel and Cornell. When both men answered in the affirmative, he said, "And are you prepared for your closing arguments?"

"I am, My Lord," Cornell replied, a barely contained smugness contorting his mouth.

"And Mr. Pitt?"

"I have two more witnesses, My Lord."

Not for the first time during this trial, Cornell nearly catapulted himself from his chair. "My Lord, how much longer must we endure these histrionics?"

The judge looked directly at Daniel. "More dramatics, Mr. Pitt?"

Daniel warned himself to remain calm, even if the words he chose belied that calmness. "My Lord, a man's life is at stake here. Does my worthy opponent prefer that I rush through these proceedings, thereby depriving my client of the best defense possible?"

One look at Judge Lambert told Daniel he had finally scored a point.

"Proceed," the judge said. "But the court expects you to—"

"I will keep this short," he said, cutting off the judge's words before he considered the consequences. "And it will be relevant."

The judge stared at him with such intensity that Daniel felt it viscerally. He had to shake off a surge of panic before announcing in the most confident voice he could muster, "I call Dr. Miriam fford Croft to the stand."

Again, Cornell could not contain himself. "For what possible reason?" he demanded. "My Lord, this woman cannot possibly—"

Daniel turned and faced the prosecutor. "*This woman*, sir, is a leading pathologist, fully qualified to give expert testimony, a scientist with impeccable credentials."

"Who happens to be your wife!" argued Cornell.

Daniel could not suppress a smile. He was enjoying Cornell's little playacting reaction and was tempted to praise the man for his thespian gifts. Instead, he said affably, "Mr. Cornell, choosing an unsuitable husband should not be held against her."

The tension in the room was broken; there was laughter all around. Cornell scowled, which pleased Daniel greatly. He gave a quick glance to the judge, who appeared to be putting little effort into masking his amusement.

Miriam entered the witness box and was sworn in.

"Dr. fford Croft," Daniel began. "Could you please tell the court what qualifies you to stand in this witness box and testify about scientific information that plays a vital role in these proceedings?"

He did not bother to glance in Cornell's direction to know that he was about to object. And why would he not? The expression on Miriam's face informed everyone in that room that she was about to sink the prosecutor's entire case against Peter Ward.

"My Lord," Cornell said, "I renew my objection. Must we be subjected to more of Mr. Pitt's time-wasting ploys?"

"Mr. Pitt?" the judge said, looking over his pince-nez glasses.

"My Lord," Daniel responded, and then turned and spoke directly to Cornell. "This witness is far too busy to be called on a whim, I assure you."

The judge nodded. "Proceed."

Daniel turned back to face Miriam. "Allow me to repeat the question, Doctor. Please tell the court what qualifies you as an expert witness."

Over the next few minutes, Miriam listed her credentials, from university studies to her postgraduate work in Holland, and then her role in the laboratory used often by the London police for forensics evaluations. She closed the list of her credentials with, "And, of course, I've had the honor of working under the guidance of Dr. Evelyn Hall."

"Considered one of the leading pathologists in London, is she not?" Daniel said.

"In London, yes, and perhaps the United Kingdom."

"Could you please tell the court what you've uncovered in your research into the death of Alexandra Stanton?"

"That Miss Stanton was one of many young women murdered in a similar fashion."

"When you say many, Doctor, are you saying three . . . four?"

"At least six others, with Miss Stanton the seventh."

"What else have you concluded, Doctor?"

A stillness hung over the courtroom, the only sound that of the creaking wood of benches as spectators leaned forward, not wishing to miss even one word of what was promising to be high drama.

"Based on the pathology and police reports, they were all killed by the same person, or perhaps more than one person . . . but working together."

"Seven young women murdered? And all by the same killer or killers?"

Miriam nodded, and then said, "Yes."

Daniel gave a quick glance at Cornell, surprised that he was not objecting, but the man seemed as mesmerized as the spectators craning to catch every word.

"And in your examination of the pathology reports, what were the similarities that led you to this conclusion?"

Miriam shifted again, this time to take hold of the railing around the witness box. "All of the victims were women, most of them young. They all died a violent death, and . . ."

When she paused, Daniel stepped a bit closer. "And?"

"And all of them suffered the same mutilation." Without giving Daniel the chance to ask for an explanation, she said, "As Dr. Ornshaw testified earlier, each one of these women had a patch of skin removed. Skin from the pubic area. That alone is cause for deep concern, but then we learned—"

Miriam paused again, but this time Daniel recognized that she was controlling her anger. Whatever she was about to say, he trusted that she would deliver the information clearly, scientifically, and using words that would cause everyone in the chamber to take notice.

"We have been facing a very complex—and might I add disturbing—situation."

"Disturbing," Daniel repeated, taking care that he said the word without emotion.

"The first thing we discovered was that significant scientific information had been either deleted or never included in the police reports."

A buzzing sound ran through the room, growing in volume as comments were shared among the spectators. There was no silence until the judge wielded his gavel and rapped it several times.

Daniel spoke to the judge. "My Lord, I would like to call another witness, and reserve the right to question this witness again."

The judge turned to Cornell. "Do you wish to question this witness before we proceed?"

Cornell remained silent, as if deciding how to proceed. He pressed his palms against the table, preparing to stand, and then shook his head.

"You are testing my patience, Mr. Pitt," the judge said.

"This witness will provide significant information, My Lord. In a sense, he will fill in many of the blanks we've been alluding to throughout these proceedings."

The judge nodded, and then leaned back, his hands folded and resting on the table before him.

Daniel gave Miriam a nod. She stepped out of the witness box and crossed to where Ian was seated.

"My Lord, I call Detective Chief Inspector Ian Frobisher."

Daniel felt tension all around him, from the gallery and across the main chamber, and most especially from Harold Cornell. Daniel knew too well how no lawyer wishes to spend weeks, even months, preparing for trial, only to discover that the other side holds potentially explosive information. He prided himself on being fully prepared, as he was certain did Cornell, but it was nearly impossible to predict those dramatic moments—they were like sticks of dynamite, carefully timed to explode. In any trial, the one thing both defense lawyers and prosecutors dreaded was the element of surprise, that moment when the dynamite is ignited. Daniel harbored a powerful wish that Ian was about to light the damn fuse.

Ian stood in the witness box. He appeared relaxed, confident. Daniel could not determine how his friend was actually feeling, but he imagined Ian's mind was whirling as he tried to second-guess Daniel's questions. With no time to prepare, and Ian there based solely on Miriam's promise that his testimony could very well change the course of this trial, Daniel was going on a great deal of trust . . . and no small amount of faith.

"DSI Frobisher, you are the lead inspector in the Alexandra Stanton case, is that not so?"

"One of the lead inspectors," Ian said. "I was brought in only days ago, after the investigation began."

"Could you please explain why this decision was made?"

"The Stanton case was not in my jurisdiction. However, when other similar cases came to light, and one of them was, in fact, being investigated out of my station, I was assigned."

"And what has been your focus these past few days?"

"We have been putting together two lists." When Daniel remained silent, he went on. "One of those lists includes the dates and places of parties attended by the seven victims mentioned by Dr. fford Croft. The second list includes everyone who attended those parties."

"Everyone?" Daniel asked, anticipating an objection from Cornell.

"Everyone whose names were provided by the hosts. Of course, there were guests who were not invited, but came with friends who were. Nevertheless, we were able to identify almost all of the attendees."

"Before we explore those lists, DSI Frobisher, there seems to be some confusion regarding the victims, and the . . . souvenirs . . . taken from them. Have you any explanations for this?"

"The police reports did not mention the patches of skin removed from the young women."

Daniel stepped away from the table and approached the witness box. "And can you explain to the court why such vital information did not appear in any of the reports . . . and we had to learn about these through autopsies and the pathologists' testimony?"

A heavy silence filled the room. Daniel felt a tightness in his chest. His entire case was now in Ian's hands.

Ian looked directly at Daniel, his eyes wavering not a fraction. "Police officers from several stations deleted this information from their reports."

Before Cornell could object, Daniel rushed ahead. "This is a very serious allegation, DSI Frobisher! Are you saying that . . ."

"No one wants to admit such treacherous behavior," Ian interrupted. "But we have written statements from those officers . . . and formal proceedings against them are being prepared as we speak."

This time, Cornell rose, but he unfolded his large frame so slowly that to Daniel he brought to mind a worm, a dramatic departure from the man's normally jackrabbit-like movements. "My Lord, this sounds like a classic case of second-hand information, utter hearsay."

"Hearsay based on what, sir?" the judge asked.

"How can we accept this testimony when it comes not from the culprit himself, but from a senior officer? Is our good DSI Frobisher misguided enough to believe we will not pursue this after the trial has concluded?"

The judge turned toward Ian. "Are any of your officers willing to testify to this?"

"Yes, My Lord, one man. He is someone I've trusted for years and who understands that his testimony might very well end his career."

Daniel felt blindsided. Was it possible that Ian was referring to Sergeant Gorman? Judging by the grief he saw in Ian's face, that was a logical assumption.

"My Lord," Cornell said, more than a hint of pleading in his voice. "Again, I must protest. This is more hearsay, pure and simple, Mr. Pitt's desperate attempt to confuse the jurors and influence the court. Until this mystery man appears, takes the oath, and testifies to his heinous deeds, nothing can be put into the record."

The judge thought about this for a moment, and then looked to Ian. "Your man has been identified as having done something highly unethical, this I understand. But what was the incentive for . . ." He paused, as if expecting Ian to fill in the name of this scofflaw.

Daniel leaned forward, while at the same time trying not to appear interested. Unlike Peter Ward, who was nearly out of his chair.

"My sergeant," Ian offered, not mentioning Gorman by name, and said with his face so devoid of expression that Daniel knew he was working to control his temper.

Daniel nearly spoke, but he feared he would be accused of leading the witness, and he certainly did not want to give Cornell good reason to dress down the younger lawyer yet again, and in front of the jury. There was another reason for his restraint: Ian was a frequent witness in court proceedings and knew very well when and how to respond, and that included protecting his men. He could only shield Gorman to a point: the man would be made to suffer sufficiently, even without his name being brought into this trial. Daniel felt a pang of sadness. He was now quite certain it was Gorman. He liked the man and there was no doubt but that he would be dismissed from the force, along with other officers who felt they had the right, whether due to compassion or not, to falsify police reports.

Daniel had several more questions for Ian, but he hesitated. His friend had just opened Pandora's box. As soon as they delved further into these reports, more questions and accusations were sure to arise, bringing a new level of chaos to this trial. A thought raced across Daniel's mind. What other reports had been affected over the years? He tried to turn his mind against this possibility. It would not be a matter of who was responsible, but which closed cases would have to be reviewed . . . and perhaps retried. A few? Dozens? Would someone on the force be given the task of reviewing all past reports written by these offending policemen, especially those cases that resulted in a trial and a conviction? How many lawyers representing these men and women found guilty would use that loophole to demand a new trial? Even more serious, how many guilty men and women would be set free, based solely on this appalling technicality?

He pulled his attention back to the judge, whose voice rang throughout the cavernous room.

"DSI Frobisher, how did your sergeant justify carrying out this deception? Or have you not yet had the opportunity to question him?"

Ian began to speak and then stopped, as if realizing that his response might alter the future for more than just his sergeant. He looked at Daniel for a long moment, and then spoke. "For the same reason, My Lord, that the other officers altered the files of these victims: to protect the memory and the dignity of these young women. And to give their families a bit of peace."

The judge did not respond, nor did Cornell. Daniel wanted to see this as two powerful men able to put aside their arrogance and yield to the needs of both the victims and their families, but he had been at this game long enough to know that compassion could be fleeting, especially when displayed by those intent on winning. And for the man seated at the prosecutor's table, his intent was always the same: to win at any cost.

Daniel stood to his full height and walked right up to the witness box, as close as the layout of the room allowed. He glanced over to where Miriam was seated and she gave him a little nod. He wanted to create a dramatic moment for the jurors, but also for the judge and prosecutor. He knew Ian, knew him very well, and recognized that his friend was holding something back. Not a secret to be kept from these proceedings, but some vital information that would be revealed when Daniel asked him the right question. He sensed what that question was, and felt uncomfortable that it must be asked. If it resulted in nothing, he would deal with the humiliation later. Cornell had already judged him to be among the lower order of lawyers, so he had nothing to lose.

"DSI Frobisher, you were asked about the motives for these policemen, the men who falsified the reports pertaining to the seven young women."

Ian moved as if trying to find a comfortable position, as comfortable as one could be while being questioned with the same relentless determination as he would interrogate a suspect of whose guilt he was certain.

"You mentioned compassion and respect for their families."

"Yes, that's correct."

From the corner of his eye, Daniel detected a figure moving in his direction. Turning, he was surprised to see Toby. He was even more surprised when Toby sat down at the defense table. He expected Cornell to complain, but the judge's voice stopped any possibility of that.

"I see our Mr. Kitteridge has rejoined counsel."

Toby gave the judge a nod, but remained silent.

The judge returned his nod, a fleeting expression of kindness crossing his face, and then he gestured for Daniel to continue.

As if on cue, a policeman entered the room. Without asking approval from the judge, he strode up to the witness box and handed a piece of paper to Ian, his superior officer.

Ian unfolded the paper and read the message. He became suddenly pale.

Daniel noticed this at once. Had others in the chamber seen it as well? Quickly picking up where they left off, he said, his voice even, "But there is more, is there not?"

Ian and Daniel, two longtime friends, stared at each other as if they had suddenly become adversaries. Daniel had every faith in Ian to be truthful, but he was keenly aware that there was the truth . . . and then there was the entire truth. In the witness box, there was no room for choice. The whole truth . . . and nothing but the truth.

"Yes, there is," Ian said, and so quietly that even Daniel, standing only feet away, strained to hear him.

There was no need to look behind him to know that Cornell was suddenly more alert than only minutes earlier.

"Would you please tell the court what more you know . . . and how you know it? And please speak so the entire room can hear you."

Ian tucked the paper into his jacket pocket and then ran his hand through his hair, a gesture that struck Daniel as his friend's need to slow the pace, perhaps give himself a bit of time so he could decide how to present this information. Whatever Ian was about to say, Daniel sensed it would change everything.

"I have just received information that answers one of our most pressing questions," he said. "We now know who was responsible for the deaths of these young women, Miss Alexandra Stanton among them."

Cornell shook his head, his face reflecting disbelief, sarcasm. "First you admit that your men are not only dishonest and unethical, a black mark on policemen everywhere, and now you attempt to shift the blame to some blackguard whose identity is suddenly revealed? This is the Old Bailey, Mr. Frobisher, not the amateur production of some Bernard Shaw play."

Daniel was tempted to correct Cornell, reminding him that Ian was a policeman who had earned both respect and rank, but he said nothing.

"I can only report what intensive investigation has revealed," Ian said, looking directly at Daniel, as if Cornell had never spoken. "After studying the lists of parties our victims attended, and comparing those events to the names of the men in attendance, we have come up with one name, one man who attended every party with the victims, and can only be the man who committed all of these crimes."

As he spoke, Daniel looked over to where Peter Ward was seated. It was as if the world had forgotten that it was Peter Ward whose life was in jeopardy. Young Ward was now leaning so far forward that Daniel wondered if he might fall from his chair.

"DSI Frobisher," Daniel said, "would you please tell the court who committed these crimes?"

Ian looked into the crowd seated behind Daniel. "I believe he's seated in this courtroom," he said, his announcement causing everyone in the chamber to search the room in an almost frantic effort.

"Do you recognize him?" Daniel asked, joining the spectators as they tried to find the culprit.

"I don't know him by sight," Ian said. "But I was told that he's here, and has been throughout this trial."

Daniel took a few steps closer to the witness. "DSI Frobisher, his name?"

As if needing to be certain beyond doubt, Ian removed the paper from his pocket, unfolded it slowly, and then announced in an emotional voice, "Martin Flynt."

There was an immediate reaction, but not at all what Daniel had expected. He would have thought there would be a roar, a cataclysmic tumult, but there was only silence. An eerie silence. He looked around him and saw confusion. Martin Flynt? The son of the famous Sir Anthony Flynt? It must be a mistake! Children from families of great wealth and social stature do not commit crimes, and especially crimes of violence against young women.

And then, as if the truth finally registered, there was a crescendo of noise: newspapermen stampeding toward the exit, Martin Flynt leaping to his feet and shouting, "That's a damn lie!"

Two uniformed officers rushed to the young Flynt, their boots pounding against the old wood-plank floorboards. Before they could take him into custody, he stood up, turned, reached out for his father, who had been seated beside him, and grabbed him by the throat.

"Get off me!" Sir Anthony called out, grappling with his son, pulling at the young man's arms.

"It's your fault!" Martin screamed into his father's face, and then he turned to the judge, his hands still gripping his father. "You think he's so important? He's not, he's a damn fraud! All those charities? His . . . his generosity? Ask him what he did to me? How he swore that we Flynts never had to worry about the law; that all of those laws were made for everyone else. Or how I broke those damn laws over and over and I never had to pay the price. Ask him what he did to my mother! Ask him about the beatings, about telling me every day of my life how I disappointed him, how I don't deserve the family name. Ask him!"

At that point the guards reached the pair and pulled Martin away, leaving his father gasping for breath.

Sir Anthony remained in his seat, rubbing his neck and looking away from his son. When he began to speak, the voices in the chamber fell silent. "He was always trouble," he said, his voice shaking with emotion, regret. "I've spent his entire life trying to keep him out of danger, protecting him from himself."

Daniel felt a pang of compassion for the man. He did not like him—that is, the man he believed him to be—nor did he respect him, but he sympathized for this father forced to watch the public arrest of his son, and for crimes that would lead him to the gallows.

As the guards noisily dragged young Flynt from the courtroom, he twisted around to face his father. "You made me do this, you maggot! Yes, I killed them, all of them, and guess what? You'll spend the rest of your life with their blood on your hands!"

Someone opened the door so the guards and Martin could pass through. As his parting shot, he wrenched free, turned and announced to the judge, "Ask him about Suffolk, too! Ask him why he shot that lawyer's parents!" He pointed to Toby, his gesture so uncontrolled it gave him the appearance of a madman.

The guards got him back under control and he was forcefully removed, his fury audible long after the heavy doors were closed and he was hauled away.

Daniel told himself not to look at Flynt's father, but he could not resist. Five minutes earlier he was known as Sir Anthony Flynt. But now, only minutes later, he would forever be identified as the father of the man who murdered at least seven young women, and was now a murderer in his own right.

Flynt sat there, his face ashen, his jaw shifting side to side, hands clutching his knees.

Daniel's earlier compassion for him was immediately driven away. This was the man who killed Delia Kitteridge and left her husband for dead. Toby and Alberta had lost their mother; Alberta's children would never spend another day with their grandmother.

Sadness washed over Daniel and he had to force it away. There was more to come. He looked at Miriam and saw grief in her face, in the way she pressed her fist against her mouth. Their eyes met and they shared the moment.

The judge used his gavel to call everyone to order. "It seems we have our man," he said, addressing Daniel and Cornell. The two men nodded, but said nothing. "The court will now turn its attention to Mr. Peter Ward."

All eyes in the chamber turned to the young man standing before them.

"Mr. Ward, there are times, as unfortunate and disturbing as they are, when the wrong man is accused. The court apologizes for the ordeal to which you have been subjected. Pursuant to regulations regarding the completion of judicial paperwork, you will be free to leave this building."

Daniel took a few steps nearer the judge. "My Lord, in the face of these dramatic occurrences . . ." His voice trailed off for a moment. "There is more to this case. As coincidental as it seems, we believe there is a link between the death of Miss Stanton and the attack on the parents of my colleague, Mr. Kitteridge. We are aware that this is out of our jurisdiction. Therefore, we will provide all of the documentation to the court, which can then be transferred to the police in Suffolk."

Daniel expected Cornell to bellow about accusations of grandstanding, but he remained as silent as those people filling every nook and cranny of the courtroom.

For the first time since Martin Flynt's outburst, Daniel looked at Toby. His face was blank, devoid of all emotion. Daniel wanted to sit with him, put an arm around his shoulder and reassure him, remind him that it was over, but his friend seemed to be elsewhere, far from this chamber.

"DSI Frobisher," the judge said, "I believe you have additional information for this court. Before your testimony was interrupted, you were explaining why these officers falsified reports, omitting a distasteful bit of information. You said it was because they were honoring the dignity of these young women."

Ian, still in the witness box, tipped his head to one side, as if trying to evade the question. "That was certainly one of their objectives."

"Was there another?"

"Yes, My Lord. What I've learned after questioning them is that they were threatened."

Daniel waited for another eruption, but the silence continued, as if no one at the Old Bailey dared to breathe, lest they miss another earthshaking revelation.

"Threatened . . . how?" Daniel asked.

"Yes, how?" repeated the judge, as if wishing to take the lead away from Daniel.

"They were told that they either removed any mention of the skin cut from the victims, or else someone they loved—a wife, child, parent—would get hurt."

Daniel had expected something dramatic, important, bribes or promises of advancement. Why else would Ian choose to remain in the witness box? But he had not expected this. Threatened? He knew that he must pursue this, ask the one question everyone was waiting to hear, but how to gird himself for what he knew would be yet another chaotic scene?

He glanced around him and was surprised to see two different police guards standing at the door leading into the corridor. Whatever Ian was about to reveal was not only dramatic, but sensational, and he had known this before taking the stand. Why else would he have ordered these guards?

"Please, sir," Daniel said. "What have you learned?"

Ian nodded, as if relieved to be given the opportunity to reveal his discovery. "All of these officers named the same source. That is, the person who had his bully boys threaten them and their families. Blackmailed them all."

"And can you tell us his name?"

Ian looked beyond Daniel, as if seeking out a specific person. He pointed into the group of spectators. "There," he said. "Sir Anthony Flynt. The man who had my men threatened into silence to protect his son, and the man responsible for the death of Mr. Kitteridge's mother." Everyone in that vaulted chamber craned to see.

There was no doubt that it was Sir Anthony to whom he pointed; the man's face went from pale to a shade nearly crimson. And yet, as if drawing from his years of impeccable reputation, of his good deeds throughout England, he sat up straighter and lifted his chin in what Daniel saw as defiance, arrogance.

"Rubbish," Sir Anthony responded. "Tragically, my son is disturbed, a psychopath. One look at him and you can see that he wants to destroy me. And these policemen? Small men, small minds." With that, he stood and moved toward the exit.

Daniel saw Ian give a nod to the two policemen standing nearby. The moment Sir Anthony reached the door, the men stepped forward and grasped his arms.

"Unhand me!" he demanded.

Someone in the room laughed, calling out, "Cut the dramatics, Tony!"

He struggled to wrest his arms free. "Have you any idea who I am? Who I . . . know? Dine with? Play cards with?"

The policemen looked at Ian, as if uncertain this was a wise move on their part.

"He's under arrest," Ian said. "Take him to the station. And no matter what he threatens, he goes into a locked cell. And not with his son," he quickly added. "They must not be held together."

"And he'll hang for it, he will!" shouted a man seated behind Daniel's table. "Two Flynt killers, swinging from the ropes . . . and I'll be there to watch!"

Daniel jumped when Toby stood and insisted, "No!" His voice was more commanding than Daniel could remember ever having heard it.

As if responding to the anger in his own voice, Toby directed his next comment to the judge. "Please, keep him here, Flynt, in the chamber. Put me on the stand."

"Are you certain?" Daniel asked, and then began to move closer to the judge. "My Lord," he said, "could we meet in chambers?"

The judge looked first at Daniel and then at Toby. "I think that's wise." He stood and began to leave the room.

"What are you about?" Daniel asked, urgency in his voice.

"Trust me, please," Toby replied, and then followed the judge.

When they were settled in the judge's private office, the three men seated, Daniel spoke. "Toby, I do know how important it is that Flynt is brought to trial for his attack on your parents, but—"

"Young man," the judge said to Daniel, cutting him off with impatience, "where is this going?"

Before Daniel could speak, Toby explained, "As you're aware, My Lord, my parents were shot. Until this morning, we had no idea who had attacked them. What we did learn, thanks to Miriam—Dr. fford Croft—was that two guns were involved, so we assumed there were two shooters."

Daniel watched his friend speak, a sadness filling him as Toby described the terrible scene.

"And what happened this morning?" the judge asked, his voice no longer that of an arbitrator guided by the law, but that of a kind, concerned man.

"My father is now able to speak, and he has described my mother's killer. Even more, he was able to remember what this man said, what he revealed."

"Why would he do such a thing?" the judge asked. "That is, reveal his motive?"

"Because he was going to kill both of them, which meant no one could repeat what he said."

"And what was that?"

"He was determined to protect his son—he knew that Martin had killed those women—and protect the reputation of his family as well. By shooting my parents, I would be taken off the case, which meant a greater chance of Peter Ward being found guilty." He immediately turned to Daniel. "Not that you aren't a brilliant lawyer."

Daniel managed to smile, although he felt the sting.

"He went to the rectory with a gun. I'm not sure he intended to kill anyone, but the police have determined that everything went quickly awry. My father was alone in the house and my mother was in the garden. When he saw a stranger approach the front door and carrying a gun, he rushed upstairs and retrieved his old military pistol. He said it took less than one minute, but when he came downstairs, that man, Flynt, was holding Mother at gunpoint. From what he recalls, there was a flurry of panic and Flynt shot my father." He paused, emotion overcoming him, and he held up a hand, as if to ask for their patience.

"Take your time," said the judge.

Daniel reached across and gave Toby's arm a gentle squeeze.

"And then . . ." Toby continued. "And then he turned the gun on my mother, but it jammed, so he grabbed Father's gun and shot her."

The office was quiet. What more could be said? Daniel felt his friend's sadness, a heavy blanket draped over both of them.

"That's why I wanted Flynt to remain in the courtroom. Not only to face the truth, but to see that protecting his son, or even more important to him, the family name, has destroyed lives."

The judge took a deep breath and released it slowly. "Had you managed to get him into the witness box, there would have been hell to pay later."

Toby looked at the man, his brow creased. "But . . . why?"

"It's a different case," Daniel explained. "The deaths of these young women and the attack on your parents are linked, we now understand this. But father and son will be tried separately, for separate crimes. Any attempt to extract a confession from Sir Anthony today could cause irreparable damage to the prosecution's case later."

Toby sat with this and awareness softened his face. "I understand, My Lord, thank you." That wasn't the lawyer speaking; it was the grieving son.

Daniel and Toby rose and thanked the judge for his time and his generosity. They returned to the courtroom, where the judge ended the proceedings, and then joined Miriam and Ian. Together, they left the building.

"Come home with us," Daniel said to the others, while raising his arm to attract the attention of a passing taxi. "Miriam needs to be with you, as do I . . . please." He placed his hand on Ian's shoulder. "None of this would have happened without you."

Daniel looked at Toby. His face was pale, his shoulders stooped, a man lacking the energy to stand straight.

As they were weaving their way through London traffic, Toby said, "Ian, I don't know how to thank you."

Ian gave a little shrug. "No need. I played my part, but Miriam, Eve, and Joe were the ones who dug into the mountain of information and made sense of it."

SEVERAL HOURS LATER, Daniel and Miriam were busily preparing a meal. Or, as Miriam described, "throwing together whatever we have and hoping for the best." Together, they carried to the dining room a tray of cold roast and sliced tomatoes, followed by a large basket of bread and a bowl of fresh butter.

Seated around the table were Ian and Toby, as well as Joe and Eve, who had arrived minutes earlier.

"Daniel called the lab and insisted we come," Eve explained.

"And it's a good thing," Miriam replied with a warm smile. "There's a roast that needs to be eaten and some very good wine that insists on being enjoyed."

The meal was consumed with little conversation. There was no need to acknowledge that the final day of any trial—when the jury comes in with its verdict or the identity of the guilty is revealed; and especially those trials like this one, where innocence and guilt are revealed not just amid tumult, but with high drama—leaves those involved completely depleted. Nevertheless, Daniel announced boisterously, "We got through this, yes? A young man has been spared the gallows, the real killer will go to trial, and we watched our man Cornell eat crow. Now we move on."

"Some of us will," Toby said, his voice low, unsure.

"And your sister?" Miriam asked.

"She knows the truth and is greatly relieved," Toby said. "She even acknowledges that our persistence cleared our father's name. To be honest," he added, "I feel a wall of ice coming down."

Miriam reached across and placed her hand on his arm. "It will happen," she said. "It takes time."

AFTER THE MEAL, the six of them moved to the sitting room, where Daniel stacked a few logs and got a fire burning, while Miriam passed out wineglasses and filled each one with the good Burgundy they kept for only the most special occasions.

"I've made a decision," Eve said, looking at each of them, one at a time. "I'm going to retire."

Miriam was about to speak, but Eve silenced her with one of her piercing looks. It was so unexpected that Miriam laughed, as did the others.

"I'd like to do the traveling I've longed for. And no," she quickly added, "I want no sympathy!"

"Why would we be sympathetic?" Daniel asked, as if truly confused. "While we're here slogging away, you'll be running your toes through the sand on the Amalfi Coast."

Eve looked at all of them, her face reflecting their love and kindness. "But you're not off the hook," she said. "Are you imagining that a little card wishing me luck and bon voyage will do?"

"Here it comes," Joe said. "Silly me to think we'd get off so easily."

"You're right there, my friend," Eve said. "I expect a bona fide retirement gift."

Ian laughed. "And why am I thinking that you already know what that gift will be?"

Eve raised her eyebrows and offered Ian an impish grin. "Because you are a very clever man," she said.

"So, what is it?" Miriam asked. With Eve seated next to her, it took no effort to give her friend a little nudge with her shoulder.

"So glad you asked, my dear," Eve said, her cheeks rosy, her eyes bright. "I expect to receive very swanky luggage. Finest leather. With my initials etched in gold."

"In gold, you say?" Daniel asked.

Eve laughed. "So say I . . ."

Miriam leaned over and kissed Eve's cheek. "So say us all!"

AFTER THEIR GUESTS had left, Daniel and Miriam washed the dishes and returned to the sitting room. Daniel threw another log on the fire and they settled together on the loveseat, holding hands. With a sizzle and crackle, the log ignited and they were surrounded by warmth.

Miriam slipped off her shoes, stretched her legs, and leaned into Daniel. "Do you think Toby will remain in London?"

The idea of his friend leaving had not occurred to Daniel. "He might feel the need to be closer to his father," he said. "Still, I would hate to see him go."

Miriam moved closer to Daniel. "It won't be the same without him, but it's splendid that he and Alberta have made peace."

"Perhaps tenuous, for the moment, but a beginning. I'm sure this pleases his father."

Miriam turned a bit, so she could see Daniel's face. "So, all in all, we have managed to bring a successful end to two seemingly impossible cases, yes?"

"We have," he agreed, giving her hand a squeeze. "But this was certainly not the ending we had expected."

"It rarely is, my love."

Daniel raised her hand and kissed it. "Perhaps the next case will be less fraught with drama."

For the next few hours, they sat quietly, watching flames flicker around the logs, sharing in their contentment as friends, lovers, equals, certain that whatever the storms, the trials, dark times or bright dawns, they would face the future together.

AUTHOR'S NOTE

It was April 20, 2012, when I first met Anne Perry. She was signing her new novel at Book Passage in Marin County, just north of San Francisco. A few weeks earlier, I had asked a mutual friend to contact Anne about the two of us getting together for tea after the reading. I admired her work and looked forward to meeting her. Since she was an international figure, I expected she would decline. Instead, she responded that she would like that very much. On the day of the reading, I called the store's owner, my friend Elaine Petrocelli, to tell her that I would be coming and ask if she would like to join me for lunch. She replied that she had come down with a terrible cold, and would I introduce Anne in her place. Introduce Anne Perry? *The* Anne Perry? I had read most of her novels, but could I pull this off with two hours' notice?

Unlike so many author intros I'd heard and even delivered, I tossed out all the usual "she has sold millions of books" and "she's been on the *New York Times* list so many times," and instead talked about Anne's characters. I asked the audience, and then Anne, if it was Lady Vespasia, the elegant and outspoken older character from the Thomas Pitt series, who most resembled her. She just smiled.

After the event, I offered to drive Anne to her San Francisco hotel. "Is there any place you'd love to see before we head for the city? Muir Woods? Point Reyes?" Her response was, "I'd love to go shopping." I took a deep breath and replied, "You seem like a very nice woman, but I don't like you well enough yet to go shopping—I hate to shop." Nevertheless, she convinced me, we shopped, and I even bought lipstick. Upon glancing at the receipt on the way out the door, I discovered that I had just spent nearly sixty dollars. For lipstick.

The next day, I drove Anne to the airport, and during that brief drive I realized that this was not only a brilliant woman, but a woman with a big heart that overflowed with kindness. And . . . she was funny! In that short time together, we shared some great laughs. A friendship was being formed.

Several months later, I was planning a trip to London and emailed Anne. I knew she was there often to see her agent, Meg Davis. She responded that she had no meetings planned and suggested I take the short flight from London to Inverness, near her home. Those three days in the village of Portmahomack, in the northeast highlands of Scotland, cemented our friendship. Me, the liberal and quasi-observant Jew, and Anne, the devout Mormon.

She had wanted to live in Southern California for many years, and it had finally seemed like the right time. That winter, she moved her entire life to West Hollywood, a six-hour drive from my San Francisco home. It was a journey I would make often over the next dozen years, both for the pleasure of visiting my friend, and because we had begun brainstorming her upcoming novels together. I'm not sure how it happened, but I became her personal editor, working with Anne on at least ten novels and five novellas, from concept to final draft.

Anne made our collaboration a joyful experience. If I happened to suggest a new plot or character twist, or a change to one of her ideas, and if she saw its merit, she embraced the change. There was no ego involvement. She knew that we were working toward the same goal: the very best novel possible. She may have tossed out some (or many) of my ideas, but she did so with such grace that I never felt the sting. (And in her most gentle way, she never let me forget who was writing these books!)

Anne loved talking on the phone. She often called me three or four times every day. These calls usually started with a discussion about a plot or character idea for the next novel or Christmas novella, or a particular passage or plot related to the novel she was outlining or writing. After the writing part was covered, our chats evolved into politics, religion, social justice, and those everyday topics friends share. Whatever we discussed, and especially when we did not agree, our responses always reflected the mutual love and respect of two friends, older women living alone, counting on the other always being there, and celebrating our friendship.

Anne wrote two novels and a novella every year. From William Monk to Thomas Pitt, her heartwarming Christmas novellas, and then her two new series led by Elena Standish and Daniel Pitt, I loved hearing her excitement as she described ideas for characters and plots. She was especially connected to Elena Standish, the feisty young photojournalist and undercover agent making her way through 1930s pre-war Europe. I often thought that Elena was Anne's doppelgänger. Planning and discussing Elena's next adventure, or young Daniel Pitt's infatuation with Miriam fford Croft, a woman nearly fifteen years older and his eventual wife, brought her great joy. These were the times when her voice rang out with pleasure . . . and youth! Her passion for writing was always evident.

I loved being Anne's personal editor, but I did have one problem. Anne wrote her novels in longhand, and there are perhaps five people on the planet who can read her scrawl . . . and I'm not one of them. Although she avoided anything technological, she finally agreed to install a voice recognition system, allowing her to write the entire novel in longhand and then read her work aloud and have it duplicated into a Word document. Thanks to her friend and tech guru Keith Stern, I could become fully engaged.

Anne had a brilliant mind and the most remarkable memory. If I asked about a scene in a book I was editing, it was not unusual for her to say, "Oh, you'll find that in chapter four, halfway down page sixty-three." At her favorite writer's conference held in Surrey,

British Columbia, and coordinated by her dear friend Kathy Chung, someone asked Anne if she was familiar with the poetry of W. H. Auden. She smiled and recited several of his poems . . . by heart.

I'm obsessed with politics, and have been since I was a child, but it was Anne, a citizen of the United Kingdom, who knew the names of every U.S. senator and perhaps half the members of Congress.

I always found it fascinating that she was not only a devout Mormon but also an ardent feminist, yet she saw little conflict between those beliefs. (After I delivered the eulogy at her funeral service, her bishop stood before the congregation and thanked me, addressing me as *Sister Victoria.* I can still see the look of surprise on his face when I told him, "Bishop, this might be the first and last time that a Jewish kid from Compton is referred to as *Sister Victoria* in the Mormon church.")

In late 2022, Anne began writing this novel, the seventh in her Daniel Pitt series. She was tired, frustrated by her lack of energy, but she soldiered on, working six days a week, often eight to ten hours a day. On an afternoon in early December, she called me to announce that she had just finished the rough draft of chapter nine. I told her she was a marvel, considering how little energy she had, and I promised to drive down soon for a visit. That night, before midnight, I received a call informing me that she had suffered a heart attack.

Over the next four months, as her health deteriorated, I spent many nights in Anne's guest room, which allowed me to be there when she was home, as well as sitting with her when she was hospitalized. As her health worsened, I brought my laptop to her room in the ICU and played opera, another one of her passions. Even when she could barely open her eyes, the soaring voices of her favorite artists, Monserrat Caballé and Mario Del Monico, made her smile.

On April 10, 2023, when it was certain that Anne's life was coming to an end, she was finally freed from the ventilator and dialysis machine. A roomful of friends came to say goodbye. Several hours after they departed, she died. I will be forever grateful that I was with her, holding her hand and reminding her how she was loved, and what a wonderful legacy she was leaving through her extraordinary body of work and her unending generosity.

The following week, before I left for home, I gathered those nine handwritten chapters of her seventh Daniel Pitt novel, as well as the detailed outline, and brought them with me. I knew that her work was being archived at Brigham Young University, but I was concerned that someone might accidentally throw away those pages before they could be delivered. At the time, I never dreamed I'd be given the honor of completing the novel, but I felt a strong need to get those indecipherable chapters into a Word file. It was my great fortune that Anne's dear friend Nicola MacDonald could read her writing and transcribe those pages.

This journey has been rich with emotions and the unparalleled support from people who loved Anne, helped me along the way, and shared my dedication to this project. Let me introduce you to a few of them.

Meg Davis was Anne's UK agent for decades. They shared so much more than a love of books and Meg's astute notes on all of Anne's drafts. Meg also made sure Anne was well represented worldwide, where she was translated into fourteen languages and was a bestseller in several countries. Anne trusted her as a dear friend and mentioned often that it was Meg who not only launched her career, but made her the writer she came to be. Saying that I thank Meg for her support and valuable guidance through this project seems inadequate. I thank her, too, for her friendship.

Donald Maass was Anne's longtime U.S. agent. Anne counted on Don's exceptional input regarding plot and character development, from the first draft to the final. To date, he has published seven books on how to write a novel, and his contribution to this one was significant. Their relationship went back decades, and Anne never failed to tell me how important Don was to her growth as a writer. Equally important, he was her beloved friend and confidant.

When this project was launched, Meg and Don were there to give me encouragement, direction, and kindness. My gratitude is immeasurable.

Susanna Porter and Anne had a remarkable history. It's rare for an editor to work alongside a writer through nearly the entirety of that writer's career. As Anne's editor at Random House, Susanna did just that. Anne told me often about her love for Susanna, and how Susanna and Kim Hovey, senior VP at Ballantine and a woman close to Anne's heart, "circled the wagons" around her through some difficult times, never wavering in their support and kindness. When Susanna asked me if there was "any chance in the world" that I would consider writing the remaining chapters of the unfinished Daniel Pitt novel, I believe my response was something like, "And is there any chance in the world that you would love golden light and glitter to drift from the sky and bring joy to everyone in your life?"

My thanks to Anusha Khan at Random House for her infinite patience and editorial gifts.

Ken Sherman was Anne's U.S. film and TV agent. More important, he was her beloved friend. Rarely did she express greater joy than when describing their evenings out, often for a film screening. Their friendship spanned decades and I know how much she cherished it. When I accepted the offer to complete Anne's novel, Ken was there to encourage me. Those emails of "You can do this!" gave me more confidence than he could have imagined.

Diana Howie, founder and executive producer of Ridgeway Film, has been a champion for getting Anne's books to the screen. Their collaborations in developing these projects led to a loving friendship, and I have had the pleasure of sharing in that friendship.

Rob Daly began as Anne's realtor, a relationship that evolved into a close friendship. As my longtime friend, Rob has been invaluable in supporting me in many of the responsibilities I've managed since Anne's death. My affection and gratitude are heartfelt.

Aviva Layton has been beside me through nearly every writing project, a dear friend and superb editor.

Darlene Chan, my agent from the Linda Chester Literary Agency, has been a source of patience and support along the way. My thanks and appreciation are without limit.

Maria Hernandez and Samira Fahmi brought peace and security to Anne's life. During her illness, their presence as her caregivers, often around the clock at home and in the hospital, chased away her fears. Knowing they were always there and she was never alone meant so much to Anne, and to everyone who loved her. Samira was with me, holding Anne's hand, when she died. Later, we were able to smile about the scene: the Jew and the Muslim saying goodbye to our Mormon friend.

I am forever grateful to the MacDonalds in Scotland—Anne's beloved friend Meg and her children, Simon and Lorna—for their encouragement and affection through some difficult times.

Anne enjoyed the support of her family, Jonathan and Sylvia Hulme, Frances and Henry, and the kindness of friends Clay Bunker and Christina Hogue.

I thank my family for encouraging me through this project: my daughter, Alisa, and Mark Askanas, and my granddaughters Olivia Law and Sophia Law; my son, Matthew Sosnick, and my grandchildren Lily, Liam, and Joshua. And to my sister, Michele Zackheim, and brother-in-law, Charlie Ramsburg, always there to remind me that I can do this, thank you.

And so here you have it, my gift to Anne. And, in so many ways, her gift to me. As readers of Anne's work, you will undoubtedly agree when I say that her voice was unique. I've done my best to write this novel in her voice.

I would like to leave you with this thought: more important than her astounding intellect, her writing gifts, and her devotion to God, Anne Perry was the kindest person I've ever known, a woman with unlimited compassion and humor, and a profound belief in the goodness of everyone.

Anne, this novel is for you, with love.

ABOUT THE AUTHORS

ANNE PERRY was the bestselling author of two acclaimed series set in Victorian England: the William Monk novels and the Charlotte and Thomas Pitt novels. She was also the author of a series featuring Charlotte and Thomas Pitt's son, Daniel, as well as the Elena Standish series; a series of five World War I novels; twenty-one holiday novels; and a historical novel, *The Sheen on the Silk*, set in the Byzantine Empire. Anne Perry died in 2023.

VICTORIA ZACKHEIM is the author of two novels, including *The Curtain Falls in Paris*, and editor of seven anthologies. Zackheim is an essayist and playwright and teaches creative nonfiction in the UCLA Extension Writers' Program. She is a frequent conference speaker and writing instructor.

anneperry.us
victoriazackheim.com